W9-BBQ-203

When She's Bad

ALSO BY LEANNE BANKS

Some Girls Do

When She's Bad

LEANNE BANKS

WARNER
FOREVER

WARNER BOOKS EDITION

Copyright © 2003 by Leanne Banks
All rights reserved. No part of this book may be reproduced in any form or by any electronic or mechanical means, including information storage and retrieval systems, without permission in writing from the publisher, except by a reviewer who may quote brief passages in a review.

Cover design by Shasti O'Leary Soudant
Cover photograph by Jethro Soudant
Book design by Giorgetta B. McRee

Warner Books, Inc.
1271 Avenue of the Americas
New York, NY 10020

ISBN: 0-7394-3876-X

An AOL Time Warner Company

Printed in the United States of America

*This book is for all you wonderful readers
who told me you loved SOME GIRLS DO
and wanted to read Delilah's story
and for us sometimes-bad-girls who know
that being a little bad can be a lot of fun!*

Acknowledgments

Special thanks and acknowledgments to the amazing Karen Kosztolnyik for continued guidance, Michele Bidelspach for terrific responsiveness, and to Diane Luger for creating the best cover art on earth. Thank you to Tony and Alisa for enduring deadlines and picking up take-out meals. Thank you also to some special people in my life who continue to encourage and inspire me: Cindy Gerard, Donna Kauffman, Pamela Britton, Millie Criswell, Marilyn Puett, my creative consultant and Mom and Dad. I am so blessed.

When She's Bad

Deathbed promises are a pain in the butt.
                                    —DELILAH'S DICTUM

Chapter 1

$\mathcal{T}$onight's the night.

Full of hope and anticipation, she told herself that tonight would be filled with lazy, sensual pleasure that would sate her body and soul. A night that would provide release from the frustration that had built to unbearable levels during the last two weeks.

Restless hunger burned inside her, building with each passing moment. Her need had risen to fever pitch and it pounded inside her like a primitive drumbeat. She slid her hand over her body with a comforting stroke. Soon, she told herself. She wore cotton, the fabric of babies, but this lover wouldn't mind the absence of silk and satin. She would seduce this lover in other ways. In fact, she had already begun with a champagne cocktail, a long, warm scented bath surrounded by candles, and now with secret, expectant darkness.

What she wanted was a satisfaction as old as time.

What she wanted was a freakin' full night of sleep.

More than anything, all Delilah Montague craved was a peaceful, uninterrupted night of sleep. She needed it to forget for just a little while that her best friend in the world had died one month ago. She needed sleep to ease the ache in her heart and head. She needed to pretend that eventually everything would work out and she wouldn't always be the object of disdain and distaste. She needed it so she could keep a razor-sharp clear head in the morning, especially since she'd inherited a large interest in the spa.

She'd been told she had a smile that opened doors and a body that made men want to empty their pockets and lower their zippers. With a father who was a fire-and-brimstone preacher and a mother who had won more wet T-shirt contests than all the Baywatch babes combined, Delilah had a lot to live up to . . . or live down, depending on one's perspective. She knew she wasn't a good candidate for marriage or motherhood, so it was easy to focus on her career. She hadn't, however, grown accustomed to the new responsibility Howard "Cash" Bradford had bequeathed her yet.

Delilah would trade her most treasured possessions for one night's sleep; designer shoes, a perfectly mixed champagne cocktail, perhaps even her secret stash of M&Ms. She would even trade her body except her poor body was too tired for anything more than intimately melding itself with her mattress.

"It's not too much to ask, is it?" she muttered to the sleep gods as she flipped her pillow over to press her cheek against cool Egyptian cotton. Her mattress was the perfect degree of firmness, a far cry from the cot in the homeless shelter where she'd slept a few years ago. Her duvet provided the exact weight and warmth to ease her trip into Lala-land.

A professional interior decorator had furnished her boudoir as a sanctuary of peace from the harsh outside world. She kept waiting for the day when *she* felt comfortable in her own condo. Until now, she'd felt as if she were walking on eggshells, afraid of messing up the white carpet and ivory leather furniture, afraid of messing up everything and ending back on the streets.

Her heart raced at her thoughts and she tried to take a calming breath. As director of Spa DeMay, the most elite spa in Texas, she worked in an environment where she pulled knives out of her back on a daily basis. No one believed she truly had a lick of business sense. No one thought she would last more than a month after her mentor Howard Bradford died. Everyone believed she had achieved her present position by lying on her back for Howard Bradford. Only she knew the real truth, and it was her job to keep the truth a secret.

Delilah pushed the hated plugs into her ears as protection from her neighbor, whom she was convinced had been hatched from some alien species which didn't require sleep. That was the only explanation she could think of for doing renovations in the wee hours of the morning.

Sighing, she closed her eyes and began to count backward from two thousand. *One thousand nine hundred and ninety-nine. One thousand nine hundred and ninety-eight . . .*

Howard lay in his large bed, a cigar in one hand, a glass of scotch in the other, his heart medication on his bedside table.

Tsking in disapproval, Delilah took the cigar and scotch away.

"Hey! Give that back!" he protested. "I'm a dying man. You shouldn't deny me my meager pleasures."

"You wouldn't be dying if you didn't indulge your pleasures so much. You just had your third heart

catheterization and I know the doctor didn't recommend scotch and a Cuban as part of your recovery."

Howard sighed, but smiled his wily winning grin. "You know I'm in love with you, Delilah."

"Me and fifty others," she said. Delilah couldn't resist smiling in return at the ornery multi-millionaire, but she tried not to show that he scared her to death. His complexion was gray and she didn't want him to die. She wanted Howard Bradford to live forever. He had transformed her life when he'd taken her on as arm candy. She'd expected to become his lover, and for a time, she had wanted that, but then she'd learned the truth Howard was determined to hide. Howard might be one of the most wealthy and powerful men in Houston, but he couldn't quite, shall we say, lift his crane. His sexual difficulties were such an embarrassment to him that he made it a practice to keep a young woman on his arm at every public opportunity.

He'd showered Delilah with gifts, clothing, an informal education and the opportunity to prove herself. She'd gone from shampoo girl to executive director of Spa DeMay, and she had "Cash" to thank for it. He'd introduced her to the arts and she'd introduced him to the World Wrestling Federation.

For all their playful arguments, both he and Delilah knew there wasn't anything she wouldn't do for him.

He coughed and his grin fell. His eyes turned serious. "There's something I need to tell you."

She offered him a sip of water and sat on the edge of the bed. "You should rest instead of talk."

"You're a bossy woman."

She cracked a sassy grin. "You helped make me that way."

He laughed and absently rubbed his chest. "So I did." He sighed. "I need you to do something for me."

"Anything except the cigar, scotch and Viagra," she said, knowing none of the three mixed well with his heart condition.

"The evil trinity," he said wryly, then turned serious again. "If something happens to me—"

Delilah's heart contracted. "It won't."

"Don't be a sissy about this," he said with an edge to his voice. "I'm surrounded by enough hysterical idiots. I'm counting on you to be sensible."

Delilah stiffened her lip. "Okay, what can I do?"

"If I die, I'd rather you not tell anyone the truth about my, uh—" He cleared his throat. "My condition."

Realization hit her. Male pride, one of the strongest forces in the universe. Even in the face of death, Cash was concerned about his image. "If anyone asks me, my response will be that you were so virile I couldn't keep up with you."

Cash chuckled. "Whatever happens, Lilly needs to be protected. I want you to keep an eye on her."

"She may not like that."

"I'll talk to her," he said.

"I'm not sure that will help," she said, suspecting that Howard's daughter, Lilly, wasn't overly fond of her.

"Let me handle it. There's something else,

though, that's very important to me. It's not a small request and it won't be easy for you."

Delilah wrinkled her brow in confusion. "What—"

A knock sounded on the door, interrupting them. Miguel, Howard's longtime housekeeper, stepped into the room. "Sorry to interrupt, Señor Bradford, but Señorita Lilly is on the phone."

Howard's eyes lit up. "I'll take it, Miguel. I must have forgotten to turn the ringer back on," he said, picking up the receiver. He covered the mouthpiece. "We'll talk tomorrow. Okay, darlin'?"

Still worried, Delilah forced a smile and kissed his forehead. "Sure thing," she whispered, wondering what he had intended to tell her. "Get some rest after you talk to Lilly."

Tomorrow, tomorrow, tomorrow . . .

A buzzing sound permeated her brain. Delilah frowned. She covered her ears, but it felt like a bee was buzzing inside her head. She desperately tried to go back to sleep. If she stayed asleep, maybe Howard would tell her what he wanted her to do.

Tomorrow had never come for him. He had passed away in his sleep.

Refusing to open her eyes, afraid of looking at the clock, she buried her head under her pillow.

The buzzing continued.

Her heart sank. *Not again!* She peeked out from under the pillow at her alarm clock and scowled. The luminescent numbers mocked her. 2:37 A.M.

Frustration and impotent fury raced through her. She threw the pillow against the wall. "Stop!"

The buzzing continued.

Not certain whether to cry or scream, Delilah pulled the remaining earplug out of her ear. Who knew where the other plug had gone? The buzzing sound reminded her of a trip to the dentist. Pushing back the covers on her bed, she stomped to the wall she shared with her neighbor. "I'm in hell," she muttered to herself. "That guy Cash told me about, what's his name? Danny, Dan, Dante? He left out a level of hell and I am in it."

She'd tried to keep her exchanges with her mystery neighbor civil up until now. She'd left polite little notes at his door, but she couldn't handle another night of sleep deprivation. She pounded on the wall. "Stop it! For God's sake, stop it, stop it, stop it!"

The buzzing miraculously ceased. Delilah slumped in relief.

"Did I wake you?" called a muffled male voice from the other side of the wall.

Delilah rolled her eyes. *Only every night for the last eighteen days.* "Yes. Please stop," she called back.

"Sorry. I didn't know you could hear me," he yelled.

"Yeah, right," she murmured darkly.

"Are you sure it was my drill that woke you? It's a silent drill."

"It's not silent. It's a giant man-eating termite."

"Are you sure you don't have a problem with insomnia?" he asked, as if the buzzing sound was all her imagination.

Surely he wasn't patronizing her, she thought, her temperature rising even more, which meant it would be impossible for her to go back to sleep. "I definitely have a problem with insomnia and you are it," she yelled.

"Me?" he yelled in astonishment.

"Your nighttime renovations."

"I do quiet renovations at night."

"Not quiet enough, Mr. Tooltime. Put your weapons of destruction away," Delilah yelled in return. "My best friend in the world died a month ago and I really need my sleep."

Silence followed, then a mumbling sound.

"What?" Delilah asked, pressing her hands against the wall as she craned to hear.

"I said I'm sorry. I quit my job and fiancée. I've been trying to keep busy."

"All night?"

"Can't sleep."

Even through the wall, she could feel his regret in admitting he couldn't sleep. She couldn't escape a stab of sympathy for the guy. She understood far too much about losing. Sighing, she felt an odd sort of connection with her insomniac neighbor.

She thought again and shook her head. "That's wack," she muttered to herself. "I'm sorry about your problems, but you need to find something quieter to do at night."

"Like what?"

She rolled her eyes. Why was she supposed to solve his problems? "Bowling. The bowling alley is open all night," she said and headed for the bathroom.

With his ear pressed against the wall he shared with his neighbor, Benjamin Huntington III would have replied if he hadn't heard a shriek of frustration followed by the sound of his neighbor's shower.

Pulling back, he glanced down at his high-tech silent drill, then eyed the wall again with skepticism. The woman's shriek still rang in his ears. *Great*, he was living next door to the Wicked Witch of the West.

His fingers itched to continue drilling. After all, *Broom Hilda* was still in the shower. She wouldn't hear him. Muttering, he unplugged the drill. The renovations were supposed to be therapeutic. So far, they'd been working. Even though he'd made a few mistakes and sections of his condo resembled the apocalypse, he liked the feeling of progress. He liked working with the tools and his hands.

The renovations helped him deal with his own insomnia and disillusionment. In one week, he'd lost both his dream job and the fiancée he'd thought was his dream woman. As if it had just happened an hour ago, Benjamin remembered his confrontation with the managing partner of the most prestigious law firm, Fitzgerald and Lewis, in Connecticut.

Benjamin had been sickened to learn that one of the other attorneys had bribed a judge on behalf of one of his clients. Fitzgerald's words still rang in his ears. *"Keep it quiet. This is the son of one of our most prominent clients."*

Benjamin had quit on the spot and he'd thought his fiancée Erin, an attorney at the same firm, would join him in Houston without batting an eye. But Erin hadn't. She'd told him the bribery was all part of the game. He was overreacting.

So now he was back in Houston, teaching law instead of practicing it. His blood pressure rose at the thought. That would change in due time, he told himself, brushing off his hands and heading for the den.

His father was urging him to join the family firm here in Houston, but Benjamin had never been comfortable being his parents' "chosen one." That had been part of the reason he'd stayed back East after he'd graduated from law school.

His brother Robert was finally coming into his own, preparing to run for public office, and Benjamin refused to steal any of Robert's thunder.

He sank down onto his overstuffed couch and drummed his fingers over his plaster-dusted jeans leg. He closed his eyes and the familiar edgy restlessness tripped through him, making it impossible for him to sit still. He needed to hammer a couple of boxes of nails into the wall or drill all the way to Dallas. Anything to escape the damned-if-you-do-and-damned-if-you-don't feeling in his chest. If he had been able to play the game as his fiancée had suggested, he would still be in Connecticut now with his rising position at the firm and his marriage plans intact.

He wouldn't have been able to look at himself in the mirror. Benjamin had been told by more than one person that his deep-seated sense of integrity would cause him unending heartburn if he practiced law. He just hadn't known it would cost him his dream job and future wife. Since he'd followed his convictions and made the right decision, the least he had expected was the ability to sleep at night, but he had too many unanswered questions about himself, about his future.

He glanced in the direction of his neighbor's condo. And now he'd learned he was living next door to a woman with a shriek that could make his skin crawl. Where were a good hammer and board when you needed them?

Champagne cocktails and M&Ms are the real necessities of life.

—DELILAH'S DICTUM

Chapter 2

"Take a message. I'm not paying him or seeing him," Delilah told her assistant, ignoring the niggling uneasiness underneath her skin at the mention of Guy Crandall.

"This is the third time he's called this morning," Sara Cox said calmly. Sara was always calm except when her almost-ex-husband, Frank, called to harass her. The woman's determined calm was the reason Delilah had hired her. That and the beaten-down dejectedness Delilah saw Sara trying to shake. Delilah knew a little too much about being beaten down herself.

"The answer will be no if he calls ten more times," Delilah said, still fighting that itchy discomfort. Cash had warned her about Guy. Cash had also told her to *just pay him*, but Delilah wanted to expand the business and in order to expand, she needed to trim unnecessary costs. Guy Crandall didn't appear to do a blasted thing, so she'd cut off the weekly payments for his nonexistent consultation services.

Leaning over her cherry desk, Delilah studied the expenses for the business for the zillionth time and felt a cautious spurt of optimism despite her lack of sleep. If everything went half as well as she planned, she could open a new location in Dallas in twelve to eighteen months.

If she was successful, she would effectively shut the mouths of all her detractors, and heaven knows, she had a lot of detractors. Her stomach burned and she reached for an antacid as she shook off the drowsiness that still plagued her. A little peace would go a long way in soothing her ragged nerves, but Delilah suspected peace wasn't in her future today.

"Coffee," she murmured, noting her empty cup. Sometimes she wondered if she lived on coffee, antacid, and her secret stash of M&Ms in her bottom desk drawer. The staff nutritionist would be horrified, but Delilah left the herbal tea that reminded her of stinky socks for the clients that streamed in the door of Spa DeMay paying astronomical sums for everything from sea enzyme treatments, mud wraps, microdermabrasion, and permanent makeup to a highly coveted spot at the exclusive Botox parties held after hours. The only concession she had made to being healthy had been to quit smoking, and that was in direct response to her eleven-year-old half-brother living in Pennsylvania. Rising from her leather chair, she strode into the greeting area for coffee while her assistant fielded another call.

"Frank, I've asked you not to call me at work," Sara said in a shaky voice. "I've already told you I'm not going to quit my job and come back to you."

Delilah wrinkled her nose in distaste at the way Sara's ex tried to manipulate her.

"You're wrong. I can hold down a job," Sara said, her voice cracking. "I may not have a lot of skills now, but I'm learning."

If there was one thing Delilah couldn't stand, it was a

bully. Her stomach burned as if she hadn't just swallowed an antacid tablet. Swinging around, she gently pulled the phone from Sara's hand. "Pardon me," she said to Sara, then lifted the receiver to her ear. "Frank, this is Sara's boss. Stop calling the office or I will arrange for someone to remove your testicles and Sara and I will have to fight over who gets to wear them for earrings."

She hung up the phone and met Sara's startled gaze. "Hope you didn't mind."

Sara shook her head in tiny movements that barely disrupted her carefully coiffed red hair. She cleared her throat. "Do you really know someone who would remove Frank's, uh—"

"Testicles," Delilah supplied, certain Sara was too lady-like to say the term aloud herself. She returned to the coffeemaker and filled her cup. "Yes, I do." She'd met a lot of interesting people through Howard Bradford.

"Well," Sara said in a voice that evoked images of melted butter and honey on a flaky biscuit. "If you happen to get Frank's *earrings*, I'd like to wear them first."

Delilah chuckled in approval. When Sara had first shown up for her interview, she had been a shadow of a woman, painfully meek. Although Delilah was known for her ball-breaking attitude, there had been a time when she'd been vulnerable and unsure. Even though she'd interviewed more assertive applicants, Sara had haunted her and she'd sensed hiring her would be the right thing to do. So far her instincts had proven correct. With each passing day, her assistant seemed to get a little stronger. Until Frank called. "Does he call you much at home?"

"I don't pick up."

"Good." Delilah sipped the hot brew. "Have you started dating yet?"

Sara blinked. "Dating? A man?"

Delilah laughed. "You can use the plural form. You'll be single any day."

Flustered, Sara shook her head. "I haven't thought much about it and I'm not ready, and if I were, I haven't met anyone who would ask me and—"

"They're not all like Frank," Delilah said.

Sara took a deep breath. "So I've been told."

"But you obviously haven't experienced," Delilah said, speculatively. She'd matched up more than one couple at Spa DeMay. She was good at managing everyone's love life except her own. That quality seemed to run in her family. "You know what you need? You need a young stud muffin who will provide you with pleasure while you retain the control."

Sara's cheeks turned scarlet. "I can't imagine—"

"Well, you probably should."

Sara folded her hands. "Miss Montague, you've done a lot for me. I'll never be able to repay you for helping me find a safe place to live and for giving me this job when I know I wasn't the prime choice, but I cannot accept your offer of providing me with a sexual—" She cleared her throat and lifted her hand nervously to her neck. "A sexual stud muffin."

"Well if you change your mind," Delilah ventured.

Sara's lips twitched. "I'll let you know, but I'm not like you. You're experienced and confident. Men want you."

Not the way she wanted to be wanted, Delilah thought, but quickly brushed the thought away. Oddly enough, her relationship with Cash had provided her with a future at the same time that it had painted her as a floozy. Her mother had been a floozy. Like mother, like daughter. Delilah told herself for the hundredth time that she didn't care if the world thought she was a floozy, as long as she was a smart floozy. If she had anything to do with it, she wouldn't end her days dirt poor in a trailer in Nowhere, Texas.

A tall, gorgeous, buff blond man strode through the doorway. Delilah felt a rush of pleasure. There were very few people at Spa DeMay who didn't secretly or not-so-secretly disdain her. There were very few employees at Spa DeMay whom she genuinely liked. Paul Woodward, the spa's most popular massage therapist, was one of them. He was the kind of guy who crackled with masculine energy and wore his strength with ease. He had a ladykiller grin. With his good looks, he should have been cocky as hell, but he wasn't. She could love him. Like a brother.

"How's my favorite Woody?" she teased.

He gave a half chuckle then shook his head. "I'm fine, but I've got bad news, Miss Montague. Helga made the new esthetician quit."

Delilah groaned. Helga, the spa's most talented and renowned esthetician, was easily threatened. "I need a strong second when Helga's not available. I don't know what it's going to take. I'll go pull her hair," she said. "Or talk to her if I can get rational by then."

"Let me know if you want a neck rub after you're done with her," Paul teased.

Delilah gave a fake pout. "No full body massage?"

"You're the boss."

Delilah laughed and waved him away. "Go make me some money."

"You can't say I didn't offer," he said and nodded in Sara's direction. "Mornin' Miss Cox. You're lookin' pretty today."

Sara's cheeks colored. "Why thank you," she said in an astonished voice.

Delilah smiled as Paul treated them to the sight of his broad back and tight butt as he left the outer office. "He's so fun to flirt with. He almost distracted me about Helga."

Sara gave a disapproving sniff. "He gives the impression that he's quite accustomed to distracting women with his body."

"You're not being snooty, are you? Do you really believe Paul isn't a genuinely kind person?"

Sara gave a quick shake of her head. "No. I'm not at all snooty. He's just—" She shrugged. "He's just so good-looking it's a bit overwhelming."

Delilah nodded. "With looks like that you'd expect him to be a real jerk. But he's not." She sighed and made a face. "As enjoyable as it is to talk about Paul, I really need to talk to Helga. Page me if there's an emergency."

"Good luck," Sara said with a nod.

"I'm going to need it," Delilah muttered and walked out of the office.

A receptionist immediately flagged her. "Miss Montague, Mrs. Manning says she's desperate to get into the Botox party scheduled for tomorrow night."

Mrs. Manning's husband was president of an oil company. Like most of the women who walked through the elegant front doors of the spa, she was trying to hold off plastic surgery as long as possible. "Tell her we'll squeeze her in, but she must sign the releases before she can attend."

Delilah skimmed the front desk appointment book for Helga's schedule and saw that she was on break. Probably smoking in her office, Delilah thought and turned down the hall. She gave three raps on the door then opened it. Helga scrambled under her desk, no doubt trying to conceal her cigarette. Helga kept a fan running in her office at all times.

There was a strict no-smoking policy at the spa that Helga ignored. Helga was a stern, tall, blonde fifty-one-year-old woman with a streak of paranoia that rivaled the width of the Mississippi river. She was a pain and Delilah would have cheerfully fired the woman if she weren't the most talented and famous esthetician in the west. Women were willing to pay a great deal for one of Helga's facial treatments.

"Good morning, Helga. What happened with Cynthia?" Delilah asked, already knowing the answer.

Helga poked her head above the desk and lifted her chin in regal distaste. "She didn't know what she was doing. I gave her suggestions and she became hysterical. She was no good."

"Helga, according to you, all of the estheticians are no good."

"I have high standards for my clients," Helga said with a shrug.

"But you do understand that we need at least two more estheticians to satisfy customer demand."

"It is better for the customer to wait. Then they appreciate the service more. If they must wait, then they believe they have received something special. Which they have if I have performed their treatment."

Delilah sighed. She'd held this conversation with Helga too many times to count and she was ready to try something drastic. *Everybody works harder if they have something on the line*, Howard had told her, and he was right. "You know that I would like to start another location of Spa DeMay in Dallas?" Delilah began.

Helga looked down her nose at Delilah. "You do not know enough about the business to do such a thing."

Delilah bit her tongue. "Actually Howard thought it

was a good idea. So do the accountants. I've been thinking you are such an integral part of Spa DeMay that I would like you to take on a larger role."

Helga perked up with a mixture of skepticism and curiosity. "What do you mean larger role?"

"Well, Helga, you must know that when it comes to facial treatments, you are the Queen. Anyone we hire will be second choice."

"Yes," Helga agreed, relaxing a centimeter. "What does this have to do with a larger role?"

"In order to expand, we must hire more estheticians. I would like for you to oversee them."

"I already do that," Helga said dismissively.

"If we can keep two estheticians for one year, then I'll give you a bonus."

Delilah could practically see the wheels of Helga's mind begin to turn. "What bonus?"

"Two percent silent ownership in the spa."

Helga blinked. "Ownership?"

"Two percent silent ownership," Delilah emphasized.

"I could not be silent."

"You may serve in an advisement capacity, but I will make final decisions. But if you're not interested," Delilah said as if she were pulling a platter of cookies from the table.

"I did not say that," Helga quickly said. "I will agree." She gave Delilah an assessing glance. "Perhaps you are smarter than some thought."

Damn right, Delilah thought, but smiled instead. "Who would have known? Go ahead and write the want ad advertising the positions." She extended her hand to seal the deal then headed for the door, knowing she'd just made an agreement with someone who would love to see her fail.

A deal with the devil. Delilah had a gnawing feeling it wouldn't be her last.

On the way back to her office, she slowed at the sight of Lilly Bradford at the front desk. She felt an odd pang at the sight of Howard's only daughter from his long-dissolved marriage. He had loved her so much, and would have moved heaven and earth to protect her from his secrets. Now Delilah was in charge of protecting Lilly. Overhearing the receptionist tell Lilly they were booked for the day, she intervened.

"I'm sure we can work something out," Delilah said to the receptionist.

"But we're slammed," the receptionist protested. "I've already had to work in—"

"We're never too slammed for Miss Bradford," Delilah said firmly, looking at the book. "What can we do for you today, Miss Bradford?"

Lilly didn't quite meet Delilah's gaze. Come to think of it, she never really had. Lilly had been a plain, painfully shy adolescent who was now desperately trying to be seen as a desirable marriage partner for Robert Huntington. She'd successfully straightened her teeth and Howard had been more than happy to pay for laser vision correction surgery that meant she no longer had to wear glasses. Her hairstyle covered ears that stuck straight out just like Howard's had, but anyone with a smattering of women's intuition could see that Lilly suffered from a dearth of self-confidence. "I-uh have a special dinner date for tonight. I need my hair done," she said, absently stroking her shoulder-length highlighted blonde hair. "A manicure and makeup."

"Is Sharon okay for your hair?" Delilah asked.

Lilly nodded, still not meeting her gaze.

Delilah felt a strange tug in the region of her heart. "Big night planned with Mr. Huntington?"

Lilly's eyes widened in surprise. "Yes," she said. "Perhaps. I'm not sure."

Delilah smelled an engagement coming. Or at least Lilly's hopes for one. "We'll have you looking so beautiful you will bring him to his knees."

Lilly swallowed and if her face could talk, it would have said, *I can only hope.* She could practically feel the woman shimmer with nervousness. "Call these clients and reschedule their appointments. Miss Bradford's services are on the house as always," she said to the receptionist. "Come this way. Would you like a glass of wine during your manicure?" she asked Lilly.

Lilly hesitated then nodded. As they rounded the corner, Howard's daughter came to an abrupt stop and she met Delilah's gaze with a fierce anger her demure, uncertain appearance had completely belied.

"Don't bother trying to make nice with me," Lilly said. "You can't bribe me to like you. You may have been able to sleep your way into getting my father to care for you and give you control of the spa, but I can't stand the sight of you. And I never will."

Delilah blinked in shock as Lilly whirled away. She shouldn't feel hurt. It was natural for Lilly to dislike her. Everyone in Houston had believed Delilah was Howard's mistress and he was her sugar daddy. It had been her job to make everyone believe. Unfortunately, even though Howard had died, it was still her job. She sighed. Deathbed promises were a pain in the butt.

*Flirting is one of life's least expensive pleasures
and it can sometimes get you free dessert.*
—DELILAH'S DICTUM

Chapter 3

After a tough day at work, Delilah was looking forward to relaxing at home—and hoping that just maybe her dreadful neighbor would take a break from his renovations.

As she dragged herself to the elevator, Delilah heard the sound of fist pounding flesh and winced. The unsettling noise echoed from just two car rows away from her in the underground garage of her high-rise condo and reminded her of a different time in her life when she'd lived in a different, less safe neighborhood. She wished she could turn the other way. After her crappy day at work, every fiber of her was begging for a little peace.

Muggings weren't supposed to happen here. This garage had video security surveillance. She glanced toward a camera and shook her fist, wondering who was sleeping in front of the monitor right now.

She heard a groan of pain, and helplessness shot through her. One step away from becoming a basket case, she couldn't bear the idea of death. She glanced heavenward in dismay and whispered, "Don't you know I'm not a good choice for this duty?"

If only she wasn't plagued with this damned belief in

responsibility. There was a reason she was here at this minute, and she'd better not screw it up or she would be paying for it forever.

Her stomach turned as she felt the unwelcome noose of responsibility tighten around her neck. Her mind whirled with crazy possibilities. She wasn't packing a pistol and she wasn't Superwoman. She glanced down at herself in a futile search for a weapon. In her short designer skirt and high heels, she was dressed to slay men—metaphorically speaking—and inspire women, not kill thugs. What was she supposed to do? Stab the bad guys with one of her heels? Her mind wandered. There had actually been that time when she'd had to stomp the instep of an over amorous client. She thought about her thong underwear. Thongs were usually a very effective distraction for men, but—

She heard another punch and couldn't stand it. Time for a lie. Ducking behind a car, she covered her eyes and at the top of her lungs screamed, "Fire! Fire! Thank God there's the police! Fire! Fire! Officer, over here! Help!"

When she took a breath, she inhaled with her pulse pounding in her ears. Out of the corner of her eye, she caught sight of three hoodlums scurrying out the far exit of the parking garage. She tentatively stepped forward and peeked around the corner, spotting a man slumped on the ground.

She scrambled toward him, praying no thugs remained and swearing under her breath. "Are you okay?" she asked, poking gingerly at his shoulder. "Please be alive. Are you conscious?"

He gazed up at her and grimaced. "I think," he said in a slurred voice. "Who—"

"We've got to get out of here. Be quiet and get in the

elevator," she said, dragging his tall frame to his feet and trying to support him as she urged him to the elevator. She felt muscles bunch beneath the tweed wool jacket he wore and she wondered if he had tried to defend himself.

She clumsily shoved him against the side of the elevator and punched the button for the floor to her condo. She would figure out what to do with him later. Now, she just needed to get them away.

She stepped closer to peer at his wounds, touching his face, half of which was unmarked. Strong jaw, chiseled bones, he looked about thirty with dark hair and the one eye that was open seemed to look right through her. A good soul, she instantly concluded with the confidence of a woman who'd graduated with a PhD from the school of hard knocks. Her ability to read a man through his eyes had saved her butt more times than she could count. Her heart still hammering a mile a minute, she bit her lip as she took inventory. She started to chatter and couldn't make herself stop. "Your left eye looks terrible. Swollen shut and red already. What's your name?"

"Benjamin, Benjamin Hu—"

She made a *tsk*ing sound. "Oh, Benjamin, your mouth is bleeding. And your cheek—"

Benjamin didn't know which was making his head spin more—the throbbing in his brain or the woman's nervous talk. Just after his assailants had fled, he'd wondered if he was going to die. The next thing he remembered was spotting the most shapely pair of legs he'd ever seen in his life, quickly followed by a wild-eyed woman who'd dragged him into the elevator. He had the impression of being blown away by a hot Texas wind.

"Did they punch you in the stomach?" She touched his

chest, then her hand fell to his belly, and he instinctively sucked in a sharp breath.

"What if you're bleeding internally? You should go to the emergency room. Are you feeling dizzy or nauseated? You could have a concussion."

"I-jus-got-back-from—" He swallowed and closed both his eyes.

"Omigod. Your voice is slurred. You could have a concussion. Your brain may be swelling. We have to—"

"—dentist," he said, and pulled gauze from his mouth. "I just got a root canal."

"Oh." She grimaced in sympathy. "Helluva day."

He stared at his rescuer with his good eye. There was something vaguely familiar about her, but he couldn't place it. He watched her brush a dark lock of her hair away from her eyes. She gnawed on her full bottom lip and his gaze traveled downward over curves he suspected had caused many masculine meltdowns. Her top fit her shapely breasts like air and her skirt was too short, too tight. She was the antithesis of every conservative well-bred New England woman he'd dated since he'd entered Harvard Law School.

The woman looked like sin. With heart.

The elevator dinged, signaling the end of their ride. His floor, he thought. How convenient. He could collapse on a clear spot in his condo if he could find one. His do-it-yourself renovations were supposed to provide him some sorely needed do-it-yourself therapy. After he collapsed, he planned to knock out a wall.

"Come with me," she said. "I can at least get some ice on your eye while we figure out what to do next."

"But I'm right down the—"

"Don't argue with me. We need to figure out whether

to call the police first or take you to the emergency room," she said, nudging him down the hallway and unlocking the door to her condominium. "Take the sofa. I'll get the ice."

This was his *neighbor*, he realized. The woman who had shrieked at him last night? *The Wicked Witch of the West? Broom Hilda?* Surely more than one person lived here. He'd barely sunk down onto her ivory leather sofa before she returned with a frozen bag of peas. She gingerly lifted the bag to his eye.

He sucked in a quick breath.

"Sorry, but you'll thank me in the morning," she said in a husky voice.

If his head weren't splitting in half, he might enjoy a few fantasies about how to spend the kind of night that would make him thank her in the morning. Instead, he met her gaze with his good eye. "I don't have to wait. Thank you for screaming."

"You're welcome. What about your stomach and ribs? Do you think anything is broken?"

He slid his hands over his trunk and slowly shook his head. "I don't think so."

"We should call the police," she said. "And make sure whoever is monitoring security tonight gets fired," she added in disgust. "You just know that if someone had been having sex on the floor of that garage, those security dodos would have been plastered to the monitor. Heck, they'd probably be making copies of the videos for their friends, but what happens when someone gets mugged and—"

She broke off as Benjamin clutched his ribs.

"What's wrong?" she asked, instinctively reaching out to him.

"Please don't make me laugh," he said in a voice that surprised her with the tinge of sexiness.

She blinked and took a quick reassessment. A different kind of assessment this time. He was just over six feet tall judging by the way she'd had to look up at him in the elevator. He had nice dark hair, although a bit mussed at the moment. Dark eyebrows framed his brown eyes. Expressive eyes. Well, one of them was expressive. She liked that. Great bones, she thought, taking in his chiseled facial structure, and she was trained to notice. Couldn't tell a thing about the mouth since it was swollen and bloody. Broad shouldered, but lean with muscles. A runner, she guessed, or swimmer, looking at his shoulders again. She allowed her gaze to sweep past his thighs, down to his feet. Large feet. *Oh, my.*

Sense of humor, good dresser, and he had a good soul. Interesting man. She wondered if a woman would be able to keep him in line.

She met his gaze and felt a surprising punch. He knew exactly what she'd been doing. Well, damn. Intelligence could really ruin the mix.

"I don't think I've ever been strip-searched more thoroughly by a woman," he said, sounding flattered.

She almost felt embarrassed. After all, the man had just taken a beating. She shrugged and shot him a smile that she knew had knocked at least a few men off-kilter. "I'm nothing if not thorough. Lean back, I'll get you something to drink. Hard or soft?" she asked, thinking it might be fun to get him hard.

"Whiskey sounds good, but I'd probably better not mix the dentist's meds with alcohol. Just water."

Sensible too, she thought, as she walked to the refrigerator and pulled out a chilled bottle of spring water. What

an interesting man. She liked his voice. She liked the way
he smelled. She liked the one eye that wasn't swollen
shut, but his intelligence would likely cause problems. Intelligent men were harder to control and Delilah liked
being in control.

"Here," she said, unscrewing the cap on the water bottle and giving it to him. "I'll get the phone. You can call
the police."

"What's your name?" he asked as she turned away.

"Dee Montague," she said, smiling to herself as she
wondered what he would think of her given name. It never
failed to provoke a reaction. "Delilah, actually."

He paused. "Delilah?"

"Yes," she said, glancing over her shoulder.

"It suits you," he said slowly. "So how do I thank you
for saving me?"

"I don't know," she said, dialing the number for the police. After speaking with someone, she returned with the
phone to sit beside him on the couch. "Maybe we can put
our heads together and come up with something later," she
said, pleased to regain her ingrained ability to flirt. "In the
meantime, you should talk to the police."

"I'll return the favor," he said, surprising her with his
solemn tone. "I promise, if you ask me for something, I'll
do it."

Delilah got a funny feeling in her stomach. She wasn't
accustomed to solemn promises from men. She wasn't accustomed to believing promises many men made, but she
had a strong sense that this one might keep his promise.

She held the bag of peas against his eye while he re-
ported the assault in the garage. Listening to him with half
an ear, she tried to place his aftershave. A man had de-

signed it, she decided. It was the kind of aftershave created to make a woman hungry and wet.

"Benjamin Huntington III," he said. "My address is Waterstone Towers, 533 Cary Street, unit 1428."

Dee frowned. Puzzled, she wrinkled her brow. Had she heard correctly? The back of her neck tightened. As soon as he turned off the phone, she took it from him. "Did I hear you say you're in unit 1428?"

He nodded. "That's right," he said with a half-smile that managed to be sexy even though half his face was pummeled.

She could have pummeled the other half.

Huntington. Unit 1428. Huntington. Unit 1428. Delilah felt her chest tighten with resentment. The Huntingtons were one of Houston's most prominent and wealthy families. Lilly was hoping to marry one of them. Delilah barely stifled the urge to shriek. On top of the trauma of the evening and everything else she'd been through during the last few months, this was just too much. She felt her composure begin to crack and pointed at him accusingly. "You're my neighbor?"

"Right next door." He lifted the bottle of water to his lips.

"And a Huntington," she said in disgust. "I should have known it was some overgrown trust baby being so inconsiderate of neighbors. As a Huntington, you're probably not used to having neighbors."

"Now wait a minute—"

Delilah shook her head in disbelief. "You are the new neighbor who starts hammering or using some kind of loud machinery at six P.M. every evening and you don't stop until well after midnight."

"I'm renovating—"

She didn't want him to explain. She wanted him to stop torturing her. "And you are the new neighbor who plays some kind of music that sounds as if the building is being stormed by torch bearers bent on destruction."

He looked perplexed. "Russian opera?"

"And you play this music full blast despite the fact that I've left several notes requesting you to turn it down," she said, gritting her teeth. "And it's so loud I can't even escape it when I take a shower."

"Notes? What notes?"

"Oh, right," she said in complete disbelief. "Just like you didn't know your *renovations* left me without electricity when you went out of town weekend before last."

He stared at her with a blank expression. Delilah didn't believe it for one minute. The man had caused her untold misery. More than ever during the last month she had craved the solace of home, but for all the disturbance he had made, he might as well have brought a wrecking ball inside her condo instead of his. No one could be that ignorant. Then again, maybe this meant he wasn't intelligent after all. Too late, she thought. She knew the truth. He was the most annoying neighbor on the planet, and like an idiot, she had rescued him.

"Why do you have such a bad opinion of the Huntingtons? What did we ever do to you?"

"Nothing," she said. "You just exist." She pulled the bottle of water from his hand. "Get out. Go get your own water."

He stood, looking at her as if she were crazy. And although Delilah would die before she admitted it to him, she *was* a little crazy right now. Since Cash had died, she still hadn't figured out how to solidify both her professional and financial future and keep her promises to Cash, and the Power Tool Prince currently staring at her as if she had a screw loose, that he no doubt could tighten, was partially responsible. She couldn't sleep, therefore she couldn't think, therefore she hadn't figured out a solution for keeping the vow she'd made and cementing her future.

"Get out," she told him, shooing him toward her door. "After a long day at work during which I pull about a half dozen knives out of my back, I don't want much. All I want is a little peace and quiet. All I want is to lose myself in a hot shower, but I haven't been able to do that because of you," she said, shaking her finger at him as he backed through her doorway. "That's bad enough, but I waited two years to get my cleaning lady to clean on Fridays. Two years. I was gone for two weeks and you waltz in and I'm back on Tuesdays because my cleaning lady is cleaning for you on Fridays."

He shook his head. "I had no idea."

"Well I'm giving you an idea," she shouted. "You've destroyed any chance I have for peace in my home, then you have the nerve to get mugged just as I'm arriving home, so I nearly have a nervous breakdown trying to save you. Give me back my peas," she said, snagging the bag from his hand before she slammed the door in his astonished half-handsome, half-pummeled face.

The sound of the slamming door reverberated in his already pounding head as Benjamin stared into space with one eye, wondering what had just happened. He'd gotten a root canal. He'd been robbed and beaten by thugs. He'd been rescued by the reincarnation of a mad Mae West. He wasn't sure which was the worst.

Lilly Bradford was so nervous she was afraid she was going to lose her dinner before she ate it. She patted her ears to make sure they were covered by her hair then patted the romantic pastel dress she wore. She hoped Robert would find it romantic, so romantic he would ask her to marry him. Or at least go to bed with him. She would die before she admitted it, but this was one time she wished she possessed one-tenth of Delilah Montague's sultry sexiness. There was a woman who brought men to her knees. A bitter taste filled Lilly's mouth. Delilah had even brought her father to his knees. As much as she detested Delilah, she couldn't help wishing she had more know-how in the game of seduction/romance.

Lilly glanced up from the table where she waited for Robert and saw him across the room of one of the most romantic restaurants in Houston—The Brownstone. Her heart dipped. He was shaking hands as he made his way across the restaurant. Robert Huntington was quite simply the man of her dreams. He was handsome, intelligent. *Houston Magazine* had named him one of the city's top ten bachelors the past two years running. Lilly still couldn't believe that he had asked her out. She, who'd once had buck teeth, thick glasses, and a lisp. The lisp still crept into her speech every now and then when she was especially angry or upset.

She took a deep breath, reminding herself to remain calm. She didn't want to blow this. After all, this was Houston's most romantic nightspot. Tonight could be the night everything changed for her.

She loved everything about Robert, his ambition, his ideas, his gentleness with her. She envied the closeness his family shared and hoped she could be a part of their inner circle. She sensed his mother and father approved of her. She'd yet to meet his brother, but she knew the entire family held Benjamin in high esteem. When Robert's father spoke of Benjamin, he puffed out his chest and described him as a chip off the old block. Robert seemed to admire Benjamin. He often talked about seeking his opinion.

Lilly wanted to be one of the family, to spend holidays with them, to be included. When her father had left her mother, she'd never really felt as if she belonged to anyone. Her mother had always been strict, but once her father had left, she'd become nearly impossible to please. Lilly was ashamed of the relief she'd felt when her mother had remarried just a few years ago and moved to New York, but she'd sensed this was, at last, her chance to make a life for herself—a life *she* wanted. More than anything she wanted to belong. To be needed.

Lilly looked at him again as he smiled his heart-turning smile and looked intently at each person he greeted. His brown hair was cut short, his strong jaw shaven, his shoulders broad beneath his well-tailored suit coat. Her stomach jumped again. Oh, Lord, she hoped she didn't get sick. She resisted the urge to stand up and wave. She was never sure whether he saw her or not. He usually found his way to her side at functions they'd attended, but he was so passionate about his intent to run for public office that she feared he was looking through her or past her, but not quite at her.

She crossed her fingers by her side. Maybe he would do more than look tonight.

She held her breath as he finally turned to her and sent her reeling with his smile. "Hi," she said breathlessly.

"Lilly, you look beautiful," he said and brushed his mouth over her forehead.

She tamped down a spurt of frustration. Sometimes she craved a more overt display. It was probably unreasonable, but she couldn't help wondering how he would react if she gave him a French kiss in front of all these people. He would probably be shocked. And never call her again.

"Sorry I'm late, but I have something important to discuss with you. I think you're going to be excited about this."

Her heart raced in her chest. "I can't wait."

He smiled. "Just a little longer. Here's the waiter. Do you know what you want?"

A proposal, she thought, *decent or indecent.* She waved her hand. "Why don't you order for me?"

"That I can do," he said. "We'll start with a bottle of Dom Perignon, we'll share bruschetta as an appetizer, Caesar salad for two, Filet oscar for me, rare, and Shrimp provençale for the lady."

Lilly stifled a sigh of disappointment and leaned closer to whisper to him. "I'm allergic to shellfish "

"Oh, I'm sorry. I forgot. Chicken marsala?"

"Fine, thank you," she said. She could forgive him. It was just a little glitch. Sure, she'd told him she was allergic to shellfish several times, but Robert had more important things crowding his mind. Tonight the proposal could have him distracted.

She laced her fingers tightly together in her lap and waited for the waiter to leave. "So tell me why you're so excited?" she asked with a smile and hoped he didn't notice her slight lisp.

He leaned toward her. "I wanted you to be the first to know. After my parents, anyway," he said with a low, intimate tone. He opened his hand on the table in a gesture of invitation.

Lilly rubbed her damp palm against her dress and placed her hand in his. "This sounds important."

"Trust me. It is."

Lilly's pulse pounded so hard she feared he could hear it. "Tell me."

He looked from side to side and cleared his throat. "I have just received the endorsement of the Texas Cattlemen's Association and the *Houston Chronicle*."

She nodded. "And?"

He laughed. "This is huge. Do you realize what kind of influence these endorsements could give me? This has to be my biggest breakthrough so far."

She nodded, still sitting on the edge of her seat. "That's great news. Great news. Was there something else you wanted to tell me?"

His eyebrows furrowed together. "What do you mean?"

"I mean was this what you wanted me to be the first to know?" she asked, praying that it wasn't.

He beamed. "Yes, it was. I knew you would be as excited as I was." He released her hand and pointed. "Look. Here comes the waiter with the champagne. Great timing."

"Incredible," she murmured, numb with disappointment. She felt like an idiot. She wondered if there was a neon light flashing *stupid* on her forehead as she watched the waiter pour the champagne.

Robert swirled the bubbly liquid in his flute and sampled it, then lifted his glass to her. "Join me in a toast."

Trying to muster some enthusiasm, she dutifully lifted her glass and kept her smile plastered on her face.

"To good news," he said, clinking his glass against hers. "And good friends to share it with."

"Cheers," she muttered and gulped the champagne. *Good friends*. Her ego was flattened. She lifted the glass and gulped it again. *Good friends, ol' buddy, ol' pal.* Another gulp and she was finished.

Robert raised his eyebrows in surprise. "Careful Lilly, you don't want to get lightheaded in public."

"Why not?" she asked, feeling waspish.

"Well you wouldn't want to embarrass yourself."

"I'm curious," she said, wishing she had the nerve to get roaring drunk. "When is it appropriate to get lightheaded?"

"In private," he said in a low voice. "With someone who won't take advantage of you."

What if I want to be taken advantage of? She opened her mouth, looked into his eyes, and promptly lost her nerve. "Congratulations on your news," she said and saw the light return to his eyes. Her reminder of his success had made him happy. His happiness should have made her happy, but she was miserable and now she had to sit here and hide it through at least three courses.

Chapter 4

*S*he'd had that blasted dream again.

Even after she'd poured herself a champagne cocktail and sank into her mini-Jacuzzi with her rubber ducky, it had taken her forever to get back to sleep. When she had, she'd been transported to a dark room with a floor of eggs. She had to get to the other side without breaking any eggs.

Delilah was no shrink, but she knew the way she felt about her life. If she made one false step, she could end up covered with slimy eggs and lose everything, which was part of the reason she was convinced marriage and mother-hood weren't for her. What made this dream more wacky than ever had been the appearance of her neighbor.

Who would have thought that she could have rescued the man who had seemed bent on torturing her for the last few weeks? Worse yet, who would have thought she could have found him attractive, even if only for a moment of complete ignorance? And he was a *Huntington*.

Her stomach burning with the thought of it, she fished inside her tiny purse for an antacid as she walked through the door to the spa. It was so early there weren't many people around and she distantly noticed the click of her heels on the Italian tile floor. It was a sound she didn't usually hear due to the high activity level.

First things first. She started the coffeemaker, flicked on all the lights and tapped her foot impatiently as she waited for her third dose of caffeine. She cheated and shoved her mug directly under the rich brown liquid, then returned the carafe to its rightful place. She gave the cup a few quick cooling breaths and sipped.

"Well, well, if it isn't the infamous Delilah Montague, Howard Bradford's protégée."

Startled, Delilah whipped around and strangled on her coffee, dumping some of the hot liquid on her leather jacket. She glared at the man standing in the doorway. Short with shifty eyes like a ferret and too much gel in his hair. Slimy, she immediately concluded.

"Who are you?" she asked, reaching for a napkin to dab her spill.

"Pleasure to meet you," he said, extending his hand, which she didn't accept. "I'm sure you've heard of me. Guy Crandall."

Delilah's stomach tightened, but she instinctively feigned ignorance. "I don't recall the name."

His smile stiffened. "Are you sure? Howard and I go way back."

She shrugged. "I met several of Howard's close friends."

"Howard and I were business acquaintances. I was on his payroll."

"For what?"

"Consultation services," he replied.

Delilah knitted her brows in confusion. "I don't recall receiving any consultation services from you."

Guy made a sound of exasperation. "Who do you think

you're fooling? You know what I'm talking about. It was a cover."

"Cover for what?" she asked and this time she didn't have to pretend ignorance.

"I can't believe you don't know," he said, glancing over his shoulder.

"Well, I don't."

"I have information that could cause a lot of trouble for Lilly Bradford's romantic future. If you don't start paying me, I'm going to sing like a canary. And trust me, Miss Delilah, things will get messy."

Delilah lifted her chin. She wasn't afraid of messy. She'd dealt with messy her entire life. The only thing that kept her from decking Guy was the thought of Lilly. Lilly had been protected. Lilly hadn't been forced to deal with messy. Delilah bit her tongue.

Sara glided into the office and stopped with a start. "Oh, good morning. A visitor so early?"

"Excuse me," Guy muttered before he slithered out of the room.

Sara stared after him. "His voice sounds familiar. Who was that?"

"Guy Crandall."

Sara's eyes widened. "Oooh. What did he want? It didn't look pleasant."

Delilah poured herself another cup of coffee and took a quick sip, barely flinching at the quick burn. "It wasn't," she said, not elaborating as she walked into her office.

Blackmail. Guy Crandall's visit must have something to do with Cash's last request, she thought distastefully as she closed the door behind her. Guy must know something about Cash that even Delilah didn't know. Something that could hurt Lilly.

It was a perfect set-up for Guy because Lilly was Cash's Achilles' heel. He would do just about anything for her, including pay a slimeball like Guy to do nothing.

Delilah made a face. She didn't want to pay Guy. Everything inside her rebelled at the idea of letting someone like Guy extort money from her. She had more backbone than that.

She wouldn't do it. She absolutely wouldn't do it.

If she hadn't promised Howard.

By the end of the day, Delilah's head was pounding. She made a mental plan for her evening as she drove through the vestiges of rush-hour traffic. Chinese food, a soothing CD, a bath, a couple of cocktails and if the sleep gods were kind, she would dissolve into her mattress for eight hours with no eggs in sight.

She placed her order for Chinese and sank into the tub, listening warily for sounds of Armageddon from her neighbor, but she heard nothing. After a long soak, she reluctantly left the tub and wrapped herself in a white terrycloth robe. Her doorbell rang and she grabbed the money for her Chinese dinner.

She opened the door to a frazzled teenage girl and a screaming baby.

Not her Chinese dinner. The poor girl must have the wrong address.

"Are you Delilah Montague?" the girl asked.

Delilah paused, getting an unsettling feeling in her stomach. "Who wants to know?"

"I do," the woman said and cocked her head toward the baby. "And Willy, here."

Willy. Delilah looked at the red-faced baby and felt a spurt of apprehension. "I'm Delilah Montague, but—"

"Good," the woman said with relief. "I'm Nicky. Nicky Conde. Howard said he told you about me and Willy."

"Howard?" Delilah echoed.

The woman gave a loud sniff and stared at Delilah with sadness in her dark eyes. "He promised!" she wailed.

"He promised what?" Delilah asked, not at all sure she wanted to know.

"He promised he would tell you about me and Willy. I told him I couldn't handle the baby. I mean, I love 'im, but he's just too much for me to handle. I'm too young. I have my whole future in front of me," she wailed, sobbing. "Howard gave me money, but I can't keep Willy anymore. You have to."

"Me?" Delilah echoed in horror. "Why me?"

"Howard promised you would keep him if I couldn't. He promised. There are papers in the diaper bag and everything."

Delilah held up her hands. "No, no, no. I didn't hear anything about this baby until now. And I can't see any reason why I should take on the responsibility of your baby."

"But Willie is Howard's son," Nicky argued.

Delilah felt the hallway tilt. She shook her head. "He can't be Howard's son. Howard couldn't—" She broke off, reluctant to disclose Howard's problem even though this woman may have helped cure him.

"He used this little blue pill—"

"Oh, absolutely not. Howard's doctor strictly forbade him to use Viagra."

Nicky shrugged. "He used the pill and when I showed up pregnant, he told me he wasn't using it anymore because it made his chest hurt."

Delilah's headache returned with a vengeance. "How old are you, Nicky?"

"I'm nineteen and I wanna be a model. I'm leaving Willy with you and going to Paris. Howard said you would take care of Willy."

Delilah's breath locked in her chest. This couldn't be happening. "For how long?" she asked, dread locking around her feet like twin anchors.

Nicky tossed the diaper bag at Delilah's bare feet. "He'll be your son."

Benjamin couldn't ignore the commotion in the hall-way any longer. He opened his door to the sight of Delilah standing in her robe, holding a screaming baby while a teenager turned and ran for the elevator.

"Wait! You can't leave. You can't—" Delilah stared at the baby as if it were the anti-christ. "Omigod."

"Delilah?" Benjamin said.

"What in hell am I going to do with a baby?"

"Delilah?" Benjamin repeated.

"What in hell am I going to do with a baby?" she muttered, not appearing to hear him.

"Let me help you get this stuff inside your condo," he said, picking up the stroller and overstuffed diaper bag.

Delilah looked at him as if she were in a daze. "In my condo? Do I have to?"

"I don't think you want to stay out here the rest of the night," he said over the sound of the baby's cries as he nudged her inside her condo.

Still in shock, she jiggled the baby and paced, mutter-ing to herself. She looked at the squalling red-faced infant in disbelief.

Her jiggling and pacing failed to comfort the baby, and

she emanated enough nervous energy to power the space shuttle. He impulsively pulled the baby from her arms. "Get a drink. Let me try."

She looked at him blankly for a moment then moved her head in a circle and headed for the kitchen. He heard the tinkling of ice cubes in a glass as he turned out the lights and spoke to the child in a low voice. "She's only partly crazy. She'll calm down and you'll be okay. Are you a boy or a girl? Blue," he said, looking at the infant's blue sweater. "Boy. I bet you've had an eventful day, so you just need to relax and go to sleep. Don't try to understand women. That will just upset you more. Trust me, if you learn this lesson now, you'll be saving yourself a lot of grief."

The baby hiccupped and shuddered and stared wide-eyed at Benjamin. Quiet. He kept up the low-voiced monologue, switching to the subject of corporate law. Within minutes, the baby's eyes started to droop. Another few minutes passed and the baby was asleep.

He felt Delilah's curious gaze as she came to his side. "How did you do it?" she whispered.

"I turned out the lights and bored him to sleep. Pull the cushions off the couch and I'll put him down."

"Down?" she echoed.

"To sleep," he said. "Hopefully for the night."

Still feeling as if someone had hit her with a baseball bat, Delilah pulled the cushions off the couch and arranged them in the corner of the room. Her mind whirled. Howard. Nicky. Baby Willy. *Viagra*. Delilah shook her head. If Howard weren't dead, she'd kill him.

She glanced at Benjamin, surprised at how easily he'd calmed the baby. It was almost as if he had the magic touch.

Which she clearly did not possess. "Thank you."

He shrugged and set Willy down on the cushions. She darted for the diaper bag and pulled out a blanket. A bunch of papers came out with it. She winced at the sound, hoping it wouldn't wake the baby. Benjamin nabbed the blanket and put it over Willy while Delilah looked through the papers.

"Oh my God," she murmured, her blood turning to ice. The papers granted her custody of the little banshee. "This can't—"

"Want me to look at those?" Benjamin offered.

"No," she said, stuffing the ones with legal mumbo jumbo back into the bag and skimming a letter that contained instructions for Willy's care. Her stomach sank. . . . *allergic to disposable diapers . . . delicate stomach, prone to digestive problems . . .* "When am I going to wake up?"

"Delilah, are you okay?" Benjamin asked.

She met his searching gaze and forced herself to nod.

"Who's the baby?"

"Willy," she said with a smile that felt brittle as she stuffed the instructions back into the diaper bag. She turned off the lamp closest to the baby in hopes that he would remain asleep until she could figure out how to handle this situation. "It's Willy."

"Who's the mother?"

"Um, Nicky."

"Who is Nicky?"

Hell if I know. She couldn't confide in Benjamin. She couldn't confide in anyone. "Um, my cousin," she invented, telling herself it wasn't a bold-faced lie. Her mother had always said that in some way everyone in the whole world was related.

"How long is she leaving Willy with you?"

Forever. Delilah felt as if someone had taken away her future, locked her in a cell and thrown away the key. She opened her mouth, closed it and tried to concoct a reasonable, believable explanation. "Nicky's having financial problems." The baby made a rustling sound as he moved in his makeshift bed and Delilah froze, lowering her voice to a whisper. "We have to be quiet."

He nodded his head in the direction of the kitchen. "Let's go in there."

Delilah's heart sank. His questions were going to continue and she wasn't sure how to answer them.

"Why doesn't the father of the baby help her?"

Delilah was certain the father of the baby *had* helped. Howard Bradford was a lot of things, but he'd always been conscientious about his financial support of Lilly. Delilah knew Howard had done the same for Willy. She just didn't know exactly how. "Willy's father is dead," she said. "Nicky doesn't feel like she can handle the baby by herself and I had agreed to be the godmother in case both parents died."

"But both parents haven't died," Benjamin said, looking at her as if he didn't quite believe her.

Delilah resisted the urge to squirm. "That's right, but, uh—"

"So you shouldn't be legally responsible."

"That's probably true, but—"

"Does Nicky have other family? Maybe—"

Delilah waved her hand. "It's a long sad story. I'm really the only—" She choked over her words. *Damn Howard Cash Bradford and his Viagra.* How was she supposed to take care of a baby and the spa? Hadn't Howard known she would be a horrible mother? After all, she'd lost her mother when her father had taken custody of her.

He hadn't even allowed visitation. What did Delilah know about mothering? She felt sure of defeat. "I'm the only one."

He frowned. "But it's obvious you didn't expect this. It's very strange."

"Yes it is. But that's my family for you," she murmured, oddly grateful that her last statement was true. For some reason, she didn't like lying to Benjamin. He seemed like he had more integrity in his little finger than most men had in their entire bodies. But that was probably an illusion, she told herself, and she didn't know him very well.

He studied her again and she held her breath, wondering what he saw. Did he know she was a flaw-filled scaredy-cat? Ridiculous, Delilah told herself and forced herself to breathe.

He shrugged. "If you're willing to accept responsibility for him, then you must know what you're doing. Let me know if you want me to get some referrals for nanny agencies," he said and started toward the door. "Good ni—"

Panic froze her feet. Adrenaline sent her dashing to her door to stop him. "Wait!" She plastered her back against the door. "You can't leave."

He lifted one of those dark sexy eyebrows. "Why not? Everything seems to be under control here."

For this second, she thought. What if that baby woke up? What was she going to do with him when he needed something? What was she going to do with him when she needed to go to work tomorrow?

Delilah swallowed a scream and a healthy measure of pride. "Not exactly."

He rested his hands on his hips. "Not exactly how?"

"I mean I'm not prepared to take care of this baby."

"Then give him back to his mother."

"But I have to take care of him because I made a promise."

That stopped him. He understood promises. He sighed and raked a hand through his hair. "Then you need to get ready to be a single parent."

"And I will, but I, uh, uh—" The words stopped in her throat. She forced them out. "I need your help."

"Mine?" he asked in an incredulous voice. "What can I do?"

"Well, you've already helped. You got him to go to sleep and you remembered that I'm going to need to hire a nanny. And I was hoping you might help me juggle things until I can make arrangements." She took a deep breath and waited and waited. Delilah was desperate. She knew he probably wouldn't come through. No man in his right mind would agree to giving her what she wanted.

But heaven help her, she needed help. Terror clawed through her. She put both hands on his shirt collar and drew his face toward hers. "I saved your butt. You promised if I asked for something, you would do it." The promise he'd made to her hung between them.

Realization crossed his face. "This is what you want in return?"

She nodded.

"Exactly what do you want?"

"Help."

Benjamin's ingrained truth meter was clanging at top volume. Delilah Montague wasn't telling the truth, the whole truth and nothing but the truth. He'd stake his license to practice law on it.

The baby had been dumped on her, however. He'd witnessed that with his own eyes. She clearly hadn't been expecting the dumping. And just as clearly, she was determined to take care of the baby even though she didn't have a plan.

If he were smart he would find a way to extricate himself from the situation. After all, he was supposed to be using this time to figure out what he was going to do with his life. He needed the soothing drone of power tools, not the ear-rattling scream of a baby or the hormonal disruption Delilah generated by her mere presence.

If he hadn't made a promise to her . . . There went his damn conscience again. It had cost him a great job, his fiancée. If he wasn't careful, it would cost him even more.

Sighing, he pushed back his sleeves and moved toward the diaper bag.

Delilah stepped in front of him. "What are you doing?"

"You said you needed help. There were some papers—"

She tensed. "You don't need to see those."

Benjamin ground his teeth. He liked having all the facts and right now he didn't. When a man didn't have all the facts, there was often a rattlesnake waiting to strike. He'd learned this the hard way. "Was there any information on caring for the baby?"

Delilah blinked. "Oh." She rummaged through the diaper bag and gave him a crumpled sheet of paper.

Benjamin skimmed the instructions and grimaced.

"What?"

"No disposable diapers," he said, shaking his head. "That requirement will eliminate half the nanny prospects."

Delilah bit her lip. "Don't say that."

"They're not gonna beat down your doors to use cloth diapers. You have the yellow pages around here?"

She nodded. "I'll start calling."

"Let me call my mom first," he said, pulling out his cell phone. "She has the inside track on this kind of thing." Feeling Delilah's gaze on him, he checked his watch and dialed the number for his parents' house. "Hey Sadie, this is Ben. Is Mom around?"

The housekeeper answered affirmatively and he waited until his mother came on the line. "Hello Benjamin, how are you, dear?"

"I'm fine. I need a favor. I have a friend who is in need of a good nanny. Can you recommend some agencies?"

Silence followed. "A *friend*?" his mother repeated. "What *friend*? How long have you known this *friend*?"

Benjamin heard the I-want-a-grandchild tone in his mother's voice and could have kicked himself. "Don't get your hopes up, Mom. It's just a neighbor. I only met this person since I moved back to Houston."

"Oh," she said, her voice full of disappointment. "Well, is this neighbor female?"

Benjamin stifled a groan. He knew his mother too well. If he wouldn't give her an instant grandchild, then she would take a prospective daughter-in-law who could provide her with a grandchild. "Mom, this is just a kindness for someone who suddenly has custody of a cousin's baby."

"What happened? Was there a death?"

Great. She wanted the details. "Yeah, it's a sad situation."

"How old is the baby?"

"The baby's age is—" He looked at Delilah.

She lifted six fingers.

"Six months."

"Aw, what a shame." His mother made a *tsk*ing sound. "And your neighbor is going to take care of the little thing. Boy or girl?"

"It's a boy. Mom, about the nanny agencies—"

"And your neighbor is female, right?" she asked, hope creeping into her voice again.

"Mom," he said in a warning tone.

"Well Benjamin, we've been so worried since your engagement fell apart, and you haven't been out with any women even though I've tried—"

"Mom, we can talk about this another time. I need nanny agency recommendations right now. Can you help or not?"

"Well, of course I can," she said, mildly offended. "All the daughters of the women in my bridge club use Nanny Finders. All the daughters of the women in the Women's League use Nanny Connection. Either of those should work. Are you coming to dinner tomorrow night?"

Unwilling to face the well intended grilling and manipulation, he shook his head. "I can't make it tomorrow night. More renovations on the condo."

His mother made a sound of frustration. "Why you insist on doing it yourself when you could easily pay for it, I'll never understand. For that matter, you could move in here—"

Never in a million years. "Mom, you're an angel to offer, but I couldn't accept. Thanks again for the nanny refs. I'll talk to you soon. Tell Dad I said hi." He hung up, feeling Delilah's curious gaze on him. "She gave me two names. You might want to go ahead and give them a call tonight, leave a message on voicemail and follow up in the morning."

"Did she ask if the baby was yours?" Delilah asked bluntly.

"She was hoping. She wants grandchildren and I've dashed her hopes since my engagement broke up."

Delilah's lips lifted in a smile that held a hint of longing. "It might seem like a pain, but it's nice to have someone who cares that much for you."

"She's a mother to the core," he said, then stopped at the expression on her face. "What about your mother?"

"She passed away a long time ago. I didn't live with her after I turned nine."

He gave a low whistle. "And your dad?"

She grimaced. "That's not a great bedtime story." She bit her lip. "So what were the nanny agency references?"

"Nanny Finders and Nanny Connection," he said, watching her as she fanned through the phone book and picked up the phone. As she left her messages in a voice edged with a sultry huskiness, he couldn't help studying her. Her terry robe gaped to reveal her ample cleavage. The bulky material failed to hide the curve of her waist to her hips. Her brown hair skimmed over one eye, giving her a sexy, slightly dangerous look. The style was choppy and hip, rebellious.

Benjamin had always preferred long hair. Delilah was so different from his ex-fiancée. Erin had been blonde and slim, cool and classic.

"Done," she said, hanging up.

He nodded. "I'll take the first shift," he offered.

"First shift?"

"With the baby. If he doesn't sleep well, we could end up staying up all night. It'll be easier to take turns. If you give me a blanket and a pillow, I'll camp on a chair in your den."

Surprise crossed her face. "You're going to stay here tonight?"

He shrugged. "Part of the night. Unless you'd rather handle Willy on your own."

"Oh, no!" she said quickly, panic slicing through her gaze again. "No, I think shifts are a great idea. I—" She cleared her throat as if she were swallowing another helping of pride. "I appreciate your help. Let me get you a pillow."

She disappeared down the hallway, her scent teasing his nostrils even after she left. He wondered what it would be like to follow Delilah down the hall into her bedroom and spend the night drowning himself and his general frustration with his life in her lush curves and bad-girl mouth.

She returned with the pillow and blanket and he watched her place them on a chair. "Would you like a beer?" she asked.

He nodded. "Might as well."

She turned toward the refrigerator. "I think I have about three left from when Cash was still—" She broke off abruptly and pulled out a beer. "Here," she said, handing it to him.

He popped the top. "Who's Cash?"

"Best friend I ever had. He died."

"I'm sorry."

"Me too," she said, her gaze flitting away from his as if the subject were painful for her. She stepped toward the den. "I guess we should get you set up at your post. I hope you'll be able to doze."

"I've lost sleep over less important things than this."

She met his gaze with a half-smile. "You and me both."

Benjamin had been thinking he'd lost sleep over law

briefs and his broken engagement. From the expression on her face, he got the impression that Delilah had lost sleep for a much more pleasurable past time.

She lifted the blanket with one hand and pointed to the chair. He sat down and she covered him. The gesture was oddly nurturing. "Thanks," he murmured.

She nodded and moved to a chair next to his, propping herself on the arm of it.

"Why don't you go to bed?"

"I will soon. My head's too busy right now."

He glanced at the baby. "Big responsibility."

"Yes, he is," she said.

Silence hung between them in the darkness, a comfortable silence with a hint of something electric he couldn't name.

"What was she like? Your fiancée?"

Oddly enough, he didn't feel the supreme irritation he usually felt when someone mentioned his ex-fiancée. Delilah's question didn't have anything to do with the current situation, but he felt like answering. He would have to figure out why later.

"She graduated at the top of her class at Yale. Very bright, ambitious, but beautiful and classy. A pedigree that dates back before the Mayflower."

"Perfect," Delilah murmured.

"I thought so," he said. "She said our life was going to be perfect." And he'd been so proud that he'd done it all, climbed the ranks at the firm and wooed Erin without help from his father and away from the influence of the family name.

"Reality bites. Nobody gets perfection. At least not here on earth."

"You say that as if you know."

"Let's just say I can speak with confidence on the subject of perfection."

"What are your qualifications?"

"My father is an evangelist and he required perfection."

Something in her eyes gave Benjamin an uncomfortable feeling, but now that he was going down this road, he couldn't stop. "What happened when you weren't perfect?"

She shrugged. "The usual. That's not important. What I learned *is* what's important. Don't expect perfection of yourself or anyone else and you'll be a lot happier."

"If you don't shoot for perfection, then what do you aim for?"

"Pretty damn good," she said. Something told him that she gave everything a pretty damn good effort and that her pretty damn good effort left a lot of others in the dust.

Beware of men who are know-it-alls. Dealing with them can bring on PMS-like symptoms.
—DELILAH'S DICTUM

Chapter 5

*D*elilah awakened to a loud cry and her body stiffened. She jerked upright in bed, mentally slapping her brain to attention. Baby. Willy. Her shift.

Her heart pounding a mile a minute, she jumped out of bed and raced to the den. Her legs moving on auto, she nearly plowed into Benjamin's broad back. She blinked at the sight of him holding the baby. What was he doing here? She was supposed to have taken over a second shift, but neither he nor Willy had woken her.

Benjamin turned around and looked at her. "Good morning."

Willie howled.

"I'm guessing he needs to be changed and fed."

"Changed," she echoed, still not operating on all cylinders. Then it hit her. "Diaper," she said, not looking forward to the task.

He nodded.

She held up her hand. "Just one minute. Give me just one minute." She grabbed the paper with the instructions, hurried to the kitchen and opened one of the cans of formula she'd unloaded from the diaper bag last night. She dumped it into a bottle and put it in the microwave for fifteen seconds.

Before the microwave dinged, she returned to the den, grabbed a fresh diaper and the pack of wipes. She looked around the room. "Let's do this on the cushion," she said and Benjamin placed Willy on the cushion, screaming at top volume.

She bit her lip. "I don't think I've changed a cloth diaper before, so you're gonna have to cut me some slack," she said to Willy as she pulled off plastic pants and unfastened the pins. "I just hope it's not a mess— omigod," she said in dismay. "How is it possible for such a small being to produce such a large quantity of—"

"You might not want to leave him uncovered," Benjamin suggested.

She shot him a quick glance of confusion. "What do you mean?"

He pointed. "He might—"

She glanced down and a tiny fountain of baby tinkle sprayed onto her nightshirt. She covered his spigot with a diaper, then looked up at Benjamin. "Could you please bring me another diaper?"

He brought her another and she began to wipe up Willy, none too efficiently. Willy cried louder and Delilah grew more flustered.

"Just keep him covered with the diaper while you clean him up."

"I am," Delilah said.

Willy reached for his diaper area.

"Watch his hands. I think I had a cousin who said she doubled the diaper in the front."

Delilah frowned, trying to coordinate the task. "How do you know so much about cloth diapers?"

"I don't know that much, but I have a lot of cousins who have participated in a great deal of procreation. Maybe he wouldn't cry so much if you talked to him."

Her head pounded. "Talk to him? I can't hold a conversation while I do this, especially with him screaming."

"Make sure you stick the pin away from him, and you need to—"

Delilah swore under her breath. "You're talking too fast."

"Stick the pin," he said in a slow drawn-out voice that indicated he thought she was mentally slow. "Away from—"

Delilah jammed herself with the second pin and swore again. She waved her hand for him to stop then scooped up the baby and stood. "I really appreciate your help," she said, meeting his gaze head-on. "I also recognize that you may be more educated than I am in several areas, but just because I'm not a member of Mensa does not mean I'm a member of Densa."

Benjamin stared at her and cocked his head. "I can honestly say the terms mensa and densa never entered my mind."

"Hmm." Skeptical, Delilah scooped up Willy and carried him to the kitchen. Benjamin joined her as she pulled the bottle out of the microwave. She shook the bottle and tested the temperature of the formula. Willy squirmed and lunged for the bottle. "You're a hungry little bugger."

"Are you suggesting that I'm an intellectual elitist?"

"Yes," Delilah said without pausing. She braced the bottle with her hand while Willie noisily sucked down the liquid.

"Do you always convict without a fair trial?"

"Only when I'm right," she said with a smile.

He rested his hands on his narrow hips. "What makes you sure you're right?"

"Where did your best friends attend college?"

"Harvard and a few from UT."

"How many got advanced degrees?"

"Most," he admitted grudgingly.

"How many did not graduate from college?"

"None, but—"

"I'm not done. How many women have you dated who didn't graduate in the top ten percent of their class?"

He met her gaze. "None, but—"

"Case closed," she said.

"You couldn't convict me on the basis of those answers in a court of law."

"But we're not operating in a court of law. We're operating in Delilah's court."

"You're wrong."

"Am not."

"Yes you are."

"Not," she said and chuckled, remembering the retort she and her childhood friends had given each other years ago. "Till infinity."

His lips twitched. "Your maturity astounds me."

"You just wish you'd thought of it," she sparred.

Willy tossed his bottle on the floor and let out a loud burp.

Surprised at the volume, she gaped at him. "How does such a little person—"

"You asked that earlier," Benjamin said.

She nodded absently. Willie gave a huge grin and chortled, and it was as if the sun came out from behind a cloud. A strange warm feeling tugged at her heart.

Another warm feeling leaked down the side of her

nightshirt. It took her a moment to comprehend the source of the second one. She groaned. "Damn diaper leaked on me. I've got to change him again. I need to take care of that messy one. What do people do with messy cloth diapers anyway?" she muttered.

"My cousin rinsed them in the toilet," Benjamin informed her.

"But how?" She pictured swishing the diaper around with a stick.

"With your hand."

Disgusted, she shook her head. "Absolutely not. There's got to be a better way. I'll get gloves. Or maybe he'll grow out of his allergic reaction."

"A dream is a wish your heart makes," Benjamin said cryptically.

Disliking his tone, she frowned at him. "You know, I asked for your ongoing help with Willy and it occurs to me that you haven't changed his diaper yet."

"No. I took your second shift so you could sleep."

Delilah opened her mouth then shut it. Well, damn. She couldn't argue with that.

"You wanted to say something?" he asked with an arched eyebrow that managed to be both impertinent and sexy. His face was still bruised from his adventure in the garage.

Delilah frowned further. He was a snotty trust-fund baby intellectual elitist. He wasn't supposed to be sexy. She wasn't supposed to feel anything remotely sexy after a six-month-old had just peed on her.

Sighing, she glanced down at Willy. "What are we going to do with him until we get a nanny?"

"I've got lectures this morning. I could take him at lunch."

"So I just have to keep him until noon. Maybe I can go in late if I work late. If I'm lucky, I can interview a couple of nanny prospects this morning."

His lips twitched. "How lucky are you usually?"

She made a face. "Don't rub it in."

He gave a mock salute. "See you noonish."

"For a nooner," she said, the words popping out of her mouth of their own accord. "Sorry. I wasn't serious. I used to flirt a lot with Cash and—" She shrugged. "Bad habit."

"Sounds like you and Cash were pretty close."

"Yeah, we were," she said, not wanting to expound. She was surprised at herself. She didn't trust men easily. It had taken Cash a long time to win her trust. Why was she letting down her guard with Benjamin?

She glanced down at Willy and found her answer. Sheer desperation.

After a harried hour of getting herself and Willy dressed, Delilah put the baby into her car, drove to Walmart and cleaned out the baby department. She almost couldn't fit the playpen in her car, and the swing jutted out the passenger side window. Wal-mart no longer had any more cloth diapers or plastic pants. Despite the fact that she'd bought several pairs of plastic gloves, Delilah had a strong sense that some of his diapers were going to be so bad she would toss them.

As usual, security was nowhere in sight, so she hauled as much as she could upstairs with Willy whimpering for another bottle. When she tumbled into her door, she heard the phone ringing. Dumping the baby paraphernalia in the foyer, she dashed for the phone.

"Yes," she said breathlessly.

"Miss Montague?" her assistant, Sara, asked.

"Yes, what do you need?" Delilah asked, jiggling Willy as his whimpering turned to a fussing sound.

"Is that a baby?"

"Yes, it's a long story. I'll explain another time. What did you need?"

"You have to come to the office. The accountants are here."

"Now?" Delilah couldn't keep the wailing tone from her voice. "Why?"

"They want to talk to you immediately." Sara lowered her voice. "There's also a representative from the executor for Howard Bradford's estate."

Delilah's heart sank. "Oh, shit." She glanced at Willy and felt a slice of guilt. She probably shouldn't swear in front of the baby. "Spit," she amended. "Oh, spit."

"Miss Montague?"

"I'll be there as soon as I can."

By the time Delilah heated up Willy's bottle, he was at full volume. She set him on the floor while she pulled the playpen out of the box. Thank goodness he could sit and hold his own bottle. The playpen required very little assembly. As soon as it appeared stable, she plopped him into the pen and ran to take a three-minute shower. She wasn't sure she got all the soap out of her hair and decided to gel it. Maybe on the way in the car.

Deodorant, yes. Teeth brushed, yes. Black suit. She always wore black when dealing with accountants. Any other color seemed to make them suspicious.

She found Willy in the pen wearing a happy, nearly inebriated expression. The bottle had been tossed out of the pen the same way a beer can was tossed out the window of a car.

Bracing herself, she changed his diaper, but it was just

wet. "I need you to stay happy and quiet for about an hour. Work with me, Willy. You can do it."

After grabbing the diaper bag and driving her infant-mobile to the office, she parked further away from the building than usual. She didn't want to call attention to the swing still poking out of her window.

She hauled Willy and the diaper bag into the office.

Sara gaped at her.

"This is highly unusual, and I don't have time to explain, but could you please watch Willy while I meet with the accountants?"

Sara blinked and slowly rose from her desk. "Well, of course."

Willy chose that moment to let out a loud, wet burp.

On the shoulder of her black suit.

Delilah looked down at the beige formula smeared on her black suit and panicked. "Oh, sh—" She stopped herself

"Wipe it off in the bathroom," Sara said, removing the scarf she wore around her neck. "Then put this on, but be quick. They're waiting for you in the conference room."

Oh, goody. She met Sara's kind gaze. "Thank you."

Sara nodded and took Willy from her arms. Delilah dashed to the ladies' room and was appalled to see a stress rash climbing her neck. She looked at Sara's ladylike scarf and rolled her eyes. She needed a blanket or a sheet to cover the splotchy red of her neck. She looked in the mirror. "You've got to get hold of yourself," she whispered sternly as she wiped off the formula. "What can they do to you besides take away the best opportunity of your life?"

Delilah choked back a moan and stiffened her spine. "Hey, your dad beat you and you've lived in a homeless shelter. You can survive anything."

Taking a deep breath, she jerked a knot in the scarf, lifted her chin and marched toward the conference room fighting the thought that the flames of hell were about to consume her.

She opened the door to the conference room and lifted her lips in a determined smile to the three men attired in black suits. "Good morning. I appreciate your visit," she lied through her teeth.

All three men rose and cleared their throats, before they returned her greeting.

"How can I help you?" she asked.

"Let's take a seat," Jerry Reubens, the senior accountant said.

Delilah had a strong sense that this was going to be bad news. If possible, the men's faces were more sober than usual. As she perched on the edge of her seat, she balled her fists together so tightly her fingernails bit into her palms.

Jerry nodded toward one of the executors of Howard's estate. "Bill, why don't you start?"

Bill cleared his throat. "Miss Montague, as you know, a silent partner by the name of Lone Star Corporation owns nearly half interest in the spa. Since Mr. Bradford's death, the members of this corporation have elected to sell their shares to one member. This member would like to take a more active role in the business decisions concerning the spa."

"But I still own majority interest, don't I?" Delilah said, cursing her lack of foresight in forking over those two measly percentage shares to Helga.

"Yes, but in the interest of a smooth operating business and avoiding conflict, you may want to include the silent partner in future business meetings and decisions."

Delilah frowned. "If I have majority interest, then why do I need to cow-tow to a silent partner who has suddenly decided to become a nosey, noisy partner?"

The men exchanged sideways glances.

Jerry tented his fingers together like a church steeple, not a comforting symbol for Delilah. "A silent partner has the right to request audits and question the ability of the current management. The silent partner may request weekly reports on everything from inventory to safety procedures to clean bathroom checks."

Delilah's stomach knotted. "So what you're saying is I could be nitpicked to death."

"I'm afraid so. Your best course would be to cooperate with the silent partner."

She sighed. "Okay. Who is my silent partner?"

A knock sounded at the partially opened door and Lilly Bradford appeared in the doorway. "Hi there. You don't mind if I come in, do you?"

Jerry glanced at Bill then both men looked at Delilah.

Oh, no. No, no, no, Delilah thought, gazing desperately at Jerry. But Jerry gave a slight nod of his head and Delilah saw the awful truth written on his face.

"I have some thoughts on the current expansion plans," Lilly said coolly as she entered the room. "Good morning," she said to the men, then glanced at Delilah without extending her hand or a greeting. "You've informed Miss Montague of my partnership status, haven't you?"

The room began to spin.

She'd become the guardian of a six-month-old baby last night and the person who hated her more than just about anything, Lilly Bradford, had just become her business partner. Somebody up there was having way too much fun at her expense.

Lilly sat down and opened a folder. "The first thing I'd like to review is your educational background."

A very sore point for Delilah. She stiffened her spine. "When I was hired, I was told my experience was more important."

"And what was your experience when you were promoted?" Lilly asked in a snippy voice.

Delilah wanted to grab her by her Dumbo ears and jerk her into a knot. "I had already worked at Spa DeMay for a few years. As you know, I was trained by your father," she said boldly, daring Lilly to make a snide comment in front of the accountants.

Lilly's cheeks turned pink. Her eyes sparked with fury. "But your education."

"My education is three years of training from your father. I have five years of experience at this spa. What kind of work experience do you have?" Delilah asked, turning the tables on Howard's daughter with a silent uplifted apology. *Sorry, but your princess is getting out of hand.*

Lilly opened her mouth, but nothing came out. "I—I—"

"You have a college education, don't you? What was your major? How does it relate to the spa?"

Lilly began to sweat. When she'd gone to bed by herself again last night, she'd vowed that she would be the perfect choice of a bride for Robert Huntington. After her appointment with the executor of her father's estate yesterday, she'd concluded that one of her first duties as prospective fiancée was to get the trash out of her life. Delilah Montague needed to go.

Even now, though, the woman made her feel uncertain. Lilly had every reason to feel confident and in control. She owned almost half of what Delilah wanted. She could make Delilah's life a living hell while Delilah couldn't do a thing to her. Except make her feel insecure, ignorant and inexperienced.

I am an ice cube, Lilly told herself. *She can't get her claws in me.* "We're not here to discuss my qualifications."

"If we're going to discuss mine, then it's only fair that we discuss yours. What did you say your employment experience was?"

Lilly resisted the urge to squirm. "I worked as my father's personal secretary one summer and I've been active in charity work."

Delilah nodded. "So you worked for your father and for charity." She shook her head. "The problem with charity is you don't really have to make a profit, but when you operate a business, you do."

Lilly wanted to scratch out Delilah's smoldering come-hither eyes that turned men to putty. She swallowed the hard knot of her envy. "Speaking of profit, your expansion plans will cut into profits."

"For the short term, but long-term projections indicate—"

"The problem with projections is they're just projections. Not a guarantee."

"There's no such thing as a guarantee," Delilah said, her gaze womanly wise and worldly.

For a second, Lilly wondered how she'd gained that wisdom. Something told her that whatever it was hadn't been a source of pleasure. She stopped her thoughts. There was no room for compassion or any other gentle emotion for Delilah Montague. She was trash and the garbage needed to be put out on the curb to be taken away.

"I'm going to need more information before I'll agree to expansion in Dallas."

She watched Delilah's gaze turn to steel and felt a moment of trepidation. What if she couldn't get rid of her?

"Fine," Delilah said crisply. "I don't have time right now, but give me a list of your questions and I'll let you know when I have the answers. In the meantime, if you'll excuse me, I must leave."

Delilah stood and walked out of the room, leaving the three men with their tongues hanging out of their mouths. Disgusted, Lilly stood. "I'll see you gentlemen later. Have a good day," she said and walked toward the front of the spa.

As she rounded the corner, she nearly bumped into Delilah as she held a baby. A baby boy, she presumed, taking in the blue jacket and hat that didn't quite cover his jutting ears. She instinctively lifted her hand to make sure hers were covered.

The baby extended his hand to her and gurgled.

Lilly felt a vague softening inside her. She wanted babies with Robert. "Cute baby," she said. "Who does he belong to?"

"A friend," Delilah said vaguely, sighing as she hoisted a diaper bag over her shoulder.

The sight was an odd one. Delilah the vamp with an infant and for the first time Lilly glimpsed dark circles under her father's mistress's eyes. "Why do you have him?" she couldn't resist asking.

Delilah met her gaze. "Because I promised I would."

Babe In Total Control Of Herself aka Bitch.
—DELILAH'S DICTUM

Chapter 6

*A*fter feeling as if Lilly had poked her like a voodoo doll, Delilah collected Willy and drove back to the condo praying that Benjamin would be there as he'd agreed. No guarantees, she told herself. When the going got tough, rich white boys didn't always keep their promises. Her mother had learned that the hard way when two men had bailed on her after she'd gotten pregnant. Delilah's father had been one of them.

Holding her breath and propping Willy on her hip, she pushed open the door to the sight of Benjamin sitting across from a woman with a great deal of facial hair who was dressed like a bag lady.

Benjamin stood and she felt a little tickle in her stomach that he was still there. Anyone else in their right mind would have run screaming in the other direction. He met Delilah's gaze with a deliberately neutral expression. "Delilah, this is Ms. Cannady. Nanny Finders sent her."

"Oh, okay." She passed Willy to Benjamin and extended her hand to Ms. Cannady. "Thank you for coming on such short notice. Please have a seat while we talk," Delilah said, trying to form appropriate questions quickly. The woman's facial hair, however, was very distracting.

"I was just telling your man that I'll take care of the

baby, but I don't cook dinners or clean houses. And I start charging extra if you're five minutes late."

Your man stopped her brain flat for several seconds. Benjamin wasn't *her man*. She shook her head. She was desperate for a nanny. For a sliver of a moment, she wondered if Willy would mind the facial hair all that much. She inhaled and caught a strong whiff of garlic. She couldn't force that combination of sight and smell on Willy. She bit back a sigh of disappointment. "Thank you for letting me know. Can you tell me about your experience?"

"I did baby sitting for ten years for my next-door neighbors."

"Did you keep the children on an ongoing basis?"

"No, I helped out in case of emergencies, but now I need a full-time job. I can start tomorrow."

"The agency told you that we'll be using cloth diapers with the baby, didn't they?" Delilah asked.

Complete silence followed.

"Why don't you use disposables?" Ms. Cannady asked warily.

"The baby is allergic to them."

"Oh."

The woman cleared her throat and rose. "Well, uh, I might have to think about this. It's not good for my, uh, skin to be in water a lot of the time."

"That's certainly understandable," Delilah said, heading for the door. "Thank you for dropping by." She closed the door and looked at Benjamin, wanting to kiss him for being there. She restrained herself. "She was from *Nanny Finders*?"

Setting Willy into the playpen, Benjamin shook his head. "I was just as surprised as you were."

"Do you think they're all going to be like this?" she asked, horrified at the prospect.

Benjamin met her gaze. "Delilah, how many women, and I use the term loosely, have you seen who look and smell like that?"

"True. Not many," she conceded.

"The percentages are on our side. It may take more than a few interviews, but eventually a good nanny will walk through that door."

Stuck on his use of the word *our*, she blinked. *Our*, as if he was in this with her. As if she weren't alone. As if she could count on him. Dangerous thought, she told herself.

She pulled herself together. "I can only hope."

He pointed at her suit. "Looks like you've been busy this morning. You went to work?"

She nodded. "Business emergency. I also went to Wal-mart. I bought all their diapers and some other things. Speaking of which, would you mind bringing them up from my car? I'll wait here with Willy, but the swing is poking out of one of my windows and it looks like rain."

He chuckled and nodded. "No problem. How bad was the business emergency?"

"On a scale of one to ten?" she asked. "Fifty."

He lifted an eyebrow. "What could be that bad at a spa? Did someone fry somebody's hair?"

She shook her head, not wanting to reveal the fact that Benjamin's brother was dating her business partner. The connection was sure to provoke a sticky discussion. "I'm not sure I have the words for it. I don't want to swear in front of the baby. Bad habit of mine," she said, feeling oddly nervous as he moved closer to her. "One of many."

"You're a woman of many bad habits?" he asked.

Her silly heart went pitter-patter. His eyes were too

sexy. "Many," she repeated. "Swearing, eating M&Ms, drinking coffee, drinking champagne cocktails."

"Saving lives and taking responsibility for babies."

"Baby," she quickly corrected breathlessly. She could smell his aftershave. He was way too close. He should move back five feet. Fifty feet. "*One baby*."

"I haven't figured you out. Half the time you come off like you're a hard-hearted, superficial—"

He broke off and she filled in the blank for him. "Bitch," she said. "I believe the word you're looking for is bitch."

"I think that's just a cover."

Oops. A little too close. "No it's not. I'm actually a bitch."

He shook his head slightly, studying her. "No. And the bad-girl image."

"Oh that," she said, waving her hand in a dismissing gesture. "It's not an image. I was born with it. My father said I was the spawn of a devil and angel, but the devil won."

He raised his eyebrows. "Was he the devil?"

She opened her mouth then closed it, blinking at the possibility. "What an interesting thought. My father is a professional evangelist, so I'm sure he believes that he was the angel."

"Then why did he tangle with the devil?"

"Oh, it's always the devil's fault," she said, still feeling nervous about the look in his eyes. She needed to eliminate his curiosity, the almost sexual interest. It made her jittery. "He said my mother tempted him with her earthly wiles. Quick and dirty story is he was a freshly graduated frat boy who hadn't sown enough wild oats. He went into business with the owner of the local bar where we lived, fell head over butt for my mother when she won a wet T-shirt contest. His mother, however, literally suffered a stroke when she learned her boy was playing around with a single-mother floozy. Guilt-ridden, he repented of his sins by ditching my mother and entering seminary. My mother exacted her revenge by naming me Delilah and neglecting to tell him that he had become a father. So you could say I was born and bred to be a bad girl."

"Your mother was a single mother before she had you?" he asked.

Delilah nodded, certain the truth would offend and horrify him. "Yes. She was quite proli—" She searched for the word. It had been one of her words of the day last week. "Prodig—" She frowned.

"Prolific, prodigious—"

She nodded again. "Prodigious. Probably prolific too. Fertile would also work. Four children by four men."

He didn't appear nearly as shocked as she'd expected. He still had that curious, sexually intent look. She'd seen it before a million times, so she knew. "Totally different world than yours. Totally different kind of woman than you're used to," she said, heavily hinting that he should take his interest elsewhere.

"I've had a relationship with a certain type of woman and it didn't work out. Maybe I should try a different kind of woman."

She shook her head. "Oh, don't even think about it. You're used to French champagne and trust me darlin' I am domestic to the bone. Think pedigreed French poodle versus mixed breed. You wouldn't know what to do with me if you had me, and once you had me, you wouldn't be able to get rid of me fast enough."

She saw a hint of challenge light his eyes and bit back

an oath. Oh, crap, she'd awakened the sleeping giant that lurked beneath the skin of almost every proper white boy.

He leaned closer to her and touched his finger to her mouth. "You could be right that I'm used to French champagne. You could be right that I've spent too much time with pedigreed women." He rubbed his finger over her lips in a sensual motion that made her want to slide her tongue over his bold finger. Holding her breath, she resisted.

"But you could be wrong when you say that if I had you," he said in a deep velvet voice that felt far too intimate, "I wouldn't know what to do with you."

She felt her body respond in ways it hadn't responded in months. Swallowing over her surprise that a good boy like Benjamin could generate such heat, she took a step back, determined to cover her reaction. "That's not something I want or need to know."

"That could change."

Willy let out a wail. Delilah smiled. "Not likely." Not with Willy the ultimate sexual mood-killer in residence. Strange as all get out, but it looked as if Willy could protect her from the wiles of Benjamin until he felt he'd repaid his debt of honor to her and got the heck away from her.

Benjamin spent the afternoon baby sitting. When the clock passed five P.M., he got an uncomfortable feeling that Delilah would be late. The image of her going out and forgetting to return for Willy made him itchy. After all, she had emphasized that she was a bad girl. He and Willy had gotten along fine, but Benjamin didn't want to spend the night with the baby.

No sooner had the disturbing thoughts slithered

through his mind like a serpent than Delilah burst through the door surrounded by the aroma of Chinese food and carrying bags from the grocery store and Chinese take-out.

"Nothing fancy," she said to Benjamin. "But I thought you might need some sustenance after hours with Wild Willy. How was he?" she asked warily.

"One diaper change and a nap," Benjamin said with a shrug as he took some of the bags from her. "He was easy." He pulled out two boxes of baby cookies and shook his head. "You're not really planning on giving these to Willy, are you?"

"Well, I wasn't planning on eating them myself. Although I won't make any promises," she said with a mischievous grin.

"Too much sugar," Benjamin said, shaking his head again. "Bad for his teeth, bad for his mood."

"He doesn't have that many teeth yet," Delilah pointed out. "And his mood isn't that great either."

"It doesn't matter. You can rot his teeth out before they're through the gums."

She gave him a double-take. "How do you know so much about this?"

"I turned on the baby channel while Willy was taking a nap."

She gave him a look that mixed curiosity, amusement and entirely too much sex appeal. She shook her head. "Not every man could stand there and say he'd watched the baby channel and still look like a stud."

"What does watching the baby channel have to do with my—" He didn't want to say the stupid word.

"I don't know. Studs just seem to be more interested in other things on television."

"Like the World Wrestling Federation?" He laughed. "You can put the intellectual value of that show at minus—"

"I watch wrestling."

He blinked. "Why?"

"I like the bodies," she said, lifting her hands and moving her fingers as if she were stroking imaginary bodies. "Muscles. Probably a primitive thing. You wouldn't understand," she said in a smoky voice that made him want to pull at his collar.

"So that's the kind of guy you're into?" he asked. "All brawn and no brain."

"I like a man who's open to suggestion, my suggestion," she said and touched her tongue to her lip as she emptied the bags.

Her mouth was plump and rosy and it was too easy to imagine those lips of hers wrapped around his— His body reacted to the graphic image and he mentally swore. "Some women are turned on by men who can take charge."

She nodded. "That's been a weakness of mine every now and then, too, but I just keep reminding myself that taking charge can equal controlling, dominating. About the cookies, here's the deal. The cookies are here in case of emergency."

"What constitutes an emergency?"

"Stop acting like a lawyer. That's to be decided later. Do you like cashew shrimp?"

"Yes."

"Me too, so you'll have to fight me for it," she said and pulled out a bottle of beer. "Corona with a lime okay for you?"

"No Dom Perignon?" he teased.

"Not around here," she said and pulled a bottle of budget bubbly from the bag. She put boxes of rice and oat cereal along with a dozen jars of baby food on the kitchen counter, then mixed a cocktail for herself and cut a lime for Benjamin's beer.

"Isn't Chinese food and a champagne cocktail a strange combination?" he asked as he accepted the beer she offered and joined her at the small table in the kitchen.

"A champagne cocktail goes with any food, any meal. Breakfast, lunch and dinner. Dessert and in the Jacuzzi."

"Except you're not supposed to drink while you're in the Jacuzzi."

She smiled. "I'm not supposed to do a lot of things. Have you always been such a stickler for rules?"

"A lot of the time," he said, but Delilah made him rethink some of those rules on a minute by-minute basis. "Have you always been determined to break the rules?"

"Pretty much," she said. "But you must remember that a rule breaker gave birth to me. It's in the genes," she confided. The phone rang and she picked it up. "Hello?"

Her eyes widened. "Nanny Finders. You want to send over an applicant now? That's fine. But did you tell her we're using cloth diapers?" Delilah nodded. "Good. I'll be looking for her." She hung up the phone. "The answer to our prayers could be walking through that door any minute."

In fact, minutes later, a stout woman who looked around sixty-something strode through the door with an umbrella in her hand. "I'm Mrs. Heidelkin from Nanny Finders. Are you Miss Montague?"

"I am. Please come in. Willy's just waking up from his nap," Delilah said.

Mrs. Heidelkin eyed her watch. "That's much too late

for a nap. You'll have a difficult time getting him down for the night. Babies require a strict schedule."

"I'm sure you're right. We're in a transition phase right now," Delilah said as she scooped up Willy and put him in her newly purchased high chair. She pulled out a jar of baby food green beans.

Mrs. Heidelkin turned up her nose. "I make the baby food from scratch. More nutritious." She saw the cookies on the counter. "And no cookies. Terrible for their teeth and makes them hyper."

Delilah slid a sideways glance at Benjamin.

"Is this Mr. Montague?" Mrs. Heidelkin asked.

"Mr. Huntington," Benjamin corrected the woman. "I'm Miss Montague's neighbor."

Mrs. Heidelkin nodded. "I'm glad I won't have to deal with any men. Men don't know anything about child-rearing."

Delilah met Benjamin's gaze again and her lips twitched. "You have some definite opinions."

"Years of experience. Years."

"Tell me about your experience," Delilah said as she spooned the baby food into Willy's mouth.

"I raised three of my own children and have been nanny to two other children for ten years each. I thought about retiring, but Nanny Finders told me you don't need someone to stay overnight. I can't abide working with men though. I don't like them."

"Would it bother you that Willy is male?" Benjamin asked, finding the woman's antipathy toward men grating.

"Oh, no," she said sweetly. "This way I get them young and teach them the right way. My boys are just as obedient and docile as the girls."

"It's getting late. Did you want to ask Mrs. Heidelkin

anything else?" Benjamin asked Delilah, but gave a slight shake of his head.

She paused. "You're right. Thank you so much for coming, Mrs. Heidelkin. I'll be in touch with the agency if I have any further questions." Delilah passed the baby spoon to Benjamin, then led Mrs. Heidelkin to the door.

"You can't hire her. She's a man hater."

"I know. She might chop Willy's weewee off If I leave him alone with her. This nanny's agency isn't putting out like I'd hoped."

Benjamin was still stuck on Delilah's colorful description of Willy's potential emasculation. He tried to imagine those words coming from his former fiancée's mouth and couldn't.

"Maybe I should place a classified ad?" she said, taking the spoon from Benjamin. "Help wanted: Mary Poppins reincarnated. Must change cloth diapers."

"Only in Disneyland," Benjamin murmured. "Does the job require perfect pitch and a four-octave range?"

She nodded. "And a magic umbrella." She met his gaze. "Thank you for helping out today. You can leave now."

He blinked at her abrupt dismissal of him. He had the sudden understanding of what yesterday's garbage felt like. She was pushing him out the door. Curious, he pushed back. "I'm not in a rush. I can help you all night if you like."

"I don't," she said, studying the green beans. "Like," she added and met his gaze. "I think you should leave."

"Why?"

"Because Willy is my responsibility and I need to get used to it."

She didn't bat an eye, but he sensed she wasn't telling the truth. "And the real reason is?"

She scowled. "I don't know. You ask too many questions. You won't let me give Willy cookies. You make fun of Mary Poppins." She made a huffing sound. "You show signs of being a control freak. It's like I've always said, wealthy, controlling men are a pain in the butt. And they have no sexual creativity."

She shouldn't affect him. She wasn't his kind of woman. He shouldn't feel the urge to beat his chest, howl at the moon, rip off both their clothes and make love to her until she couldn't think straight. Particularly in front of a six-month-old eating green beans.

Benjamin counted to ten then did the only thing he could. He pulled the jar of green beans and spoon from her hands, set them on Willy's high-chair tray and dragged Delilah outside the kitchen. Shoving her back against the wall, he slid his knee between her legs and lowered his mouth to hers.

"What on earth are you doing?" she whispered.

"I'm sick of hearing your ignorant assumption regarding sexual creativity and wealthy men."

"Oh, yeah, and what are you going to do about it?"

"I'm going to shut you up," he said and kissed her.

Getting a man's attention is like holding a hot auction on ebay. A little competition and they're off to the races.

—DELILAH'S DICTUM

Chapter 7

*H*e flicked his tongue over her lower lip then dipped it inside with a seductive, sensuous stroke. Heat flicked to life and roared up from her feet to her cheeks. He sucked her lip into his mouth, coaxing, daring her to respond. His kiss said *give it to me, baby.*

She instinctively slid her tongue into his mouth and felt him draw it deep inside. Her nipples turned to hard buds against his tight chest. Suddenly lightheaded, she waved her hands, reaching for something solid and stable. She found his arms and wrapped her fingers around the bulge of his biceps.

He gave a low growl that vibrated inside her while he rubbed his hard pelvis against her and she felt her blood pool in sensitive places.

Her body responded to his with hair-trigger speed. Fast, hard, dizzy. *What is this?* she thought, confused. She wasn't accustomed to being out of control unless she decided it was time to roll with it. She was accustomed to being the one in control. What the—

She pulled her mouth from his and sucked in a breath

of air. "If you don't move away from me, I'm going to re-arrange your family jewels."

"You didn't like me kissing you," he said in disbelief and lowered his hand to touch one of her rigid nipples.

She swallowed a moan.

"Tell the truth."

"I can honestly say I don't like what you did to me," she said in a voice that needed far more oomph to be convincing.

"I'm teachable. What didn't you like?" he asked, lowering his open mouth to her throat.

How easy it had been for him to put her into do-me mode. She inhaled a quick breath to clear her mind, but caught a draft of his aftershave instead. Her body was begging to be very bad, but some weird sense of self-preservation was screaming to back off.

Gritting her teeth, she shifted her position slightly and jerked her knee upward into his hardened crotch. Benjamin stiffened and not from pleasure.

He swore and stepped back. "Okay," he said, dark arousal draining from his eyes. "I somewhat deserved that."

"I warned you," she said, surprised that she still felt hot and bothered.

"Yes, you did," he said speculatively. "But you kissed me back."

Uncomfortable with the truth, she shrugged. "It's been a while."

He raised his eyebrows in surprise as if he couldn't imagine her going for more than two days without sex. "Really?"

"Really. But you're *really* not my type."

"You're not mine either," he said. "Makes you wonder what would happen if we both went against type."

Delilah could almost hear the crackle of a brush fire. She'd avoided wealthy, overeducated men due to her mother's experience, although she'd harbored a forbidden curiosity.

Something thumped on the floor in the kitchen, followed by a happy shriek. Willy, she thought with a wry smile. Her sex control switch. She and Benjamin rushed around the corner to find his face and hair covered in baby green beans as he played with a scoop of the strained vegetable on his tray.

Benjamin chuckled. The sound was low and sexy.

Delilah ignored her reaction to it. "Gross," she said, heading for the paper towels. "He'll definitely need a bath."

"Have fun," Benjamin said.

When she scowled at him, he hooked his thumbs in his jeans, drawing attention to his pelvis. "I gotta apply some ice."

As she dampened the towels, Delilah rolled her eyes. "I didn't knee you hard enough to cause pain, just enough to get your attention."

"It's the first time I've been kneed by a woman, so I'll have to see."

Her lips twitched. "So I was your first? I think I like that."

"Yeah," he said dryly. "You can say you bring out the worst in me."

"If that was the worst," she began, then broke off. She glanced at Benjamin and knew she'd been caught. Well, damn.

"Who knows?" he taunted her. "I might could have

gotten a lot worse if we'd continued. Night-night, Miss Delilah."

She told herself not to watch as he walked through the hall toward the door, but she couldn't resist stealing a peek. Benjamin had a very nice backside. She wondered what it looked like naked.

Benjamin had been summoned to his father's home office for a critical consultation session with his brother Robert and his father.

His father, whose fit broad-shouldered body belied the fact that he was knocking on sixty, pulled three cigars from his desk humidor and gave one to Robert and another to Benjamin. Benjamin didn't light his. He didn't like cigars all that much. He did, however, accept the good scotch.

"You have everything going for you," William Bradford said to Robert. "But one thing would cap it off. An engagement. You need to settle down."

This was one of the many reasons Benjamin had wanted to escape Texas. He looked at his brother's expression of discomfort and knew he could be standing in Robert's shoes if he hadn't gone east for his education. In fact, when he'd first returned, his father had suggested that Benjamin take another look at politics. Benjamin had firmly rejected the idea.

"I don't know, Dad," Benjamin said, throwing his brother a lifesaver. "Robert has probably gotten a lot of mileage out of being one of Houston's top-ten bachelors."

His father tossed him a glowering look as if to say he'd been brought here to support his father's agenda. "Nonsense. The voting public likes a stable, settled man. And an engagement would bring some sparkle to the campaign. Especially an engagement to a woman like Lilly Bradford. Her father was rough around the edges, but her mother was pure Texan until she remarried and moved to New York a few years ago. Plus Lilly's loaded."

Robert moved his shoulders as if fighting a tight feeling. "Lilly's nice, and she's pretty, but—"

"But what?" William demanded. "What's not to like?"

"I don't know if I love her that way or not."

William gave a rough chuckle. "You don't have to love her now. You can grow to love her. And if you don't, then you can break the engagement and we'll find somebody else. After the election, of course."

Robert frowned and set down his cigar. "I don't know, Dad. Lilly's not very experienced. If we got engaged and I dumped her, she might have a hard time with it."

Benjamin was relieved to see Robert exhibit a modicum of consideration. It was a sign that their father hadn't completely corrupted his thinking. Robert had been polished by their father so much that Benjamin almost hadn't recognized his brother when he'd arrived home. During their growing-up years, Robert had been labeled a geek and Benjamin had gotten into more than one fistfight in his defense. It was hard to believe that Robert had once been a shy, gangly, self-conscious boy who'd buried himself in his studies and the History Channel. Once Benjamin had left, their father had turned his full attention to Robert, and an amazing transformation had taken place. Benjamin just hoped the transformation wouldn't turn out to be similar to that of Frankenstein's.

William put his arm around Robert's shoulder. "If you end up breaking the engagement, she'll get over it. They all do."

"I'm not ready to make this kind of commitment."

William gave the infamous heavy sigh designed to trigger guilt. "Robert, a lot of people have worked hard for you. You've got to be willing to make some sacrifices too."

"But marriage? I want to marry the right woman."

"Lilly is the right woman, trust me. A campaign donation from her could do wonders for the coffers."

"Did you marry Mom for her money?" Benjamin asked quietly.

William shot him a sharp look. "Of course not. I had to fight through a dozen of her boyfriends to win her. You know that."

"So you were in love with her?" Benjamin continued.

"From the first time I rescued her from a drunken Romeo at a party."

"That's what I want," Robert said. "I don't feel that way about Lilly. What do you think, Ben?"

Benjamin downed another swallow of scotch, relishing the burn. "I think if you can live without her, then you shouldn't marry her."

William made a sound of disgust. "You can't pay attention to him." His father turned away from Robert and mouthed, *you're supposed to be helping*.

Benjamin shrugged and took another swallow of scotch.

"He's jaded because his engagement just fell apart," William said, pointing at Benjamin. "And look at the bruises on his face. He doesn't even have the sense to move in with his mother and me while he gets his act together. Instead he's living in a neighborhood where he gets beat up by thugs."

Benjamin knew he was living in one of the safest neighborhoods in Houston, but because he wasn't living in the same neighborhood as George Bush, Sr., his father thought he was living in the slums. He rose to his feet. "I've imparted about all the wise counsel I can," Benjamin said. He patted Robert on the back. "You'll do the right thing," he assured his bewildered younger brother. "I know Dad wouldn't want to manipulate you into doing something that goes against your values," he said more for his father than for Robert.

"No need for you to rush off," William said.

"I'm not rushing. I'm just leaving," Benjamin said, setting his empty shot glass on the tray on his father's desk.

"Let me walk out with you," William said. "I'll be back in a minute, Robert."

Benjamin could have found the front door with his eyes closed, so he knew his father must want to say something to him privately.

William closed the door behind him. "Are you sure you won't reconsider running?"

Benjamin looked at his father as if he'd lost his mind. "I can't do that. You've gotten endorsements from groups who have pledged to support Robert. On top of that—"

"They would prefer you," William said, lowering his voice. "Everyone talks about how much they'd hoped you'd go into politics. Robert is struggling. He just doesn't have your combination of brains and backbone."

Benjamin felt nauseous. "Robert is the candidate. I'm not. I don't want to run. I never wanted to run."

"Well, what are you going to do instead? Teach?" he said in disdain. "You could do so much better. You could have been president."

Benjamin groaned, grateful he would be out the door in three more steps. "I don't want to be president. I'm not running for political office, Dad. Ever."

William wagged his finger. "Never say never."

"I didn't," Benjamin said. "I said ever. Not that you're listening. Ease up on Robert and he might surprise you. I'll see you around."

"Be careful in that parking garage. Your face looks like hell."

"Thanks, Dad. You too," he said, knowing his father would catch his ambiguous insult in a moment. He closed the door behind him and was halfway down the front steps when he heard his father's voice.

"You smartass. You just told me my face looked like hell, didn't you?" he said with a rough chuckle. "You're a smart one. You would have had them at your feet in politics, boy."

"I'll leave that to you and Robert. Take care, Dad." As he got into his car, he tried not to let his father's taunts stick in his craw. But the truth was he'd been nursing his wounds for a while. It was time to figure out what he wanted to do next.

Lilly stood outside Delilah's office, listening to her talk with her assistant.

"Two nanny applicants down the toilet. All I want is a modern-day Mary Poppins. Is that too much to ask?"

Sara chuckled. "I can keep Willy in the evenings sometime if you like."

Lilly cocked her head to one side in speculation. Nanny? It sounded like Delilah was planning on keeping this kid around for awhile. She frowned, wondering why. Delilah didn't seem the nurturing type at all. She was too busy seducing sugar daddies like her father.

Anger hardened her heart and she lifted her chin. She was here to check on things.

Just because she could.

She stepped closer, listening to the women talk.

"I'm not letting you sit home with a baby. You're a free woman now, Sara. The world is your playground. You need to get out and meet men. You need to get out and let them chase you. Men love the chase," Delilah said in a confiding tone.

Lilly paused. *Men love the chase.* Robert didn't have to chase her. She was always waiting for him.

"It's strange as Hel—sinki, but first you have to be available and then you have to be not as available," Delilah said. "Otherwise, they take you for granted. And definitely keep more than one on the string. It's like an auction on ebay. The perceived value of an item sky-rockets if more than one person wants it."

Lilly wrinkled her nose. Delilah's words were cutting too close to the bone. Shrugging them off, she strode into the office. "Hello, I'm here to check on things."

Delilah blinked as she jiggled Willy on her hip. "What things?"

"Business," Lilly said.

Delilah exchanged a long-suffering glance with Sara. "Okay. Step into my office. What would you like to know?"

"For starters, I'd like to know if your assistant is using company time to take care of that baby," Lilly said.

The baby smiled at her and Lilly had to purse her lips to keep from smiling in return.

"Sara is helping me just until I make other arrangements," Delilah said. "You don't need to worry about it."

"If your personal life is affecting your performance at the spa, then I should be concerned about it," Lilly retorted.

Delilah's eyes froze. "My personal life will never affect my performance here at the spa. If I had twelve more children and both my legs were broken, I would still be the best director for the spa. Would you like a breakdown of services we provided last week? We set a new record for Botox parties and facials. Here. Hold Willy while I locate the report on my desk." Delilah plopped Willy in Lilly's arms and Lilly stared at the baby.

Willy squirmed, reaching to tug at her hair. He yanked then beamed at her with a big smile.

"No, no," Lilly whispered, trying to unwrap his fist from her hair. He bounced in her arms, chortling, and she didn't have the heart to stop him even though he was pulling entirely too hard.

Delilah turned with a sheaf of papers in her hand. "Here's the—" She broke off at the sight of Willy's hand tangled around Lilly's hair. "Well, well, Romeo. Now we know the truth. You have a thing for blondes," she said with a smile. "Pretty, long-haired blondes. I didn't think I'd have to start watching you in that area so soon." She untangled Lilly's hair and put him on her hip. "Sorry. Here's the report," she said, handing over the sheaf of papers. "It should make you sleep better about our profits."

Unsettled by seeing Delilah with a baby, Lilly shrugged. "I'll study it carefully."

"You do that," Delilah drawled with more than a hint of amusement in her voice.

Lilly couldn't stand the woman's confidence. She seemed to have so much of it, when Lilly had none. Lilly had no doubt that Delilah had been brought up without the finer things including a college education, but she had so much confidence she fairly oozed it. Lilly resented her for it.

"I'll be checking on things from now on," Lilly told her.

"By all means," Delilah said with a careless wave of her hand. "I'm surprised you have time though. I'd have thought Robert Huntington would have popped the question and you would be busy with his campaign."

Lilly felt her cheeks heat. Delilah had to know that she had just struck Lilly at her most vulnerable point. The woman wasn't just confident. She was vicious. "That's my personal business," she said.

Delilah's eyes rounded. "Oh, well excuse me. I thought the deed was done. Robert's a bit slower than I had thought."

Lilly immediately rose to his defense. "Robert is a man of integrity and honor. He wouldn't make this kind of decision lightly."

Delilah nodded. "I guess I can see that. Probably runs in the family," she muttered. "Amazing though, it doesn't matter if they have honor or not, you can't let them think you're waiting by the phone. But I'm sure you already know that."

"Of course," Lilly said with far more confidence than she felt. "I'm sure I'll see you again soon."

Delilah gave a smile that didn't reach her eyes. "I'm sure you will." She glanced down at Willy and smiled genuinely. "Wave bye-bye, sweetie."

Willy waved and Lilly would have to have been made of stone not to wave and smile in return. Tossing her hair over her shoulder, she strode outside to her Beemer. As much as she detested Delilah, the maneater had unwittingly planted some ideas about what she needed to do with Robert.

Her cell phone rang to the tune of Beethoven's Fifth,

and she instinctively reached for it. She glanced at the Caller ID. Robert. He was probably calling her at the last minute to meet him for dinner. She wrinkled her nose. She and Old Faithful had a lot in common.

Her finger hovered over the button to answer while Delilah's words echoed in her mind, *Don't be so available*. It killed her not to answer. By the time the phone stopped ringing, she was nearly hyperventilating. She wasn't sure she was cut out to be a maneater. She didn't have the constitution for it. Just not answering the phone made her feel like she needed to run to the bathroom from nerves.

What if Robert never called again? What if he called someone else to join him for the fundraiser at the country club? Sweating, she closed her eyes and stiffened her backbone. This was ridiculous.

If Delilah Montague could wrap her wily father around her finger, then Lilly should be able to rope Robert Huntington. Perhaps he just needed a little prod.

Feeling like a conniving she-devil, she listened to the message Robert had left. As expected, he'd invited her to the fundraiser tonight. She dialed the number for the executor of her father's estate and asked if he could recommend an escort for the evening. In fifteen minutes, she had a date.

She hoped her bladder would survive the evening. She would stash a paper bag and valium in her evening purse.

The average person kisses only two weeks of their lives. If the average lifespan is 76.9 years, we're wasting a lot of time.

—DELILAH'S DICTUM

Chapter 8

Robert Huntington greeted so many people the faces began to blur until he saw Lilly. He reached for her hand and smiled.

"Lilly!" he said, with a mixture of surprise and relief. "I was beginning to think you wouldn't make it."

Her hand felt stiff and her face looked flushed.

"Is something wrong? Are you not feeling well?" he asked. That would explain why she hadn't returned his call.

"I'm fine. I didn't get your call until—" She broke off and shrugged. "I'm um here with—" She broke off again and cleared her throat. "Robert, this is Greg Weatherby. I met him through the executor of my father's estate."

Robert automatically extended his hand to the young man at Lilly's side, but his brain paused. "Nice to meet you, Greg. Glad to have you here tonight."

"I was glad Lilly could join me," Greg said, smiling at Lilly.

Somewhere deep inside, Robert felt an odd discomfort. It was as if someone had moved the furniture in his bedroom without telling him. He didn't have time to figure it out now. "You like to play golf?" Robert asked. After months of campaigning, he was an expert with safe questions.

"Always. I'm still shooting for under par three times in a row. Work interferes."

"What do you do?" Robert asked casually, aware that he was spending more than the recommended three minutes with Lilly's escort. He assessed Greg, drawing comfort from the fact that her escort was shorter than he was. Odd as hell thought.

"Estate attorney with Long & Forrester."

An attorney. Robert stood straighter. "Really? Where'd you graduate?"

"Yale. You?"

"Texas born and bred," Robert said, distracted by a strange competitive urge. "UT. You two enjoy yourselves. Lilly," he said with a nod and moved onto the next couple.

He was expected to deliver a stirring, yet entertaining speech tonight. He had also expected to have Lilly by his side. It wasn't that he had strong, overwhelming feelings of passion for her. He just depended on her. His father was always pushing, pushing, pushing. Robert knew the pushing was motivated by his desire to win the election, but his father wasn't a restful person to be around. When Robert left his father, he sometimes felt as if he needed a drink or two. When he'd been a child, his mother had attributed Robert's bed-wetting to his father's pushiness.

Lilly expected little of him. She was undemanding and adoring, and she didn't cause him one bit of grief. Being with her wasn't overly stimulating, but it was a relief.

He stole a quick glance across the room, finding her chatting with her escort as she twirled a glass of wine. The discomfort inside him twisted again, making him frown.

He felt a nudge on his back and turned to find his father at his side.

"What the hell is wrong with you, boy?" his father asked in a low voice. "You're supposed to be circulating and inspiring donations. This is a well-padded crowd."

Robert's irritation pinched him harder. "I've been meeting and greeting."

"Well, do it more. Are you ready with your speech?"

"I'm ready," Robert said, his gaze wandering again to Lilly.

"Why isn't Lilly with you?" his father demanded.

"There was a mix-up. She didn't get my message until late."

His father sighed. "If you screw up your chances with her—"

Robert's frustration spiked. "Lay off, Dad. I haven't screwed up anything," he said and decided to get himself a drink. He was supposed to be charming and persuasive tonight and he just wasn't in the mood. It couldn't be related to Lilly, he told himself as he downed a scotch. She wasn't that important to him. She couldn't be.

Robert delivered his speech with panache. He was a competitor. He may not be his brother Benjamin, and sometimes he felt like he'd spent his entire life living in Benjamin's shadow, but Robert had been dreaming and practicing for the moment when his father would finally see that he was the real choice for politics. He wasn't as good-looking as Benjamin. Heaven knew, he wasn't as naturally gifted, but he could be just as determined. Maybe more. The years of coming up on the short end of the stick during the comparisons had toughened him.

There'd been times when he'd been so jealous of Benjamin that he'd nearly hated him, but not now. Robert could tell that Benjamin truly didn't want to be in politics. He'd been a little nervous when Benjamin had suddenly returned to Houston, but Benjamin seemed intent on deflecting their father's never-ending pressure to show the rest of the world how superior the Huntingtons were. Benjamin was determined to find his own way. Robert couldn't help admiring his brother for his ability to buck their father. Even tonight, Benjamin had showed up for a few minutes to show his support then scooted away.

After Robert finished giving his speech, he cordially accepted congratulations and promises of support. The smiles and faces smudged together and he felt light-headed. The pressure of the last month suddenly settled over him like a noose. He slipped out onto the balcony and inhaled a draft of cool air. He glanced around and was surprised to find Lilly staring onto the well-lit grounds of the club.

"What are you doing out here?" he asked, moving closer to her. "I would have thought it would be too cold for you out here."

She turned and shook her head. "No. It felt stuffy in there."

He nodded. "Too much hot air."

"I didn't say that."

"No, I did," he said dryly. "It's a political function. There's enough hot air in there to fill up a balloon and send it to China."

She laughed. "It's not that bad. You did well with your speech, but you always do."

"Thank you," he said, her presence calming him. "You look nice tonight."

Her cheeks bloomed with color. "Thanks."

He thought of her date and a shot of irritation corrupted his sense of peace. "Where's your date?"

"He's putting together a round of golf, so I thought I'd catch a breath out here."

Robert nodded. "Can I call you later? After the fundraiser's over?"

She swallowed and bit her lip. "I—uh." She lifted a shoulder helplessly and her gaze skittered away from his. "I may not be home until late. Greg mentioned something about dancing."

"Dancing?" Robert echoed with a frown. "I didn't know you liked to dance."

She gave a tight smile and fluttered her hand. "You've been busy. You probably didn't think to ask."

Confused as hell by the burst of emotions circling inside him, Robert just nodded.

"We should probably go back in," she said. "It was great seeing you. You did a wonderful job as always."

"Thanks," he muttered, wondering why he felt as if he'd been kicked in the teeth.

Tilly should be pleased. It appeared that she had knocked Robert sideways with that dancing comment. It appeared that Delilah's advice was working. She should feel triumphant.

She felt like puking.

She was seriously beginning to wonder if she possessed the fortitude to be a manipulative she-devil. The beat of the music in the disco pounded in her brain. Her face hurt from smiling and her feet hurt from dancing. A slow number eased through the dance floor and Greg took her into his arms.

She allowed it, but she was miserable. She wished she were with Robert. She would rather be home waiting for him to call than dancing with Greg. Greg was nice enough, but he wasn't Robert.

Unable to stand another moment of pretending, she pulled back. "I think I'm ready to go home. I have an early appointment and I'm tired. Do you mind?"

"Not a problem. Can I take you to dinner on Tuesday?"

No, she wanted to say, but swallowed the refusal. She would like to believe that Robert would look at her differently now, but she couldn't be sure. "That sounds nice."

"Good," he said, his gaze falling over her with sensual interest. "And I promise not to discuss golf this time."

The semi-lust she saw in his eyes caught her off guard. Lilly had never suffered any delusions about her sexual attractiveness. Cosmetics, the right hairstyle and orthodontics had given her a pleasing appearance, but she was clueless and awkward at the very idea of seduction.

"I'll hold you to it," she said lightly.

"You can hold me anytime you want," he said suggestively.

Lilly blinked at the heat that rushed through her. She gave Greg a second look and sighed. She didn't really want Greg to want her. Why couldn't Robert look at her that way?

Willy let out another stream of howls even as Delilah jiggled him and paced. She was ready to start howling with him. He'd been fussing on and off, mostly on, for two hours starting at 10 P.M.

She was getting desperate. Through her sleep-deprived mind, she tried to think of anything that made Willy stop crying. Anything she hadn't tried.

The swing wasn't even working tonight. The swing, Delilah had concluded, had been invented by an angel. It usually put Willy into a drooling daze. It was so effective she'd considered keeping him there until his first birthday.

The only other time he didn't cry was in the car.

She glanced down at her nightgown, then back into Willy's unhappy face. "Okay, buddy boy. We're going for a midnight ride. I may not be able to think straight in the morning, but that won't be anything new."

She pulled on her long, black winter coat and stepped into a pair of black suede clogs. She wouldn't stop anywhere. No one was going to see her. If she could get him asleep, maybe she could get some sleep too. Grabbing her car keys, she stepped out of her door. Willy's howl echoed down the hallway and she winced. Geez, this kid was so loud she feared he might break glass.

She quickly punched the elevator button.

She heard a door open and saw Benjamin glance into the hallway.

"Where are you going?"

"For a drive," she said.

He glanced at his watch. "At this time of night?"

"The swing isn't working. He doesn't cry in the car." The elevator dinged, announcing its arrival. "Oh, here's my ride. Good—"

"I'll come with you."

She stared at him as the elevator doors whisked open. "Why would you want to do that?"

He shrugged, tossing her a look of irritation. "You forget. I can't sleep. I can't use power tools at night anymore or my neighbor will kill me."

"Ah," she said with a smile of satisfaction. "That neighbor would be me."

"I might as well come with you. Let me grab my jacket," he said.

Delilah found his offer both comforting and disquieting. She was still disturbed by her response to Benjamin two nights ago. The man made her feel weird. She glanced at Willy and the open elevator doors. "That's okay. We'll be fine," she said and stepped inside. She pushed the button for the parking garage.

Breathing a sigh of relief, she jiggled Willy until the elevator doors whisked open. She walked swiftly to her parking space and opened the locked doors of her car remotely. She opened the door to the backseat and put Willy into his car seat. The volume of his howling increased, making her fumble with the fasteners.

"Need some help?" Benjamin asked from behind her.

Delilah nearly jumped out of her skin. She whipped around to find Benjamin inches from her. "Don't do that," she hissed, her nerves rattled.

"Just keeping my promise to help," he said innocently, but she knew better. This was the same man who'd wedged his hard thigh between her legs and made her wet in ninety seconds.

"But I didn't ask for your help tonight," she said.

"You asked for my help in general with Willy until you get things under control," he said.

As if on cue, Willie let out a shriek of displeasure.

"It doesn't look like things are under control yet."

Delilah tossed Benjamin her car keys and headed for the passenger side of the car. "Okay, you may as well make yourself useful, but I get to choose the music."

"The classical music station features opera at midnight," he said, climbing into the driver's seat. He adjusted the seat to accommodate his long legs.

"There's a reason opera is featured at midnight," Delilah muttered, putting her favorite blues CD into the player as Benjamin pulled out of the parking lot. "No one who is awake wants to hear it." After she turned the heater on, she rested her head against the headrest and counted. "Bet this won't take longer than ninety seconds. One-two-three—"

"Why are you counting?"

"To see how long it takes Willy to stop crying. Four-five-six-seven . . ." She stopped at 33 when no more fussing sounds emanated from the backseat. She cautiously glanced at Willy. His eyes were closed and he was sleeping. He looked so sweet and peaceful. A strange gooey feeling pervaded her. It was probably related to lack of sleep and the electric bun warmer heating her rear end.

"New record," she said. "Thirty-three seconds."

"You want to go back and put him to bed?"

Delilah twitched at the thought. "Absolutely not. He hasn't been asleep long enough. He'll wake up again and scream until he loses his voice." She blinked. "Hey, maybe—"

"That would require a lot of screaming. Maybe more than you can stand tonight. Babies are amazingly resilient."

She returned her head to the headrest. "Then drive on, James."

"Any location preference?"

"Cancun," Delilah said, closing her eyes and going there in her mind. "Or Grand Cayman. Although Cash told me it's hideously expensive there. He said the customs agents are outfitted with high-power vacuum cleaners that suck the money out of your pockets as soon as you enter the country."

Benjamin chuckled, and the sound vibrated inside her. "Colorful guy, your Cash."

Delilah sighed. "Yes, he was." She felt a pang of longing for her good friend, but shook it off. She didn't feel like being maudlin tonight. She closed her eyes and inhaled, catching a draft of Benjamin's aftershave. "What are you wearing?"

"Leftover shirt and slacks from an event for my brother at the Country Club. I ditched the tie when I got home."

"I don't mean your clothes. I mean your—" She inhaled. "Your smell. Is it aftershave or cologne?"

"Aftershave."

"Mmmm."

"You like it or not," he said.

She nodded. "What is it?"

"I don't know."

She shot a glance at him. "What do you mean you don't know?"

He shrugged. "My fiancée had it created for me."

"That was creative of her."

He gave a short chuckle. "Yeah, except she didn't like the scent."

"You're kidding?" she asked in disbelief.

"No. Why?" He briefly met her gaze.

She felt a ripple of discomfort at the tension that seemed to zing between them then shook it off. Nothing was going to happen. They had a baby in the backseat, for Pete's sake. "Because it's yummy. It's mouthwatering."

"Is that so?"

"Yes, the scent is," she said.

"But not me," he concluded.

"I wouldn't know," she said, closing her eyes. "But you do have that handicap."

"What's that?"

"Too controlling." She waved her hand. "Now let me go back to Cancun."

"Too crowded," Benjamin interjected.

She frowned, but kept her eyes closed. "This is my fantasy. But I'm flexible. I'll take Grand Cayman. The sun is blazing. A breeze is blowing over my lazy body while I lounge under an umbrella. A waiter delivers some sort of tropical drink and a masseur arrives to give me a massage. Great hands, great body," she said with a sigh. "Great eye candy."

"But he can't smell like me," Benjamin taunted.

Delilah refused to answer, choosing instead to imagine the sound of gentle waves lapping on the shore . . . while she inhaled Benjamin's delicious scent. She drifted off . . .

An hour later, something woke her. She blinked and shifted in her seat. The car had stopped. It was parked. She glanced out the front window then looked at Benjamin. "Why are we here?"

"It's been one of my favorite places for years," he said, his seat pushed back and his head leaning on his headrest. His hair tousled in an attractive manner, he stretched his legs and nodded toward the window. "Nice view, isn't it?"

Delilah took a second look and agreed. From the top of the hill, the lights of Houston glittered like diamonds. "It's pretty. How long have you been coming here?"

"Since I got my driver's license," he said, shooting her a lazy smile.

Delilah noticed the lack of other cars around and raised an eyebrow. "Something tells me you weren't always focused on the view outside."

"Depends if I came alone or not. I haven't been here since I moved back." He shook his head. "Haven't been here in years. It's so quiet."

Delilah glanced into the backseat. "Until Willy wakes up."

"He's out."

"What makes you so sure?"

"Male thing. I just know."

She slid him a sideways glance. "Yeah, right," she said, not bothering to conceal her skepticism.

"You'll see. Quit obsessing and enjoy the view."

She opened her mouth to protest then closed it. She couldn't deny that her moments of peace lately had been nonexistent. Her mind wandered to thoughts of the spa.

"Stop thinking," he whispered.

Delilah stared at him. "How do you know what I'm thinking? My mind could be completely blank."

"Your body talked. You tensed."

Delilah met his gaze in the darkness. She had an odd feeling about this man. He wasn't totally what he seemed, and he had an uncanny ability to read her. Since he was such a smarty-pants, she wouldn't expect him to be so sensually aware.

And there was the way he'd kissed her until her kneecaps turned to water. She hadn't met anyone in a long while that made her this curious. With her increasing responsibilities at the spa, she'd had little time. She didn't have time now, but she sure had the curiosity.

She could feel her body humming like it was an electric fence. She made a rule of not getting involved with men like Benjamin. Too educated, well-bred, he was slumming. His interest would be fleeting. If she got attached . . . But she never did, she reminded herself. She was always careful not to get attached, not to count on a man, with Howard as the exception to the rule. But that had been different.

"It's gonna happen," Benjamin said.

Delilah blinked, her face heating with unusual embarrassment. For a moment she feared he'd read her mind, but he couldn't possibly.

"What's gonna happen?"

He leaned closer. "You and I are gonna happen."

Delilah gulped. She sucked in a quick breath and felt his aftershave seep into her bloodstream. She needed an antidote. "You may be going to happen, but you and I are not going to happen."

He lifted his thumb to her bottom lip. "You're right about one thing," he said with sexy wryness. "Until you and I happen together, I'm going to happen by myself."

A searing hot visual of Benjamin pleasuring himself singed her mind and made her feel as if she were burning from the inside out. She shouldn't feel aroused, She absolutely shouldn't feel aroused. "Well, don't make yourself go blind," she told him

He chuckled and the sound was low and intimate, too inviting. His tone said, *come have some fun with me.* Delilah didn't have time for fun. Since she'd left her father's house, she'd always lived by the mantra that nothing was so serious or terrible that a girl couldn't have a little fun. Between Howard's death, pressures at the spa, Willy, and sleazoid Guy, Delilah felt overcommitted and overwhelmed.

"If I had time, I might spend some with you," Delilah admitted. "But I have too much else to do right now. I don't have time to play."

"Everybody needs a little playtime, Delilah."

"I agree, and trust me, I'll get mine later." *With some man who's easier to manage.*

The memory of the pain of childbirth may fade quickly, but the memory of changing a messy cloth diaper sure doesn't.

—DELILAH'S DICTUM

Chapter 9

*R*obert checked his watch for the tenth time as the Treasurer for the Ruritan Club droned on and on. He'd invited Lilly to attend this meeting where he was guest speaker, but she'd been busy.

Robert frowned.

He'd called her at the last minute, which he supposed was part of the problem. Except it hadn't been a problem before last week.

Her voice had been breathless with apology as she'd explained that she'd already agreed to join Greg for a swim at the country club followed by dinner. It was too easy for Robert to imagine Lilly frolicking in the pool with Greg the shark. He'd probably lure her into the hot tub. Maybe they would skip dinner.

Robert felt his temperature rise. Lilly was cavorting with another man and he was stuck here with a bunch of old farts. His father would immediately correct him. They weren't old farts. They were potential voters, potential constituents.

As the president gave him a glowing introduction, Robert stifled a sigh and put on his game face. He was here to discuss social security and he would damn well do it in the shortest speech on record.

Forty-five minutes later, Robert walked through the front doors of the country club and headed for the swimming pool. He knew the club housed two swimming areas. The first larger pool was filled with competitive swimmers and two water aerobics classes. It was busy and noisy and he looked in vain for Lilly.

His gut twisted as he walked toward the smaller swimming pool. It was older, smaller, and not as popular as the other well-lit Olympic-sized pool. Heat and humidity steamed the windows to the pool area, hindering his ability to spy— To see the occupants.

Robert pushed open the door and heard low voices and feminine giggling.

"No, Greg, I really don't think that's a good idea," Lilly said with an edge of discomfort to her voice.

"It'll be fun. No one can see. Let's get back in the pool. If you're too shy, I can help you," Greg offered.

Alarm shot through Robert. He'd been right. Greg was a shark.

"No! Greg, stop! I don't want—"

Robert had heard enough. He wouldn't allow that sleazeball to pressure Lilly. Striding into the pool area, he spotted Greg crowding Lilly against the wall as she pushed fruitlessly at him. A primitive urge roared through him and he jerked Greg away from her.

Greg gaped at him. "Wha—"

"Robert!" Lilly cried in surprise.

"She said no. She said stop," Robert said and pushed Greg into the pool.

His heart pounding a mile a minute, he turned at the

sound of Lilly's gasp. He gave his jacket a sharp tug. "Are you ready to go?"

She swallowed audibly and nodded. "Yes, I just need to change into dry clothes."

He looked at the black two-piece suit she wore and noticed her nipples puckered against the clinging fabric. Her skin was white and she was slim, her legs long, her thighs inviting. Surprised at the direction of his thoughts, he grabbed a towel and pressed it into her hands. "Be quick about it. I'll wait outside for you."

As soon as she left, he turned toward Greg. "Leave her alone."

"Or what?" Greg asked. "It's obvious you two aren't exclusive. She was with me tonight, not you."

Robert's blood pressure climbed another notch. "Whether Lilly and I are exclusive or not, I won't let her be manhandled by slime like you."

"Maybe she wants to be manhandled," Greg said with a sly look.

"Not if she's saying *no*, *stop*, but I guess you're not bright enough to figure that out." Robert stalked out of the swimming area.

Pacing back and forth outside the women's locker rooms, he struggled with his reaction to seeing Lilly with another man. It had bothered the hell out of him. He'd thought of Lilly as sweet and attractive, but not overly sexual. In fact, part of her appeal was her innocence.

Maybe she wants to be manhandled.

Robert scowled. He seriously doubted that Lilly wanted to be manhandled. If any man was going to handle her, it should be him.

The thought knocked him sideways. He swore under his breath as Lilly, her hair still wet and her cheeks pink, appeared from the women's locker room. "Are you ready?" he growled.

She bit her lip. "I guess."

He escorted her to his car in silence. As he drove toward her home, she asked a few questions about his appearance at the Ruritan Club. Still disturbed, he delivered one-word answers.

"Would you mind stopping here please?" she asked.

So busy brooding, he almost didn't notice her request. He glanced at the fast-food sign. "Why?"

"I'm hungry. I didn't have dinner."

She was hungry because Greg had given her a workout. His gut twisted as he pulled into the fast-food drive-thru lane. "What do you want?"

"Single with cheese, mustard and pickles, no onion or mayo, fries and a frosty."

"That was the most decisive I've ever seen you," he said after he repeated the order to the drive-thru attendant.

She shrugged and gave a small smile. "I guess starvation will do that to you."

He gave a small grin in return then picked up her order. As he drove the rest of the way to her house, he couldn't help thinking about the many kinds of starvation a person could experience. For example, Robert's father had told him no sex until the campaign was over. Robert didn't have much sexual experience, so he was used to taking care of himself every few nights to keep himself from going nuts.

Part of the reason he'd chosen Lilly as his escort was because she didn't tempt his carnal nature all that much. He'd felt protective of her, almost the same way he suspected he would feel about a little sister. After seeing her with Greg and getting a good look at her nearly bare body, he suspected he would be thinking carnal thoughts about sliding between her legs and playing with her nipples the rest of the night. He wondered what she looked like when she had sex. Did she make noises? Did she moan?

Feeling himself harden at the forbidden visuals, he swore under his breath as he parked the car.

"Thanks for the ride home," Lilly said and unlocked her door.

"I'll walk you to your door," he said and joined her.

"Thank you again," Lilly said when they arrived at her front door.

"Would you like me to sit with you while you eat?" he asked.

Not really flickered in her eyes. She sighed. "I don't see any point in it. You're obviously angry. You haven't stopped glaring at me since you arrived at the country club tonight."

"I haven't been glaring at you."

She shot him a look of disbelief.

"Let's go inside," he said. "We need to talk."

"Okay," she said as if she weren't at all thrilled with the prospect.

He followed her past the formal foyer into the kitchen where she flicked on the light. "You could have asked your housekeeper to make something for you to eat, couldn't you?"

"She's not staying overnight anymore. Felt too much like a baby sitter." Lilly sat down and lifted a french fry to her lips.

"Go ahead and eat," he said, unsettled by the fact that she didn't want a baby sitter.

"I'd rather you go ahead and say what's on your mind."

He adjusted his tie and nodded. "Okay. Greg said something after you left that made me wonder."

"Wonder what?"

He shrugged. "Just wonder. He said maybe you wanted to be manhandled."

She turned quiet and he studied her carefully. Her cheeks heated with color and she cleared her throat. "I'm not sure I would use that term. Of course, every woman wants to be treated like a woman," she said, her gaze sliding away from his.

"What do you mean, treated like a woman?"

She lifted her hand to her throat. "Well, I want a man to find me attractive." She hesitated. "Desirable," she said in a small voice.

Robert digested her response. "Is that how Greg treated you?"

She moved her shoulders in an uncomfortable gesture. "He called me and flirted with me. He asked me out days ahead of time," she said.

He would have sworn he heard an edge to her voice with that last comment. He supposed he deserved it, he thought sourly. "Did you really like the way he was treating you?"

She bit her lip. "I might could," she said. "With the right man."

Robert felt a mini-explosion of heat race through him. Little Miss Lilly White wanted a little action. He felt an odd mix of hormones and guilt because he suddenly wanted to be the one to give it to her. "Did you want him to kiss you?" he asked, reaching for her hand and pulling her against him before she could respond.

Her eyes were wide with surprise. "I—I—"

"Did you want him to touch you? Everywhere?"

If possible, her eyes widened even more.

"I saw your nipples standing against your bathing suit," he told her.

She blinked. "I'd just gotten out of the warm water. I was getting cold."

"Do you want someone to keep you warm?" he whispered.

She met his gaze, but couldn't seem to find the words. He glimpsed a loneliness that mirrored his own at times and lowered his mouth to hers. She tasted salty then sweet when he slid his tongue inside. He wanted to taste her thoroughly, every centimeter, to feel her and to make sure she felt him. She curled her tongue around his in invitation and he felt himself grow harder. She might be inexperienced, but she was hot. His for the taking.

He felt another stab of guilt at the thought of taking advantage of her. It would be so easy. And he'd feel like crap afterward. An odd tenderness tightened his chest. He didn't want Lilly to feel used. She was sweet and so eager to please.

Maybe marrying her wasn't a bad idea after all.

The idea rocked through him like an earthquake and he immediately pulled back. Mentally swearing, he stared at Lilly. He was going to have to think about this.

"I should go."

She swallowed. "Okay."

"Don't see Greg anymore," he said then grimaced at his arrogant tone. "I'd prefer you not see Greg anymore. Will you join me tomorrow night?"

"Yes. What are you doing?"

"I don't know," he said, his head suddenly cloudy. "It's probably some boring dinner or party. Maybe we can do something afterward."

She licked her lips and he swallowed a groan. "That would be nice."

She had no idea how nice things could be, Robert thought as he walked out the door with an erection harder than the head of a hammer. But he liked the idea of being the one to show her.

"The first shipment of books has been delivered and put on display," Sara announced from the doorway.

Shifting Willy on her lap as she studied a financial report, Delilah glanced up, pleased. Since the spa guests sometimes had to wait between appointments, Delilah had decided to add a couple of racks of books. "Oh, that's great. What came in?"

"A smattering of everything. Mystery, romance, litera ture and some of the Dummy books you mentioned. You know, *The Idiot's Guide to Shakespeare*, *Opera for Dummies*."

"We're putting them at the beverage bar and in the waiting area, right?" Delilah asked, thinking she might take a peek at *Opera for Dummies* after she finished reviewing the reports and inventory.

"Just like you said," Sara told her. "Why don't you go take a look? I'll hold Wills for you."

Delilah smiled. Sara had begun to refer to Willy as Wills like England's hot prince. She stood and passed him to her assistant. "If you're sure you don't mind. Just remember you offered if he has a big royal poop."

"You forget I've been dealing with a different kind of crap for years. In comparison, this is a breeze," Sara said, nuzzling Willy.

"You should have had children."

"Not with the man I married," Sara said firmly. "Talk about bad seed."

"Did I hear a request for a sperm donation?" Paul Woodward asked from the doorway.

Sara gasped.

Delilah smiled and shook her head at the bone-melting massage therapist. He was such a flirt and she loved him for it. This was the kind of man she should date. He wouldn't give her headaches. He would just use his amazing hands and body to provide release. Oh, heaven. If only she could generate some good old-fashioned lust for him.

"There you go, shocking Sara again with your wicked innuendos. One of these days someone is going to take you up on your offers. What are you going to do then?"

His eyes glinted with mischief. "I'll try to come up with something." He glanced at Willy. "Who's my competition with Sara?"

Sara blushed and rolled her eyes. "This is Wills. Delilah is his guardian."

Paul's eyes rounded in surprise. "So you're going to have to be a responsible type now. How's it going?"

"Fighting it every step of the way. Walk with me to look at the new displays in the beverage area. I won't be long, Sara."

Delilah and Paul left the office suite. "What's with Sara?" he asked in a low voice. "She always looks at me like I'm the big bad wolf even when I say hello to her."

"She was in a bad marriage. You probably bowl her over. Like you do the rest of us," she added, flirting a little. God, it felt good and Paul was safe.

"I keep trying, but I swear I can't get the time of day from anyone in the manager's suite. I've offered complimentary massages, drinks—"

Delilah did a double take. "You didn't really offer Sara a massage, did you?"

"Well, yeah. Her neck looked a little stiff one day. I told her I could fix it and—"

She wagged her finger at him. "You probably gave her a heart attack. You have to be careful with Sara. She's not like me. She's a lady."

He stopped and looked at her quizzically. "What do you mean? You're a lady."

His insistence warmed her heart. She hooked her arm through his. "You're so nice. I just wish I wanted to go to bed with you."

He cracked a lopsided smile. "Yeah, me too. But it would feel like I was making it with my sister. Damn shame."

"Sure is," she said with a laugh. "Let's look at these books."

He stiffened slightly. "Books. When did we get books?"

"My brilliant idea," Delilah said. "Our patrons often have some down time whether they're waiting for hair color to process or getting a smoothie here at the bar. A book can make the wait a little easier. Nice touch?"

"I guess," he said.

She gently punched his arm. "It's a great idea." She nodded her head at the eye-catching display and meandered over to the *Dummy* books.

"What are you looking at?" he asked, standing beside her.

Fighting a slight embarrassment, she pointed at the books. "*Dummy* books. I'm thinking of reading one."

"But you're not dumb."

"Bless you," she said, surreptitiously picking up three

different titles. "But you could fill libraries with what I don't know."

"When are you going to have time to read those?"

She shrugged. "At night. When I can't sleep because Willy can't."

He shook his head. "I never thought I'd see the day. No more late night bar-hopping and table dancing for Delilah."

Delilah made a moue with her lips. "Stop rubbing it in. This responsibility thing is very hard on me."

"Well, if you ever need a safe, but wild night out," Paul offered.

"I know I can count on you," she said. "I always could. I better get back to Sara before Willy drives her crazy. Bye now."

Delilah found Sara bouncing Willy on her hip as she walked from one side of the office to the other. "I'll have to check with Ms. Montague to see if she can interview this afternoon."

"If it's Nanny Finders, the answer is yes, yes, yes," Delilah said.

"Ah, Ms. Montague has just returned to the office. I'll let you speak with her." Sara punched a button. "Line one."

Delilah scooted into her office and set an appointment for nanny prospect number 999. Okay, it was actually nanny prospect number 9, but it sure felt like 999. Bracing herself for another mismatch, she felt a spark of hope by the end of the interview. After Maria Leguzma left, Delilah danced around her office with Willy singing a song from *Mary Poppins*.

She poked her head out the door. "Sara, we found her! She's the Spanish version of Mary Poppins without the umbrella. Thank God—" She broke off when she saw that Sara was gone and Guy Crandall was pulling the door to the suite closed behind him.

He walked toward her. "So this is Howard Bradford's dirty little secret in the flesh."

*A man who learns your secrets can be your worst
nightmare . . . or your dream come true.*
—DELILAH'S DICTUM

Chapter 10

Delilah hid the baby from him. Guy was such a sleaze-ball she didn't want Willy breathing the same air.

"Little Willy. I guess the little knock-out mother got tired of taking care of him, huh?"

He moved toward her and Delilah scooted behind the desk. She wanted a barrier between them. A steel wall would be right in her comfort zone.

"You know, I wonder how the Huntingtons would react to Lilly's newest little brother. You think it would change her chances of getting married to Robert?"

Delilah really hated him. "Don't you have anything better to do with your time than stick your nose in other people's business?"

"Oh, I make it my business to know. Ever since Howard fired me a few years ago, I've been waiting for my opportunity to do business with him again. And Willy here has been my ticket," he said with an oily smile as he reached out to touch Willy.

Delilah backed away. "Don't touch the baby," she said. Her expression must have revealed the loathing she felt for the man because he paused mid-motion and withdrew.

"I don't want the baby. I just want my paycheck with interest."

Delilah's temper kicked up another degree. "You're not contributing anything. How can I possibly pay you?"

"Because if you don't, the news about Lilly Bradford's illegitimate brother is going to be smeared all over the papers and the great Robert Huntington will dump her so fast every head will spin . . , and every tongue will wag. Her reputation will be ruined."

"Reputation is overrated," Delilah said with a shrug. "I don't care as much about reputation as other people do."

"Maybe not about yours, but you do about Lilly's. Pay me my weekly salary plus the interest on what you withheld and my lips are sealed."

Delilah ground her teeth. She hated this. If she paid him, when would it end? Besides, she'd written Guy out of the budget. How could she write him back in with Lilly's accountants scrutinizing her every move? "This is blackmail."

"Pays the bills," he said. "Pay me and I'll leave."

Delilah put Willy into his infant seat and pulled out her personal checkbook. Her fingers cramped as she filled in the amount. "There," she said, tearing out the check and handing it to him.

"You forgot interest," he said.

"What interest?" she demanded, her impatience crackling through her.

"Interest for payment past due. Two hundred bucks," he said.

"Two hundred," she echoed. "You're crazy. No one charges that kind of—"

"I do," he said with a smile. "Pay up or I sing."

Lord, she hated him. She knew it was one of the top ten

sins to kill, but some people didn't deserve to exist on this earth. She scribbled out another check and threw it at him.

"Thank you very much, Miss Delilah. I'm glad to see you've come around to my way of thinking." He turned toward the door.

Never, she thought. "You better watch your back."

He paused and glanced over his shoulder. "Are you threatening me?"

"Just letting you know you're dealing with a different kind of person than Howard or Lilly Bradford," she said, ripping him apart with her eyes.

He wiggled his shoulders in discomfort. "White trash."

"Something like that. If you push me too far, you'll find out what I'm truly capable of."

"Just keep writing those checks. Think of me as a con-fidentiality tax that never goes away," he said with a slimy smile and left.

Delilah made a face and shuddered. He made her feel dirty, but the worse threat was that he could empty her bank account.

Delilah reworked her personal budget for the tenth time, popped another M&M and sighed deeply. This wasn't looking good. Just when she'd gotten things straight on the nanny front, Guy Crandall had showed up to create a giant sucking sound.

She was oh, so tempted to put him back on payroll, but she was still determined to open the second location. So determined she had cut her own salary.

Big mistake. Ambition was going to be her downfall. What most people didn't know was that Howard hadn't really given her the condo. He'd put a hefty down payment on it, but Delilah was stuck with a mortgage payment like most of America. The mortgage payment had felt pretty reasonable until today. She popped another M&M. The situation was almost enough to make her start smoking again.

She squeezed the bridge of her nose and listened to the complete silence. It was a sound she hadn't encountered very often lately. Willy was sleeping.

Wandering to his crib, she checked to make sure he was still breathing. He was. Her heart softened at the peaceful sight of him sleeping. Willy wasn't worried about money. As long as he felt dry and safe, and his tummy was full, he was happy. She'd been terrified of screwing up his care and she still was, but the sight of him sleeping eased something inside her. She stared at him for a few more moments and drank in the rare, peaceful sensation.

She crept out of the room and stood in the hallway, looking at the condo that had never felt like home. Dread tugged at her. It could be worse, she supposed. She could find something safe with the money she would make from selling the condo. Not as luxurious, and it probably wouldn't have a hot tub.

Delilah frowned. If only she hadn't cut her own salary . . . If only Nicky had given Delilah some of the funds she was certain Willy's mother had received from Howard for the care of his baby . . .

If onlys didn't get a girl anywhere, she reminded herself. She needed a break, just a little one. Use that Jacuzzi while she could, sip on a champagne cocktail and eat the rest of that bag of M&Ms.

Benjamin tapped on Delilah's door twice. Reluctant to wake Willy if he was sleeping, he used the key Delilah had given him. Walking deeper into the condo, he heard two sounds: pulsating water jets and feminine humming. He rounded the corner and spotted Delilah in the Jacuzzi with a half-empty champagne flute in one hand and a goblet full of M&Ms on the tile behind her. Her eyes were closed, her head leaning back on a prissy little pillow and her shoulders bare.

He suspected the rest of her was bare too.

He supposed the gentlemanly thing to do would be to back away and leave her alone. He wasn't feeling gentlemanly. In fact, with each passing day, he was feeling more and more carnal where Delilah Montague was concerned. He caught sight of a rubber duck floating next to her and swallowed a wry chuckle. This definitely gave a new meaning to the term "lucky duck."

He stepped into the bathroom and waited for her to realize she wasn't alone. She continued to hum something, interspersed with unintelligible words that sounded like an angry country girl song. When she got to the end of it, she sighed. A few seconds passed and one eyelid popped open. The other lazily followed.

"Go away."

Benjamin bit back a grin. "Good evening to you too. You're looking quite fetching. How many of those have you had?" he asked, nodding toward her flute.

"Not as many as I'd like," she said. "But I can't get drunk while I have a baby in my care. I have to be responsible." She said the word as if she found the taste of it despicable.

"A fate worse than death," he said stepping closer to the tub and stealing a glance inside. The swirling waters concealed her naked body from him.

She shook her head. "No, but this isn't what I visual-ized for myself. But enough about me. Tell me about your day, then you can leave."

"I was offered two positions today. One in corporate law. One with a friend I grew up with."

"Which are you going to take? Let me guess. The corporate position."

"No, but I'm considering the position with my friend." He chuckled. "My father will probably cut me out of his will."

Her eyes widened. "Sounds serious."

"He'll eventually get over it. I need to do what I want to do."

"No compromise, right?" she asked, popping a green M&M into her luscious, naughty mouth. "This is one of the differences between the wealthy and the rest of us. The wealthy don't have to compromise. For the rest of us, compromise is a way of life."

He glanced around the lush room. "You don't look like you're suffering to me."

She threw him a dark look. "Give me a few days. I won't be here forever," she muttered.

"What do you mean by that?" he asked, narrowing his eyes.

She waved her hand in a dismissive gesture. "For example, you want steak for dinner tonight. You get steak. I want steak. I look at my budget and sometimes eat hamburger. Another example, you want a Jaguar, you get a new Jaguar. I want a BMW, I get a used one. If I can find a good deal."

"It doesn't look like you compromised on the condo furnishings."

"Cash did that. Hired a decorator. It was a gift." She

took another sip of champagne. "Easy come, easy go. Know anyone who wants to buy a condo?"

He felt a jerk of surprise. "You're really going to sell?"

"Nannies and babies aren't cheap," she said, biting her lip.

"You make a good salary at the spa, don't you?" he asked, something not adding up.

"Good enough, but I have an unexpected expense that's going to create a squeeze."

"Willy."

"No." She shook her head. "It's nothing you can do anything about. I'm ready to get out of the Jacuzzi, so you need to leave."

"What if I don't?"

"Then you'll be sorry."

"Why?"

"Because you'll get an eyeful of what you're not getting," she said and rose from the bubbling water.

Benjamin blinked. Her skin was rosy from the heat, her breasts plump with dusty pink tips. Her abdomen was gently rounded. Her hips curved in womanly invitation, the swirl of curls at the top of her thighs tempting him. Her shapely thighs made his mouth water.

"Told ya so," she said as she downed the last sip of her cocktail, licked her lips, and picked up the goblet of M&Ms. Stepping out of the tub, she grabbed a towel and pressed it against the side of her body, heedless of her nudity. "Better leave or you'll go blind," she taunted as she walked past him into the hallway.

His body temperature soaring, Benjamin followed her with his eyes. He might turn into a pillar of salt, but what a way to go. "What an ass," he couldn't resist saying.

"Thank you," she said and disappeared behind her bedroom door.

He stood there for a full moment, with his body at full arousal. Lord, the woman made him feel as if he'd never had sex. He shook his head then took a deep breath and walked out of the bathroom. With the bulk of his blood still lodged in his groin, he missed the turn for the front door and walked into the kitchen.

He swore at the mistake and spied a pile of papers on the table. Seeing the drawing of a pirate's flag on one, he picked it up. A budget. Beside the initial G was the pirate's flag. At the bottom of the sheet it was easy to see there was more month than money. He picked up a second paper and beside the initial G was the drawing of a snake with fangs.

What or who was G?

Curious, he headed back to her bedroom door and pushed it open. In the darkened room, he heard a sniff then another. His chest tightened at the sound. Was she crying?

"Delilah?"

She sniffed again. "I thought I told you to leave," she said in an unsteady voice.

"What's wrong?"

"Nothing. Go away."

He moved toward her, his sight growing accustomed to the darkness. Her face turned away from him, she clutched the towel to her chest, leaving her remarkable rear end on display.

Benjamin tore his gaze from her backside. "Something's wrong."

"Nothing you would understand."

"Is this related to your budget issues?"

She tensed. "I don't want to talk about that with you."

"What if I could help?"

"Not unless you know someone who would want to buy my condo?"

"And if I do?"

She sniffed and met his gaze in the dark. "That would be nice," she whispered and something inside him melted.

"Do you remember the first night we met?" he asked.

She swallowed. "When you were drilling and I yelled at you through the wall?"

He chuckled and shook his head. "No. The first time we met face-to-face."

She paused and nodded.

"You changed the way you acted toward me the minute you found out I was your neighbor."

"Not just any neighbor," she said with an edge to her voice. "The neighbor who was keeping me from sleep."

He nodded. "I don't do that anymore. So why do you still wear a chip on your shoulder with me? Is it because I'm from a wealthy family and you're not?"

"Not really," she said.

"Then what is it?" he asked, stepping closer to her.

"I told you it's because you and I are from different worlds."

"And that's it?" he asked, knowing it wasn't.

"Part of it," she said, lifting her chin. "Am I allowed not to like you?"

"Sure, you're allowed. Just tell me why."

Delilah felt frustrated, tempted and lonely all at once. His gaze challenged and soothed her. She craved the soothing sensation. Her fingers itched to feel his strength flow into her. Giving into the seductive temptation of Benjamin Huntington could cause a lot of problems. Or solve a few, such as her burning sense of deprivation. Once he had her, maybe he would leave her alone.

The notion pinched at her, but she pushed it aside. Once she had him, maybe she could dismiss him. She made a split decision based on need and gut instinct. She'd learned it sometimes took a surrender to get the ultimate win.

"I think we talk too much," she said, seeing the second he correctly caught her change of mood.

"Why tonight?"

She fought a millisecond of self-doubt. She didn't want him to turn her down, not tonight. "Time to put out the fire," she said, dropping her towel and stepping closer. She lifted her arms and hooked them around the back of his neck.

"Don't worry." Stretching up on tiptoe, she pressed her mouth to his, sliding her tongue over his bottom lip. "I'll be gentle."

He gave a rough chuckle and shook his head. "You changed your mind quickly."

She felt another sliver of doubt. He wasn't like any other man with whom she'd made love. He may not like getting aroused and not being satisfied, but he could handle going home and taking a cold shower. He had a strength of will and mind that made him an uncertainty for her.

"It's a woman's prerogative to change her mind. Are you complaining?"

"No, but understanding your mind will help me please your body."

"I'll tell you what I want. A condom."

He gave in to the temptation to run his knuckles over her nipples, making them stand at attention.

She gave a sexy half-gasp. "And don't make me wait."

She tugged at his clothes and he helped, all the while their mouths meshing and parting, seeking and finding. His chest rubbed deliciously against her breasts.

He dropped his mouth to her breast and she sighed. Her body temperature ratcheted up another degree. This was what she'd needed, strong arms, an avid mouth and talented hands. Someone to hold her and make her forget for a little while.

The way he slid his hand down her ribcage, over her waist and lower made it easy to forget everything but this moment, this man. Inhaling his thigh-melting scent, she rubbed against him and pressed her open mouth to his throat to taste him. She felt the pressure of his erection against her lower belly and slid her hand over him.

He stiffened. "Not that fast," he muttered.

"But I want it—"

He took her mouth in a French kiss that stopped her protest. She savored his dark sensual flavor and felt herself grow damp in her nether regions.

He touched her between her legs and growled in approval. "You're already wet."

She squeezed the muscles of his upper arms and moaned as she undulated her pelvis against his. He found her hot spot and made it bloom. His thumb moved over her in a mesmerizing motion.

Her heart raced like a hummingbird's and she felt the tension inside her tighten unbearably. With shocking speed and force, she came, her climax an explosion of pent-up need and frustration.

She slumped against him, breathless and surprised. She pressed her mouth against the center of his chest and darted her tongue out to taste his skin. His heart pounded in a gratifyingly fast rhythm. She lowered her head and skimmed her mouth to his belly, then lower to his abdomen. She brushed her cheek against his full erection then slid her tongue over him.

Feeling him hold his breath in anticipation, she waited a half beat before she took him into her mouth. The hiss he made was the sexiest sound she'd ever heard. Emboldened by his response, she pumped him with her lips, taking him deep into her mouth.

He gave a low groan and slid his fingers through her hair to still her head.

"You can't tell me you don't like that," she said, rubbing her lips down his shaft.

"I can't," he said, backing away with a sigh then pulling her to her feet and backing her against her bed.

Not fighting gravity, she fell backward on the bed. He followed her down, giving her another secret pleasure in the dark. His weight, braced by his elbows, made her feel oddly protected.

"Why did you stop me?"

"I have a rule," he said, moaning as she wiggled her breasts against his chest.

"A rule," she echoed. She should have known he would have something stupid and irritating like a rule for sex.

"Ladies first," he said.

"I went," she said, surprised at the rush of heat that raced through her when he lifted her hand and pressed his mouth against the soft underside of her wrist.

"Three times for you," he continued. "Then one for me."

Delilah blinked. *"Three?"*

He chuckled. "One, two, three then me."

Full of skepticism, she shook her head. "Oh, you won't last. No way."

"It'll be a stretch," he admitted, swearing when she cupped his crotch. He slid his tongue from her inner wrist to her inner elbow and Delilah felt the tips of her breasts harden.

Moving out of reach of her seeking hand, he gave her other arm the same treatment. The caress was so soft, yet so stimulating she was loath to move. He ran his finger along the same path. "Do it again," she whispered when he stopped.

He chuckled and the sound was low, intimate and arousing. He slid his mesmerizing finger to the outside of her breasts and a wicked restlessness built inside her. She felt languid at the same time that her nerve endings felt like oil popping on a hot griddle.

"Like that?" he asked, winding his finger around her nipple.

She couldn't resist the urge to arch her back. "Yessss. It's just too—"

"Too what?" he asked, dipping his mouth to draw her nipple into his mouth.

Thank goodness, she thought, moaning with half-relief. He slid his hand between her legs to gently taunt her. She opened her thighs, wanting more. She knew that was a blatant invitation, but she couldn't remember feeling this much want, this much need, in a long, long time. She was already swollen again, already wet.

He lowered his mouth down her belly to kiss her thighs then pressed his mouth against her femininity. His tongue worked magic over her, laving her, pushing her, sending a buckshot of wild sensations through her. Delilah could hardly breathe.

When she thought she could take no more, he stroked her again and sent her flying. She cried out in release, shuddering and trembling.

He moved back up her body holding her close, keeping her from splintering apart. Delilah looked into his dark, dark eyes and felt a tremor shake her. She had thought she would ultimately be in control of this little game, but everything had been turned upside down. He read her body like a book. It wasn't enough for him to screw her and leave her. She could see it in his eyes, feel it in his touch.

He would do it with tenderness and care, exquisite technique, but he was going to take her like she'd never been taken before.

"That's two," he said, and she felt his erection against her thigh. "Has anyone ever told you how much fun it is to make you—"

"Not lately," she said. "I think two to one is fine."

"Not if I can help it," he said and pulled open the drawer to her bedside table. He pulled out a condom and put it on. Then he lowered himself so that he was just at her opening, tantalizingly close.

Delilah wiggled, but he bracketed her hips with his hands and shook his head. "Slower is better," he coached her and eased just barely inside her.

He started to pull back and she protested. "Noooo—"

He eased inside her again, a little further, but not far enough. Delilah groaned in frustration.

He pulled back and she bit back a sob.

He thrust all the way inside her, stretching her, taking her breath. Watching her expression carefully, he lifted his hands to hers, twining his fingers through hers. "Too much?"

The combination of tenderness and complete posses-
sion undid her. She opened her mouth to speak, but no
sound came out. Deluged with all kinds of feelings she
hadn't expected to feel, she moved her head in a circle.
"Not too much."

His gaze devoured her as he began to move in a rhythm
that made her swell and stretch. His body claimed hers.
The power of their passion swirled around her head like a
mist. Oh, she wanted him. Every inch of him. Every . . .

She strained to absorb him, rocking her pelvis into his,
taking him deep inside her, intimately squeezing him with
every stroke he took.

His labored breath matched hers. His fingers gripped
hers. His body glistened with passion. She felt the savage
wrench of pleasure inside her and gasped, her climax
coming in waves. She hit a peak then another took her by
surprise.

She cried his name out loud.

"That's three," he muttered and finally went over the
edge with her.

Delilah wasn't sure how many minutes passed before
she caught her breath. Her heart was beating so hard she
could feel it in her brain. On the lovemaking Richter scale,
that had been . . . No number seemed high enough.

Damn, she'd hoped he would be a lousy, selfish, clueless lover. Instead he had blown her away. Mentally
swearing a blue streak, she closed her eyes and nudged
him in a broad hint for him to get off of her and hopefully
go away.

He rolled over.

Thankfully, he was quiet. She stole a quick glance and

saw that he looked as if someone had hit him with a brick. She wasn't sure that was good or not.

She felt vulnerable, incredibly well-laid, and she wasn't sure when her knees would stop shaking. *It was just sex,* she told herself, but it didn't ring true. Which scared the hell out of her.

She needed to get him to leave.

Flattery usually worked like a charm. Taking a deep breath, she tried to calm herself. "You were amazing. Incredible. Whew!" She fanned herself. "I don't think I'm going to be able to find the strength to walk you to the door."

He rolled onto his side and looked at her.

She didn't meet his gaze.

"Are you hinting for me to leave?" he asked in an incredulous tone.

"Well I know how men really don't like to hang around after the deed, and I won't lie. You really did wear me out. I'm sure you're tired, too. And if you're not, you should be—"

Benjamin chuckled.

She found the sound both arousing and irritating. "What?"

"You like me more than you want to admit," he said, studying her.

"You wish," she said, throwing him a sideways glance.

"You can't believe how good it was between us," he goaded her. "You want me again."

She laughed, but the sound was slightly off-key, just a little uncomfortable. "I can absolutely promise that I do not want to make love again."

"You're sure," he said, sliding one index finger down

the inside of her arm. He knew some of her secrets now. He wanted to know the rest.

Delilah quivered then rubbed her arm where he'd touched it, as if she wanted to rub away his effect on her. He felt an odd stab.

"Okay, you want the truth? I've had a lot of frustration during the last month and you just helped me get rid of it. Thank you very much. I know you wanted the same thing—a night of hot sex. Here's more of the truth. You're slumming. Pick another girl next time. I'm sure you can find one."

Benjamin felt a surge of anger blast through him. If he hadn't seen the tinge of vulnerability in her eyes, he would have sworn at her and left. "My intentions toward you aren't totally honorable, but I'm not slumming."

"I'm not the kind of woman you usually go for."

"So maybe I've been going for the wrong woman."

"I'm not the kind of woman you would take home to meet your mother and father."

"My mother and father would bore the hell out of you. They often bore the hell out of me. Want to know the truth, Delilah? The earth moved as much for me as it did for you, but you won't admit it because you're scared."

She narrowed her eyes and jerked her chin upright. "If I'd been scared, I wouldn't have let you be with me."

"Maybe you should be scared. Maybe I should be too. I've never been with a woman like you, and something tells me you've never been with a man like me."

He was right. She'd never been with a man like him, but she would sew her lips together before she admitted it. Right now, she needed to rein herself in, and she couldn't do that if he was naked and in her bed.

Size matters in jewels flaunted below the belt and on the finger.

—DELILAH'S DICTUM

Chapter 11

$\mathcal{D}$elilah finally got rid of Benjamin, but he still succeeded in wrecking another night of sleep for her. She hadn't expected him to make love to her until she was shaking, and she hadn't liked being called chicken. Especially if there was a grain of truth in the accusation.

The following morning, Benjamin strolled through her front door as if he owned the place. He looked great. Business casual in a camel hair sport coat, shirt and tie, and slacks that emphasized his long legs. She instinctively inhaled and caught his delicious scent. His eyes glinted with a determination that made her uneasy. She narrowed her eyes at him as she hustled Willy to his high chair. He'd already downed his bottle and his rice cereal was ready.

"What are you doing here?" she asked, wishing she didn't feel blurry and muddled.

"Good morning to you, too," he said with a dry tone. He handed her some folded papers. "Here's an offer on your condo. Let me know if you're interested."

Delilah blinked. "Offer? What are you talking about?"

"You said you wanted a buyer for your condo. I have one for you."

Willy banged his fists on his high chair and made

grunting noises. Delilah spooned rice cereal into his mouth and reached for the papers. "Who—" She broke off when she read the name. "You! Why do you want to buy my condo? What do you want with it?" She glared at him. "Is this because we had sex last night? It's really not a good idea to make financial decisions that are influenced by sex."

"No. It's not about sex," he said in a long-suffering voice. "You were very good, but your sexual performance has nothing to do with the value of your condo. I invest in real estate." He shrugged. "I already own several condos in this building. What's one more?"

Delilah couldn't stop her mouth from falling open. She had known Benjamin was loaded, but he hadn't acted *that* loaded. Willy banged on his tray for another bite. Distracted, Delilah obliged. "So you can just arbitrarily decide *oh, I think I want to buy another condo today*. And it's done?"

He moved his head in a circle. "Within reason. And reason is a matter of perspective. Anyway, I've got a lecture, so I've got to go. Let me know if the offer works for you. I'll rent it to you so you won't have to move."

Delilah's stomach knotted. He was probably planning to take the rent in trade for the use of her body. *As if that would be such a hardship*, her baser side taunted her as she inhaled his aftershave again and felt herself salivate. Still, the thought of the arrangement bothered her. She shoved a spoon of rice cereal into Willy's mouth and opened her mouth to de-confuse Benjamin on the matter of her hopping into the sack with him.

"And don't get any ideas about bedding me instead of paying me," he said before she could get out even a word.

He leaned closer so that his face was a breath from hers. "I expect your rent in cold hard cash."

Shock froze her vocal cords. She worked her mouth, but no sound came out. He backed away and she cleared her throat. "Of course," she managed. "I wouldn't have it any other way."

"Good. I'll see you later. Do you want me to take Willy this afternoon?"

Still stunned, but trying to hide it, she nodded. "Uh, yes. That would be nice. Can you?"

"Yes. See ya after lunch," he said and left her staring after him.

Willy banged on the tray and she spooned another bite into his mouth. She felt as if someone had hit her in the head with a frying pan. Or her fairy godmother had waved a wand in her direction. "Yeah, right," she said, rolling her eyes. "Okay, what just happened? I got an offer from Benjamin Huntington to buy my condo and he would allow me to continue renting it. He's taking you this afternoon. There's gotta be a catch. The offer is low, rent is sky high," she muttered, snatching the papers and scanning for telltale figures.

The offer was fair. The rent was ridiculous. Ridiculously low. Tossing the papers onto the kitchen counter, she plopped down in a chair across from Willy. She spooned the cereal into his mouth. "So what do you think? Is Benjamin a good guy or not?"

Willy gurgled and gave her a smile laced with cereal. She couldn't resist smiling in return. "Oh, I should have known you guys always stick together," she teased, tickling him under his chin. His cackle lifted her mood. Even with ears like Dumbo and chronic diaper rash, Willy was a heart stealer. Although she was the first to admit that

Willy could drain every ounce of energy and sanity from a normal human being, Delilah wondered how Nicky could have brought herself to give the baby up.

Willy had a way of getting under her skin. "Sorta like a chigger," she joked, wiping his face and swinging him out of his chair.

Robert strode up the stone path to Lilly's front door. He felt a kick of excitement he hadn't felt before. After the plastic chicken dinner they endured last night, he'd taken her home and he'd kissed her good night at her front door. Her innocence had stopped him from going any further. He knew she was inexperienced and he would have felt like a heel to take her without making a commitment. His father's prodding nudged at him. His brother's caution pulled him in the opposite direction.

He knocked at Lilly's front door and she appeared with a bright smile on her face. "Hi," she said in a breathless voice that somehow made him feel lighter.

"Hi yourself. You ready?"

She nodded. "I just need to get my jacket." The phone rang. "Oops. I guess I should get that. Come on in."

Robert followed her inside and wandered into the den where she picked up the phone.

"Oh, hello Greg," Lilly said. "I can't talk. I was just getting ready to leave." She paused.

Greg. Robert fought the urge to grind his teeth.

"Saturday night?" she echoed, biting her lip. "I, uh, I don't think I can . . . Sunday?" Her eyes rounded. "I'm sorry. I can't. I'm busy both nights," she said. "Next Tuesday?"

Robert narrowed his eyes.

"I really can't talk now. I have to go. I'll be late. Bye

now," she said and turned off the phone. "Wow, he's persistent." She pushed her hair behind one of her ears and cleared her throat. "Well, I'll get my coat."

He snagged her hand when she turned to leave. "Did you want to go with him?"

She shook her head. "No."

"Are you sure?"

"Yes, why?"

"That's what I wanted to ask you. Why don't you want to go with him?"

She took a deep breath and looked down. "I'd rather be with you," she said in a low voice that got under his skin.

He felt an easing sensation inside him. Things were getting back to normal. "Good," he said. "I don't think Greg had honorable intentions for you."

Lilly gave him a blank look. "Honorable?"

Robert nodded firmly. "You deserve to be treated honorably. You should be treated with respect. Don't forget that."

"Honor, respect," she echoed and sighed. "Robert, do you think a man can't have sex with a woman he respects and honors?"

Surprised by her question, he tugged at his collar. "No. A husband can respect his wife and have sex with her."

"So you think if a man has sex with a woman and they're not married, then he can't respect her?"

Robert felt a rush of discomfort. "I didn't say that."

"Well, what do you think?" she asked, impatience leaking into her voice. "What's your opinion?"

"I think it depends on the relationship and the individuals involved," he hedged. "Why are you asking?"

She bit her lip and her cheeks turned pink. Determination glinted in her eyes and she cleared her throat. She leaned closer. "Do you ever think about having sex with me?"

Robert blinked. She could have knocked him over with her little finger. He frowned. "Lilly!"

She lifted her chin. "Well, isn't it natural to think about it?"

Robert's throat suddenly felt parched. "I guess, but I have something else on my mind right now. I have a surprise for you. I want to give you something special, but I want to get your opinion first."

Her eyes rounded. "A gift? Robert, what a surprise."

He nodded. "I think you'll be pleased. It's something I definitely want you to have."

She smiled. "You're making me curious."

"Then let's go so you can satisfy your curiosity."

Twenty minutes later, Robert led Lilly onto the front porch of a house whose owner she didn't know. She looked at him. "Who lives here? What are we doing—"

Robert grinned. "You'll find out soon enough."

The door opened and a middle-aged man looked from Robert to her and back to Robert. "Good to see you, Robert. Is this the little lady you're shopping for?"

Robert gave a big nod. "She certainly is. Lilly, meet the finest breeder and trainer of golden retrievers in the state of Texas, Richard Ginter."

Mr. Ginter chuckled. "You're gonna make me blush. Nice to meet you, Lilly. Come on in and I'll show you my little ones. They've both been housebroken and I've trained them to be good companions. We just need to find out which one you fancy the most. This way," he said, walking through the paneled den.

Lilly stared after the man, unable to move her feet.

"Go on, sweetheart. I can't wait to see your face."

Housebroken, golden retrievers, companions. Lilly had the sinking sensation this gift definitely wasn't going to be jewelry. She forced herself to take a shallow breath and followed Mr. Ginter through the den and kitchen onto the back porch where four dogs greeted them with barks of joy.

"He's not talking about—" She gulped as Mr. Ginter called two puppies onto the deck.

Robert laughed as he wrapped his arm around her waist. "She can't believe it. Aren't they gorgeous, Lilly? You've got a tough choice to make."

"This is Maxine," Mr. Ginter said. "And this is Max. Take your time. They've both got great personalities, but Robert wants you to be happy."

"And safe," Robert said, meeting her gaze. "I don't like the idea of you being alone in your house at night."

Lilly bit her tongue. She wondered what it was going to take for Robert to realize she wanted a lot more than a puppy from him.

Benjamin heard Delilah rush through the front door as he jiggled Willy and paced the length of the den. The baby had been fussy for the last hour.

Smelling Italian, he caught sight of take-out bags from a popular Italian eatery and joined her in the kitchen. "I didn't know what you would like, so I got the sampler," she said. "Sorry, no red wine. I think there's another Corona in the refrigerator. Will that do?"

"You don't have to feed me dinner," he said.

"The least I can do," she said and glanced at Willy. "Are we winding up for the arsenic hour?"

"Sounds like it. He's drooling like someone left his faucet on."

Delilah dumped the bags on the counter and made a sympathetic pout. "Poor thing. You look like you need a cookie," she said, extending her arms.

"Bad habit to start," Benjamin said, handing Willy to her.

"What am I supposed to do? Tell him to chew on a nail?" She tossed Benjamin a look of disapproval. "Nothing wrong with a cookie after a long day of teething." She pulled a box of baby cookies out of the cabinet and offered one to Willy, who immediately crammed it into his mouth. Cooing, she gave him a kiss and set him in the high chair then pulled out the take-out containers and plates. She grabbed Cheerios and reached for the Corona at the same time Benjamin did.

Their hands touched and she paused, meeting his gaze. "I'll let you get that," she said. "And I'll get my water."

"No champagne cocktail tonight?"

"No. It looks like I may be driving Willy around the block a few times."

They both sat down at the kitchen table and Delilah poured some Cheerios onto Willy's tray. The baby's face lit up and he immediately began to pick them up one by one.

"Nice trick," Benjamin said in approval.

"Thanks. A girl at work told me about it. I'm all ears on baby tips these days. And they're clinically proven to reduce cholesterol," she said, reading the claim on the box. "Balances out the cookie."

He chuckled and served himself a portion of lasagna while Delilah took the spaghetti and meatballs. "I love their sauce."

"Have you decided to accept my offer on your condo?"

"It's a fair offer," she said, taking a bite and licking her lips. She stabbed a meatball with her fork, set it on her tongue and sucked it into her mouth.

Benjamin felt an immediate, visceral response.

"The rent you want me to pay, however, is way too low."

"Do you have a better offer?"

She stopped mid-bite and swallowed. "Well, no, but—"

"The offer's on the table until midnight. Take it or leave it."

She blinked. "Until midnight?"

"Yes," he said, taking a bite of lasagna.

"Well aren't you the pushy one." She sighed, looked at another meatball and set down her fork, "This is such a bummer. I wouldn't even have to be thinking about this if—" She broke off and sighed in disgust.

"If what?" he asked casually.

"If nothing," she retorted and stabbed another meatball.

"This wouldn't have anything to do with someone whose name starts with G, would it?"

She froze. "What do you know? Have you been snooping in my personal business?"

"I saw your creative budgeting plans last night," he admitted. "The snake was very good."

"It was none of your business."

"It wasn't exactly hidden."

She lifted a bite of pasta and sucked in an errant piece. She licked her lips. "I don't want to discuss it."

"What about my offer?" he asked.

"Why are you making it?" she asked, meeting his gaze.

"Because I can."

She rested her cheek in her hand. "I think this isn't just a business decision for you."

"You're afraid I'm trying to get in your pants," he said. "You already knew that."

"Yes, but—"

"Or maybe you're afraid that I'm trying to thank you for saving my life in the garage."

She cocked her head to one side in a considering way. "That's possible."

"Or that there's some sort of fate involved between you and me. Something weird that I can't explain."

She stopped and stared at him, her gaze alternating between fear and acknowledgment.

"But if anyone said that to me, I would say that sounds like a lot of bullshit," he said. "I guess it depends on if you believe in fate or not."

"I've always thought you make your own fate," she said. "I don't buy a lot of lottery tickets."

"Neither do I."

She gave a slow smile. "You don't need a lottery ticket. You're independently wealthy."

Irritation nicked through him. "Could we just leave my financial status out of it? I'm tired of it."

She lifted her eyebrows. "Okay."

Benjamin looked at the lasagna and suddenly lost his appetite. He was sick of dealing with the status and image of the Huntington name. "Sometimes I wish my name was Smith," he muttered, pushing his plate away. "Let me know if you want to sell your condo to me."

"I do," she said, surprising the hell out of him.

"That was fast."

"You made me an offer I couldn't refuse," she said, wiggling a breadstick like it was a cigar. "Okay, it was the only offer I got, but . . . it's timely and what I need right now. Finish your lasagna," she said with a slow, sassy smile, "Mr. Smith."

He chuckled and pulled his plate back. He took a bite. "How's life in the spa business?"

"Everything's coming up Botox and books."

"Botox and books?"

"Yeah, you know Botox is that poison that freezes your facial muscles and decreases some wrinkles. The books are just an extra we've added to help our clients deal with the wait time. So far, they like it."

"Whose idea was it to bring in the books?"

"Mine, but enough about my brilliance. How's the law professor business going?"

"I'm getting bored. I want to start practicing again."

"But you don't want to be disinherited."

"This is a sticky time for my family. My father's tense about the election."

"What about Robert?"

"My father's more tense than Robert is. I wish my father would have run for political office and gotten it out of his system. It's always been his dream for us to go into politics. Parents and their dreams for their kids."

"I wouldn't know. I think my father's dream for me was to become a nun."

Benjamin chuckled. "That would have been a waste of talent. Was he that bad?"

"The message on his answering machine says, 'Turn or burn. Trust or bust. That's the message of the gospel. Leave a message and I'll return your call.' "

He swore under his breath and shook his head. "And I thought I had it bad." His cell phone rang and he glanced at it, reading the caller ID with a wince. "Do I really want to answer this?" He sighed and flipped the phone open. "Hi Dad."

"The jeweler's here. I want you to come help pick out the diamond ring for his fiancée," his father said.

Benjamin groaned. "I didn't know he had decided to propose."

"He's very close."

Benjamin had an itchy feeling of suspicion. "Just for the record, whose idea was it to bring in a jeweler?"

"Mine," his father admitted reluctantly. "But I can sense a change in Robert. He's looking at Lilly differently."

"How do you know it's not sheer terror? And why do you need me to help pick out a diamond ring?"

He saw Delilah's eyes grow wide.

"Because we just do," his father said. "Come on over and congratulate your brother. It's the least you can do. We can celebrate with a cigar."

"I'll be over in a while." Benjamin flicked the phone closed. "Looks like my brother's getting engaged. I need to congratulate him."

Delilah lifted her glass of water to her lips.

"Really? Who's the lucky girl?"

"Lilly Bradford."

She made a slight choking noise then swallowed.

"You know her?"

She shrugged. "She visits the spa sometimes."

"Dad likes her because she's loaded. Her father was Howard Bradford. He was a rascal and a ladies' man."

She nodded. "Well, you won't be missing anything here. We're watching *The Wiggles*. Another recommendation from someone at work. Cookies and TV: the keys to sanity."

"Sing him a lullaby," Benjamin said, standing, thinking he must be a sicko to prefer watching *The Wiggles* to visiting his father and brother.

"I don't know any lullabys," she said.

"Doesn't matter. Just sing something slow and repetitive."

"Uh-huh," she said as if she had no intention of doing any such thing. "Best advice I can give you for the ring is think big. Men may say size doesn't matter, but it does."

Her husky voice made him think of tangled sheets and a long hot night. She might be watching the G-rated *Wiggles*, but the visuals in Benjamin's brain were definitely X-rated.

A baby's laughter is addictive.

—DELILAH'S DICTUM

Chapter 12

*S*ara Cox walked into the Literacy Center and immediately felt a whisper of relief. She wouldn't have to sit at home alone for another interminable evening and she refused to put herself through the torture of another night at a bar. Once was enough.

Her boss, Delilah, would hound the living daylights out of her for her attitude, but she was more comfortable with books and libraries than she was with martinis and cocktail lounges. She'd completed the literacy training at another location and was now ready to start working as a volunteer. She signed in at the desk and introduced herself to the receptionist. The receptionist said she would give her an orientation packet in just a few moments.

Sara poured herself a cup of coffee and wandered around the room filled with books. Rounding a corner, she nearly plowed into a tall masculine figure. "Oh, excuse—" She stopped just in time, but her coffee splattered onto her pink sweater. "Damn, I mean darn," she quickly corrected herself, embarrassment flooding through her.

She glanced up into the face of Paul Woodward, who looked almost as uncomfortable as she felt. "Omigoodness, Mr. Woodward, I didn't realize it was you."

"Sara," he said with a nod, glancing past her shoulder. "Just call me Paul."

Stunned, she stared at him. She would have expected to run into anyone but him at the Literacy Center.

Why was he here? Perhaps the same reason she was here. Maybe he was more than eye candy after all. She grabbed some tissues from her purse and blotted her sweater. "I completed my training, but this is my first time at this location. I love reading so much. I can't imagine how people go through life not being able to read. I always wanted to volunteer, but my husband didn't want me to." Mentally cursing herself for babbling, she swallowed. "How long have you been coming here?"

"First time for me, too," he said, shoving one of his hands into his pockets.

He seemed tense, she noticed, as she observed the way his biceps flexed. He was a gorgeous man and she always felt intimidated when she was with him. She wondered how his student would be able to concentrate on reading when he was so easy on the eyes. "So what inspired you to come? Was it the new book section at the club? I think that's what prompted me."

"Yeah, something like that." He scratched the side of his chin and looked past her again.

She was probably boring him to death. She glanced down at the magazine he had balled up in one hand. "What are you reading?"

He opened the worn magazine.

"Massage Therapy: Advanced Techniques," she said with a smile. "No wonder you're the top requested massage therapist at the spa. What do you like to read for pleasure?"

He gave her a blank look. "Tolkien," he muttered.

"Classic fantasy. It's interesting how well his work has

translated to film. I haven't had an opportunity to see the latest installment."

"Me neither."

"Mr. Woodward," the receptionist called.

Paul tensed and panic crossed his handsome features. He shook his head. "I gotta go," he said and strode through the double doors of the Literacy Center.

Sara stared after him, troubled. She hoped she hadn't offended him. She wrung her hands for a moment, then followed a strange instinct and went after him. Spotting him just as he stepped into the elevator, Sara called after him. "Paul! Paul, wait."

He glanced over his shoulder and looked as if he wanted to do anything but wait on her. His innate courtesy must have won out. He pushed the door back and waited for her to enter. "What floor?" he asked.

"I, uh—" She shrugged. "Garage." She looked at his face which was turned away from her. "I'm sorry. Did I say something to offend you?"

"No," he said, looking at the numbers at the top of the elevator.

"Well, is something wrong? I mean, one minute you were waiting to tutor and the next—"

"I wasn't waiting to tutor," he said.

She wrinkled her brows in confusion. "Then what— why—"

He gave a heavy sigh and finally met her gaze. "I wasn't waiting to tutor. I was waiting to be tutored."

It took a full moment for the meaning of his words to sink in. "Oh, I didn't know."

"I'd appreciate it if you didn't tell anyone else."

"Of course not." The elevator dinged and the doors

whooshed open. He stepped outside and she followed. "But why did you leave?"

He shrugged his wide shoulders and looked away. "I don't know. It just didn't feel right."

"Is it because you ran into me?"

"I don't know."

Sara sensed his embarrassment and searched for a way to soothe it. "It's very impressive that you would try to improve your reading skills. You're so successful in most areas of your life. Most people wouldn't bother."

He nodded, still not meeting her gaze. "It's held me back," he admitted.

"A lot of us have something that keeps us from being what we want to be," she murmured.

"You don't, do you?" he asked.

"Oh yes," she said with a sad smile. "I stayed married way too long. There were a lot of things I wanted to do and now it's too late."

"Why? You're young."

"I don't feel it."

"You look it."

"Thank you," she said. "Your charm is showing."

"No really. You dress a little older, but you're pretty. Very pretty," he said, looking into her eyes.

Her heart fluttered and she felt heat rising to her cheeks. Self-conscious of her response, she bit her lip. "Well, uh, I'm new at this tutoring thing. Would you like to see if I can help you?"

He looked at her for a long moment. She could see a battle with trust and indecision. "I'm game if you are."

Delilah was so angry she wanted to chew glass. With *The Wiggles* wiggling and singing on the television and

Willy safely in his playpen, she grabbed two cartons of eggs from her refrigerator and stalked into her bathroom.

"Spoiled little bi—" Standing just outside the stall, she tossed the first egg against the wall of the enclosed shower. Lilly had pranced into the spa today and called another impromptu meeting trying to prove Delilah's inability to manage the spa, especially now that she was bringing a *baby* to work with her.

"Ungrateful, ignorant piece of—" She threw two more eggs and watched the slimy yolks slide down the wall of the tub enclosure.

"Treats me like dirt. Looks at me like I'm worthless—" She tossed three more eggs.

"What are you doing?" a male voice asked from the doorway.

Delilah whipped around with an egg in each hand. "Benjamin," she said and bared her teeth.

Benjamin resisted the urge to find a shield to protect himself. He hadn't seen Delilah this furious since she'd rescued him and found out he was her so-called power tool neighbor. Her eyes were wild with fury, her hair mussed, her cheeks high with color. She wore a slim-fitting cream top and a slimmer fitting leather skirt and heels that emphasized her curvy legs. She looked like a sexpot bent on destruction. He glanced at the shower enclosure. Destruction of her shower.

"Why are you egging your shower?"

"Because murder is illegal," she said. "Because I'm sure I would be slapped with a lawsuit and thrown in jail if I pulled every hair from her dense head, or every fingernail from her finger."

"Who is she?"

Delilah turned away from him and tossed an egg at the

shower, then another. "My not-so-silent partner. I own the majority of the spa, but she owns the bulk of the rest of it. Since she inherited her part, she wants me out of there."

"If you own the majority, she's out of luck."

"I know that and you know that, but she's got a ton of money, so the accountants don't want to upset her. She waltzes in, calls an instant meeting where she details my *inferior* performance as director, makes digs about the fact that I've brought Willy to the spa with me. Never mind the fact that the nanny starts tomorrow. Nope, this little she-devil thinks I'm trash and she's doing her best to remove me." Delilah tossed four eggs in quick succession.

"So call your own meetings," he said.

She turned and looked at him as if he were dense. "Why would I want to torture myself and waste time like that?"

"So you can have control."

Delilah opened a second carton of eggs and tossed two at the shower. She had a good arm. He noticed she wasn't fussing and fuming anymore.

"You call the meeting. You set the agenda. You say when the meeting is over. You can even tell her to present her questions to you in writing in advance of the meeting."

She met his gaze. "I can do that?"

He nodded. "Yes and if you hold a meeting every month—"

"Every month," she said darkly and tossed another egg. "I'd be happy to get it down to bi-weekly. She's in there every day annoying the hell out of everyone. Geez, she needs a distraction."

"Who is it?"

Delilah's face closed up. "I'd rather not say." She tossed another egg. "I'm not sure this will work."

"You'll have to hold the line no matter how much she complains."

"Or how much the accountants complain," she said, throwing another egg. "Well, it's worth a try." She picked up two eggs and turned toward him. "You want to throw these?"

His lips twitched. "What an offer."

"I could tell you were lusting after my—" She shrugged. "Eggs."

He chuckled. "I haven't egged anyone since—"

"I'm shocked. *You* egged somebody. I would have thought you would have been too perfect to do something like that."

The way she said perfect got under his skin. "It was an honor egging. Rival high school football captain sliced the tires of our best receiver's car."

"Yes, but do your parents know?"

He took the eggs. "I wouldn't want to give my mother a fainting spell." He tossed one, then the next, surprised at the satisfaction that coursed through him.

"Feels good, doesn't it?" Delilah said.

He glanced at her and felt the slow drag of arousal. "Yeah. Other things feel a lot better."

She took a quick breath. He saw a hint of the heat he was feeling mirrored in her gaze. She looked down at the carton. "Half a dozen left. You want an omelet?"

"Yeah," he said, and watched her squeeze cleaning liquid over the enclosure and turn on the shower head.

"Clean-up's a snap," she said. "I can dig the shells out later."

"And you don't even have to spend the night in jail."

"I bet you'll look at a carton of eggs in a whole new way," she said, heading for the kitchen.

Benjamin was currently fixated on her rear end. He couldn't help remembering how it looked naked. He swallowed a groan. He couldn't help remembering how good it had felt to slide inside her.

"In fact, I wouldn't be surprised if you don't throw a few eggs at your own shower in the future."

"Waste of food," he said. "Immature, unproductive."

She lifted her eyebrows, her face full of skepticism.

"And brilliant. I wish you had another carton."

He and Delilah fixed the omelets together, adding odd ingredients she dug from her refrigerator. She buttered the leftover take-out Italian bread. She fed Willy and talked with him. After she changed a diaper, he watched her press her lips against his belly and make a raspberry. Willy giggled with glee.

"Looks like you two are getting along," Benjamin said.

"Yeah, he grows on you. Sorta like mold," she said with a sly smile and made another raspberry on Willy's belly

Benjamin shook his head. "I never would have predicted it."

"What?" she asked, picking up Willy and standing.

"I think that baby has won you over."

"Not everyone knows this," she confided, "but I have a strong, self-destructive nurturing streak. I'm usually successful at resisting the urge, but Willy's really sweet when he's not screaming."

"You were nurturing with me," he reminded her.

She met his gaze and something powerful sizzled between them, then she looked away. "Yes, when half your face had been bashed in and I didn't know who you really were."

"And now that you know who I am," he ventured.

"You know how some people are allergic to strawberries?"

"Yeah," he said, wondering where in hell this would lead.

"Well, I'm not. I'm just allergic to men like you."

He was getting very tired of the generalization. "I wonder if all women like you are allergic," he said.

"What do you mean all women like me?" she asked sharply.

"The same way you mean men like me," he said.

Frowning, she set Willy in the playpen and crossed her arms over her ample chest. "Define women like me."

"Sure," he said. "As long as you define men like me."

She gave him a hard look and he could see curiosity and defiance battling on her face. "Okay, you go first."

"A woman like you has a PhD in Practicality. She's often, but not always, a good judge of character. She has a huge heart which she tries hard to keep hidden. A woman like you understands her sex appeal and knows a lot about pleasing a man, but could probably learn something about pleasing herself."

She lifted her eyebrows as if she didn't quite agree, but couldn't quite disagree either. "Go on."

"A woman like you has hit some rough spots and she feels like it's her against the world. She has her defenses up so high that sometimes she can't get past them, which can give her a big blind spot. A woman like you is wary of any man she perceives to be her equal."

She stood stick straight in front of him. "And I suppose you're just the man to take care of my blind spot and teach me all I need to know about pleasing myself," she said in the husky voice that made his gut knot.

"Is that an offer?" he taunted in return.

"No," she immediately said.

"Of course," he said. "Just as I said. You're threatened by any man you perceive to be your equal."

"And you're an overeducated, pampered, trust baby smart-ass," she retorted.

"But I'm not a chicken," he said. "And you are."

Her eyes rounded with anger. "Get out. Get out. I can't believe I fixed an omelet for you."

"I helped fix it," he said.

"Get out," she said, shooing him into the foyer. "I can't believe I allowed you to lure me into this ridiculous discussion. I'm not a chicken. You're just trying to goad me into letting you sleep with me."

"Who said anything about sleeping?" he said, chuckling to himself as she hissed at him.

"You know what I meant. Pure and simple, you want to screw me again." She poked at his chest, pushing him toward the door. "You're frustrated because your fourteen karat–gold fiancée turned out to have a heart made of cast iron. And you're frustrated because you're at loose ends right now. You're used to being Mr. Type A, head of the class, high-achiever, gets everything he wants. Well, you're not getting me anymore. Once was more than enough."

"It was more than once, Delilah."

"Out!" She whisked open the door.

"Cluck. Cluck," he said, then stepped outside. She slammed the door at his back so hard it created a breeze. He heard her scream of frustration and felt a trace of satisfaction that she had no more eggs. But he did.

After lunch, Robert led Lilly to the country club's courtyard. His father had insisted on milking the proposal for all the publicity they could get. *Great human interest,* his father had said. *Think of the women's vote.*

The black velvet box felt heavy in his pocket. He wondered if he was doing the right thing. Lilly had smiled and chatted throughout lunch. He couldn't remember a word she'd said. He kept visualizing a jail cell clanging closed. Then he remembered how he'd felt when he'd seen another man trying to make it with her. He'd wanted to rip the guy to pieces. Robert obviously cared for Lilly more than he'd realized. He was still adjusting to that fact. Mentally, he believed taking the next step was the right thing to do. He hadn't had many serious relationships with women and he'd always made sure not to put too much of his heart on the line. With Lilly, his strong, growing feelings for her had snuck up on him without him realizing what was happening.

Lilly shivered. "It's so cold. Are you sure you want to go out here?"

"The fresh air will do us good," he insisted, glancing over his shoulder and spotting a man with a camera. His stomach turned. "Come over here to the bench."

Lilly looked at him in confusion. "We're going to sit? Robert, we'll freeze. That wind is cutting right through my—"

Impatience cut through him. "Just do what I ask," he said more sharply than he'd intended.

Her eyes rounded and she stiffened. "Whatever you say."

Great, he thought, stifling a sigh. Now, he'd pissed off his prospective fiancée. He swore under his breath, wishing he didn't feel so nervous. He remembered what his father had said, that a man was never completely ready to tie himself down. "*It's natural male instinct not to want to commit, but there comes a time in a man's life where it's the right thing to do. If you're willing to give the girl a guard dog, you must be feeling territorial, so it's time to give her a diamond too."*

It's the right thing to do, he told himself.

Besides, there was no way out now. His father had already arranged for the news to be leaked to the press. Lilly stopped at the concrete bench and looked up at him. "Do you really want us to sit here?"

"For just a moment. There's something—" His throat muscles tightened. "There's something I want to discuss with you."

She sat down on the bench and looked up at him, her face suddenly solemn. "Sounds serious."

"It is." He cleared his throat and swallowed. "I've been thinking that you and I should form a permanent arrangement."

"What kind of permanent arrangement?"

He cleared his throat again. "Well you need to think about this because politics can be hard on a woman, but I think you and I—" He swallowed. "I think you and I would be good together in many ways."

She nodded warily. "Uh-huh."

He felt his body separate from his mind. Bending on one knee, he took her hand and opened his mouth. No sound came out. His throat was totally closed. He couldn't even breathe.

"Robert?"

He cleared his dry-as-a-desert throat yet again. In desperation, he pulled the velvet box out of his pocket.

"Omigod," Lilly whispered. "Yes," she said, pulling at his hand and jumping to her feet. "Yes, I'll marry you."

Robert pulled her into his arms and slumped in relief. Thank heaven for Lilly. He hadn't even had to ask her.

A sleeping baby can make you believe in the possibility of peace on earth.

—DELILAH'S DICTUM

Chapter 13

Cluck, cluck.

She was not a chicken. Delilah made a face as she zipped off an email to her younger half-sister Lori Jean in Dallas. Lori Jean's father would probably have a seizure if he knew his little unsoiled dove was communicating with her trashy sister. After she and Lori Jean and Katie had found each other over two years ago, they'd made a vow to keep in touch. Delilah felt uncomfortable about deceiving her sisters. She hadn't told either of them about Willy. They would want to help and then they would want an explanation and the thought of trying to explain gave her a headache. So maybe she would surprise them at Christmas.

She turned off her computer and her mind wandered again to Benjamin. His sexy, suggestive voice had echoed in her brain throughout the day, but smarty-pants Benjamin Huntington was wrong.

She'd been so angry when he'd left she'd wished she had another carton of eggs, but she would have preferred to egg his door. Or his face.

Groaning, she stole a handful of M&Ms from her stash and made a mental note to replenish it. She gathered the bags of items she'd picked up during her lunch break. At first she'd picked up formula and baby food, but there'd been a toy store next door to the grocery store.

She'd bought Willy a new pair of cute jammies and a Houston Astros outfit complete with cap. She'd also found a pop-up toy she knew he would love, a musical ball, two books, a new crib toy . . .

Delilah cradled the musical ball in her hand and smiled sheepishly. "Christmas gifts. Now I need to get him a stocking . . . " She heard her door whip open and Guy Crandall appeared like a bad dream.

His presence was a dark cloud over the joy she felt at her purchase of Willy's Christmas gifts. Delilah felt a spurt of resentment. "Why are you here? I know my check didn't bounce because the funds have left my account."

He moved closer to her desk then glanced over his shoulder as if he were afraid someone might be following him. "I need more money."

"More?" she echoed in disbelief. "I just wrote you a big check. A very big check."

His lips tightened. "You were late, which meant I was late with some of my, uh, creditors."

"But I gave you extra—"

"It doesn't matter," he cut in impatiently. "I need more. If you want me to keep quiet, write another check. Half of what you gave me last time."

Frustration raced through her. She stood. "Why don't you just do what everyone else does and get a job?"

His eyes darkened with anger. "Cut the chat, bitch, and write the check."

Feeling trapped and hating herself for being at his mercy, she sat down and pulled her checkbook from her purse. "I realize that you're accustomed to dealing with

Howard, but I'm not made of money," she said as she filled out the check. "Unlike Howard, I don't have an endless supply and I do have other responsibilities." The ball she'd bought for Willy made a musical sound as it wobbled on the side of her desk.

He snatched the check from her hand. "I'll be back in two weeks," he said and strode out of her office, leaving her with a terrible taste in her mouth and a heavy feeling in her chest. She looked at the bags of gifts for Willy and gnawed on her lip. She refused to take them back. Getting these little things for Willy had made her feel happier than she'd felt since Howard had died. She was surprised at her tender feelings for Willy. She'd always been terrified that she would be a horrible mother. Her mother had been loving, but wild and crazy, and Delilah had lost contact with her at such a young age. Her father had been autocratic and condemning. She'd never been able to measure up, and he'd been determined to stomp out any evidence of her mother's genes in her.

Delilah chuckled. Sorry, Daddy-o. Her mother's years of influence may have been cut short, but her love had lingered. Delilah thought of Willy with his sweet smile and the way his face lit up when she entered the room. Maybe she wouldn't be a rotten mother after all. Maybe she could have children and a family—

She caught herself. No trips to fantasyland allowed today. She had other pressing slimy problems to solve.

She would figure out how to rein in Guy. She didn't want to know what kind of habit would make him act so desperate for money. Something told her it wasn't a weakness for M&Ms. There had to be a way to get control of him, but she suspected eggs weren't going to help her this time.

*   *   *

That night Delilah fed and rocked Willy to sleep, singing him the song her mother had sung to her, "You are my sunshine." He smiled in contentment and reached to touch her face.

He moved his mouth and made off-key non-words as he tried to sing along. She couldn't help laughing at his cute efforts and he laughed when she did.

His body gradually relaxed and he fell asleep as she continued to rock him. It was such a peaceful moment she wanted to freeze it and bring it out to experience again when she was ready to pull her hair out. It was such a hushed calm time. This was how church should feel, she thought. Quiet, peaceful and safe.

She put his soft, relaxed body into his crib and watched him. He had screamed with glee when she had walked in the door. Silly, but she felt as if she'd lost pounds off the weight on her shoulders. Now his little bottom was hiked up in the air and his thumb sat loosely in his mouth.

A surprising sweet sensation crowded her chest. Willy felt safe. Delilah tried to remember a time when she had truly felt safe and secure. She felt a twist of pain at the spankings she'd endured from her father and dismissed the thought. No need to get maudlin.

Now that her young'un was in bed, she could enjoy the quiet of the evening. As long as she didn't think about Guy, Lilly or Benjamin. Which she wouldn't.

She microwaved and ate a healthy low-fat, low-cal, low-taste dinner and followed it up with a fudge-covered mint Oreo for dessert. She prepared a champagne cocktail, slipped a CD into her portable CD player, lit a dozen scented candles and closed the door to her bathroom.

Delilah moaned as she sank into the Jacuzzi. She

would miss this hot tub if she ever had to move. *Don't think about it*. She picked up the *Opera for Dummies* book and lazily scanned the pages.

A half hour later as she took a sip of her drink, she caught sight of something in her peripheral vision. Benjamin. She ripped off her headphones and glared at him. "The bathroom door was closed. Don't you ever get the hint?"

He loosened his tie and strolled toward her. "I was afraid you might have drowned since you didn't answer when I knocked on the door."

Delilah felt a shot of alarm that nearly sent her out of the water. "Did you wake the baby?"

"No. I tapped. I didn't bang. Isn't that what an intelligent man would do?"

"I suppose," she said grudgingly. "Well you've seen that I'm fine. I haven't drowned. In fact, I was doing very well before you entered the room. So leave," she said bluntly.

He glanced around at the candles. "This looks nice. Did you need more light to read?"

Read. Delilah remembered the title of the book she was reading and felt a wave of self-consciousness flood over her. She was stark naked, but she was much more embarrassed by the topic of her book than she was her nude body. Splaying her fingers across the cover of the book and positioning it closer to the water, she shook her head. "I put a couple of candles beside me. See?" She cleared her throat. "Now shoo."

"But your little party looks so inviting," he said.

"It's not. It's a party for Ducky and me. Three's a crowd, so go away."

"You know, Delilah, the way you're talking, I would almost think you don't want me here."

"That would be ri—"

"Not very hospitable," he said, unbuttoning his shirt.

Alarm shot through her. He actually looked like he was planning to get in the tub. "You don't understand. I want an evening of comfort and peace. You are disruptive. You are a pain in the butt. And I'm not having sex with you again. Remember?"

He tugged off his shirt and started on his belt, giving Delilah a minor heart attack. "You just haven't experienced how nice I am to have around often enough, yet."

"That's right. And I'd like to miss out on the experience of having you around tonight. Can't you just leave, already?" she asked in frustration as he pushed his slacks down.

"On my honor, I won't be a pain," he said.

Delilah rolled her eyes, then covered them. Heaven help her, this guy was persistent. She peeked through two fingers then closed her eyes. The only way she was going to get rid of him was to let him get in the tub. As much as she loathed leaving her sanctuary, he'd successfully invaded, so she would leave if he didn't. "Okay, you may stay in the tub for five minutes. Then you have to get out and you may get no closer to me than my feet."

"Deal," he said and she heard the splash of water as he stepped into the tub. "Ah."

She tossed him a dark glance, taking in the relaxed position of his head, his broad shoulders and the hair on his muscular chest. "Glad you're enjoying it. Four minutes and forty-five seconds."

"No time to lose then," he said, sitting up and meeting her gaze. "How was your day?"

"Good and bad and good," she said.

"What were the good and good?" he asked.

Delilah smiled. "Maria the wonder nanny arriving today was the first good. Buying Christmas gifts for Willy at lunch was the second good."

He nodded. "And the bad?"

"I'd rather not talk about it."

"Okay." He reached under the water and she felt his hand on her foot.

"What are you—"

"You said I couldn't get any closer than your feet." He held her foot firmly in his palm.

"That didn't mean you were supposed to touch it."

He rubbed the sole and a ripple of pleasure raced through her. Using both hands, he massaged the instep and Delilah couldn't withhold a sigh. He pressed his thumbs over the ball of her foot and she bit her lip.

He paused. "Want me to stop?"

"No," she said immediately. It felt too good and it was just her foot, she told herself. No secret feminine parts, just her foot.

He gave a low chuckle and continued to rub her foot until it turned to putty. When she'd had enough, she lifted her other foot for his attention.

"I'm past five minutes," he taunted.

"Do the other one or I'll feel uneven."

He rubbed her other foot and she rested her head against the tub. "For someone who's such a pain in the ass, you're very good with feet."

"I'm good with other parts too," he murmured. "Remember?"

Trying not to remember, she waved her hand in a dismissive gesture.

"Better watch your book. It's about to get wet. What are you reading?"

Delilah tensed and tossed the book over the side of the tub. "Nothing. Just something I picked up at the spa. We've added a book section." He continued to massage her foot and moved to her ankle and she closed her eyes. "Are you sure you didn't take a course on this or something? If law doesn't work out, you could get a job at the spa if you don't mind painting toenails too."

He chuckled. "Does that mean you'd hire me?"

She shrugged. "Maybe. Our most popular massage therapist is male. Lord, what a hottie. Nice guy, very nice guy."

"How well do you know him?"

She wiggled her hand. "I don't know his life history, and we get along. He works a full schedule, but he's always in a good mood. He's not cranky like the esthetician."

His hand crept upward to her calf and it occurred to her that he was now somewhat closer than her foot, but she couldn't muster a protest. She felt languid and relaxed.

"What's wrong with the esthetician?"

"She's territorial. Facials are her country and she doesn't want anyone moving in on her country. I had to give her a small percentage ownership of the spa to get her to hire and keep some assistants."

"Smart move."

"I got it from Cash. He was smart."

"But not too smart, because you don't like too-smart men," Benjamin said, his hands moving to her knee.

She really should stop him, and she would. In a minute. "He was too smart, but he didn't make me feel dumb."

She smiled, remembering one of the conversations she'd had with him. "He made me feel like I could do anything."

She felt his hand on hers and opened her eyes. Benjamin was much closer than her foot and he was studying her. "You can do anything you want, can't you?" he asked in a dead serious voice.

She waited for him to wink or laugh or roll his eyes, but he did none. He didn't even blink. He looked at her as if he thought she *could* do anything she wanted. Her stomach felt as if she was going down the up elevator.

"I'm still working on that," she finally managed to say, but her voice sounded husky to her own ears. "Your time's up and you're closer than my foot."

"Yeah," he said, his eyes feeling like they were blazing a hole through her.

Delilah held her breath.

Benjamin released her hand and backed away, rising from the tub, revealing his naked body. She would have to be blind not to notice that he was aroused and as he turned, he gave her a nice view of his tight rear end.

Delilah began to sweat. *Oh, wow.* She could have him back in her bed tonight if she wanted. But she didn't want, she reminded herself. She watched him towel off then pull on his boxers, slacks and shirt and gather the rest of his clothing in one of his hands. He turned back to face her. "So was I a pain in the ass?"

Hit by too many emotions to name, she shifted uncomfortably. "No," she admitted in a small voice.

"Did you like the foot massage?"

"Yes," she whispered.

He nodded. "G'night."

"Night," she said and listened as he walked out of the bathroom and through the foyer. As soon as she heard him close the door behind him, she dunked herself under the water. *Oh, wow*.

Lilly stared at the two-carat diamond ring sparkling on her finger and pinched herself. She still couldn't believe that she was engaged to marry Robert Huntington. In his darkened car, she stole a glance at him and felt her heart flutter wildly in her chest.

He was going to be her husband.

Lilly could barely contain her excitement. She sensed that Robert's feelings for her weren't as strong as hers were for him, but she was determined to change that. She would be the best wife Robert could imagine, she swore to herself. She would be exactly what he needed and that included getting the dirt out of her life—Delilah Montague.

Robert pulled into Lilly's driveway and cut the engine. He looked at her and touched her hair. "Your hair is so pretty."

Her hair colorist at the spa was responsible for that. "Thank you. You've been quieter than usual. Is something on your mind?"

"The usual," he said. "The campaign."

She nodded, trying not to feel a little disappointed that she wasn't included in his thoughts. She stretched toward him. "I loved being with you tonight."

His eyes lit. "Did you?"

He tugged a strand of her hair to pull her toward him and lowered his head. "You're so sweet," he said, brushing his lips back and forth over hers.

Her lips buzzed from the sensation. Other parts of her buzzed too. She wanted more. She pressed her mouth against his and he rewarded her with his tongue.

Lilly sighed, shyly rubbing her tongue over his in response. Robert deepened the kiss and pulled her closer. Her breasts tingled with arousal and her skin heated beneath her winter coat. Lilly heard a low moan, then another. A full moment passed before she realized *she* was making those sexual sounds.

Restless and hot, she wished Robert would touch her breasts. She wished he would rip off her clothes and make savage love to her. She wished . . .

As if he'd heard her thoughts, he cupped her breast through her coat. Lilly tugged at the coat. She wanted his hand closer. His hand slid away and she nearly wept in protest. Desperation made her bold. She lifted his hand to her sweater and his thumb immediately found her hard nipple.

He gave a low murmur of approval.

"Robert, do you want to stay the night?" she whispered, her heart beating a mile a minute.

He continued to massage her nipple until she couldn't resist the urge to squirm. "Oh, Lilly you tempt me."

Thank God, she thought. "I want you to stay the night." She gave him a thorough French kiss.

Robert groaned and pulled away slightly. "But Lilly, you're so sweet. You're innocent. I don't want to take advantage of you."

Please do. "We're engaged. How can you be taking advantage of me?"

"I don't know. Don't you want to wait until our wedding night?"

Why would she want to do that? She swallowed. "Do you?"

He leaned his forehead against hers. "Lilly, you're so innocent. I want it to be right for you."

"When I'm with you, everything is right," she said.

Twenty minutes later with her body on fire, Lilly was tearing off her clothes beside her bed. Alone, except for Maxine, who watched her warily from beneath Lilly's bed. Frustration roared through her like a forest fire and she wanted Robert to put out the flame.

Her need was overwhelming, both sexual and emotional. In her softly lit room, she glanced into her bureau mirror and looked at her half-naked body. Her eyes were black with arousal, and her cheeks were flushed. She lifted her hands to her aching breasts. They were heavy with need, the tips sensitized. She looked like a woman ready for sex.

Lilly let out a shriek of frustration and turned away from the mirror. She darn well was ready for action, but her fiancé wasn't cooperating. Lifting a hand to her forehead, she wondered if Robert wasn't consummating their relationship because he wasn't totally committed.

Lilly wanted the physical reassurance of their commitment to each other. She glanced at the diamond ring on her finger. Maybe that should be enough, but it wasn't. She wanted Robert's body pressed against hers. Then she would be more certain.

Lying awake in her bed, Delilah wondered if one more night of quick, hot, uncommitted sex with Benjamin would relieve some of the frustration that gnawed at her. Her feet were still tingling from his touch. As were other parts, she thought with a groan and flipped over in her bed again.

She was still surprised at how he'd handled her feet as if he'd known the exact spots to press to relieve tension, the exact level of pressure to bring her maximum pleasure.

It made her remember how he had handled other parts of her. And his body. She felt her temperature climb. *Oh, wow.* Delilah pulled her sheet over her head.

She wondered if she should just go ahead and hit the sack with him again. Even though he'd been Mr. Honorable Huntington nearly every step of the way with her, Delilah harbored no illusions that anything she shared with Benjamin would be more than a fling. Which was all she wanted. If she even wanted that. Then she remembered how he'd made her tremble when he'd made love to her. It wouldn't be just hot sex with Benjamin, and that really pissed her off.

"Are we done for tonight?" Paul asked Sara.

Sara nodded, glancing at the clock. Paul was probably eager to hit the singles' scene. She was certain he turned every female head when he entered a bar.

"You're making great progress," she said, rising from the chair of her dining-room table. Her townhouse was a work in progress since she'd left her husband. She didn't have a lot of money, but she never stopped being thrilled with having the choice to decorate her small living space the way she wanted.

"I have a great tutor," Paul said, rising with her, his dimple creasing his cheek.

"Thank you." Her heart skipped a beat, but she ignored it. Paul Woodward was a huge flirt. He would flirt with her ninety-year-old grandmother if he had the chance.

"I left something in the car, but I want to bring it to you now. Is that okay?"

Surprised, she shrugged. "I guess."

"Okay," he said, heading for the door. "Don't lock me out. I'll be right back."

"Okay," she said, curious. She followed him to the door.

He whipped around just before he left, catching her off-guard. She stumbled and he caught her shoulders. "Don't watch me. This is a surprise."

She couldn't resist smiling at his enthusiasm. "Okay."

"Go back to the table."

"Are you ordering me?"

"Yeah. You've given me a lot of orders, so I'd say it's my turn."

His playfulness made her feel as if someone had turned on a light inside her. "Okay," she said, returning to the table. Pressing her hands to her hot cheeks, she made a sound of exasperation with herself. He made her feel like a teenager, and he probably had no idea. Gosh, she felt silly. She'd been surprised at how often he'd wanted tutoring, nearly every other night. She dreaded the time when he decided he didn't need any more help.

Paul swept through the door with a huge grin on his face. One of his hands was tucked behind him as he walked toward her. When he stopped directly in front of her, he pulled his hand from behind him, revealing a beautiful bouquet of pink flowers.

Shocked, Sara put her hand to her throat. "Omigoodness, they're beautiful."

"You like them?"

"Of course," she said and looked at him in disbelief. "You shouldn't have."

"I wanted to. I've taken up a lot of your time and you've been so patient and encouraging."

"But it's been my pleasure," she argued. "It's been very rewarding for me to see you progress so quickly."

His handsome face turned serious. "But I've been the one who benefited. These are just a token of thanks. I want you to accept them."

"I will," she said, full of conflicting emotions. She was delighted, but also afraid. "I should get them in some water." She took the flowers from him and searched a cabinet for a vase large enough to accommodate them. Finding a white milk glass vase, she filled it with water. Her chest tightened with a disconcerting knot. Usually someone said thank-you after a favor was complete. Did this mean that Paul felt he was finished?

She swallowed hard. "They're so beautiful," she murmured to fill the silence and cover her anxiousness. "I hope they'll last a long time. You really shouldn't have—" Her voice broke and she bit her lip in horror.

"Sara?" Paul asked.

She felt him close behind her and the earnestness in his voice unraveled her self-control a little more. "They're wonderful," she said, but her voice sounded unsteady to her own ears.

"Sara? What's wrong? Are you allergic? Do they remind you of your husband?"

"No, no, no," she said, a chuckle escaping her throat that could have passed for a sob. Steeling herself, she turned around and faced him with a smile. "I'm not allergic and I can't remember my husband giving me flowers except for after I left." Her throat tightened up again, but she was determined to keep smiling. "I'm just—" She took a shallow breath. "I'm new at this and I'm very proud of you. But I didn't know we were—" Despite her determination, her voice wavered and her eyes filled. "I didn't know we were done."

"You're crying," he said in surprise, lifting his thumb to her cheek.

Cringing inwardly, she closed her eyes and felt a tear slide down her cheek. "I'm sorry. I know it's silly and—"

"Look at me," he said.

She bit her lip. "Another order."

"Please?"

As if she could turn him down. She opened her eyes and prayed he couldn't see that his tutor had a mile-wide crush on him.

He traced her tear with his thumb then moved his finger over her bottom lip. She held her breath.

He looked at her with a sensual question in his eyes that nearly buckled her knees.

"I'm too old for you," she whispered.

He shook his head, "No, you're not." He lowered his mouth to hers and took her lips in the sweetest of kisses. There was gentleness. And need. She felt it under the surface, rumbling between them, catching her by surprise.

She pulled away. "I don't think I can be like you."

He frowned. "What do you mean?"

"I mean I don't think I can be casual about—" She groped for a word. "About things as you can."

He looked at her with a sensual conviction that would have rocked her onto her rear end if he hadn't been holding her shoulders.

"I don't feel casual about you at all, Sara."

For men: How to make a woman weak in the
knees (or get her flat on her back)—treat her like
she's water and you haven't had a drink in days.
—DELILAH'S DICTUM

Chapter 14

Christmas shopping for Willy was so much fun it could almost replace sex, Delilah decided as she dressed him in his new little Santa PJs and danced with him to a song by The Wiggles. Since it was a week before Thanksgiving, she was probably rushing the Christmas thing a bit.

Her phone rang and she picked it up.

"Delilah, I was starting to wonder if something terrible had happened to you."

Delilah winced at the sound of her older sister's voice. She was usually delighted to talk to Katie, but she couldn't quite figure out how to explain everything that had happened in the last two months. "I'm fine," Delilah said. "Just obscenely busy."

Willy let out a shriek and Delilah bit back an oath.

"What is that noise? It sounded like a baby," Katie said. "Delilah, you haven't—"

"Of course I haven't. That's the television." Delilah set Willy in the playpen with a baby cookie and walked into the foyer. Willy shrieked again and Delilah stepped outside her front door.

"You're sure you're not in trouble? You sound out of breath," Katie said.

Delilah frowned. Her sister was entirely too observant and perceptive. "I'm fine. Just super busy with the spa. How are you and Michael?" she asked, referring to Katie's security consultant husband. "How's Jeremy?" she asked, her heart twisting at the thought of their young hearing-impaired brother.

"Michael and I are fine. Jeremy is here every weekend. We're starting to think about babies," Katie told her.

"Oh, wow," Delilah said, filled with a mixture of feelings. Having Willy had made her wonder what it would be like to have a baby and a husband. The thoughts had taken her off guard. "After all the parenting you had to do I thought you might wait forever."

"Me too," Katie said. "But Michael is changing my mind. He's so good with Jeremy and he likes the idea of me going to college during the pregnancy and early years. I kinda do too."

Delilah felt a slice of envy. She knew Katie and Michael shared a rare love, one that most people never experienced. Certainly one she never expected to experience.

"We want you to come up to Philly for Thanksgiving," Katie said.

Delilah shook her head. "I don't know. I'm pretty slammed at the moment."

"But it's a family holiday. You should be with family."

"I know, but the spa is so busy right now."

Silence followed. "We made a promise to stick together," Katie said, reminding Delilah of the emotional reunion they'd shared two years ago.

She felt a sharp twinge of guilt. "I know. It's just really crazy here right now. I'll tell you about it at Christmas."

"You promise?"

"I promise. Give my love to Michael and Jeremy, and tell Jeremy to keep the emails coming."

"Have you been in touch with Lori Jean?"

"Through email. She's going crazy at that girls' school where her father sent her. If he doesn't loosen the reins a little, she's going to rebel and end up on one of those *Girls Gone Wild* videos."

Katie chuckled. "He's determined to keep her pure as the driven snow."

"Yeah, well he forgets that we don't have Snow White among our ancestors." Feeling antsy about leaving Willy in the pen, Delilah cracked her door. "I should go. Thanks for calling. Keep me posted."

"I will," Katie said. "No backing out on Christmas."

Delilah's heart twisted. Having been jerked away from her sisters at such a young age, she still wasn't accustomed to the idea of family. "No backing out. Take care. Bye now." She turned off the phone and stared at it.

"Waiting for a genie to pop out?" Benjamin asked from behind her.

She glanced up at him, something inside her easing at the sight of his solid features and level gaze. "I wouldn't mind three wishes," she said, walking into her foyer.

He caught the door and followed her in. "Talking to one of your brainless boy toys?"

She threw him a sideways glance. "Why would you think that?"

"You didn't want whoever it was to hear Willy in the background."

Irritated by his partially accurate deduction, she considered letting him think the worst, but something inside her wouldn't allow it. "My sister in Philly. She has an overdeveloped sense of responsibility. She would feel like she needed to rush down here and rescue me." Every once in a while, Delilah wouldn't mind being rescued.

She glanced at Willy, who had happily smeared his face and PJs with soggy cookie, and smiled. "I see you enjoyed your cookie from head to toe," she teased the baby.

He smiled in return and bounced on his bottom.

"Don't say anything about the cookies," she warned Benjamin before he could open his mouth. "After a hard day of teething, he's due a cookie."

"What about you? After a hard day at the spa, what are you due?"

"Champagne cocktail or a soak in the Jacuzzi." She winced at her boring life. "Sleep is good too."

"I have a favor to ask."

She glanced at him warily. "What?"

"I've been invited to a small party tomorrow night. Would you go with me?"

She gaped at him in surprise. "What kind of party?"

"My brother just got engaged. My family is having a get-together of about fifty people to celebrate."

Delilah felt the smack of shock. *Engagement party.*

She blinked. "So he went through with it. Lilly Bradford?"

Benjamin nodded.

Yay, maybe wedding planning will keep Lilly away from the spa. Boo, what if Guy adds up Lilly and Robert's collective fortune and asks for more money?

"So will you go?"

Delilah blinked. "To the engagement party?" A hysterical giggle escaped her throat and she nearly strangled herself swallowing the next one. Oh, Lord, the irony would be rich. She could just imagine the number of colors Lilly's face would turn if she walked in with Benjamin.

She shook her head and cleared her throat. "No. I can't. I don't think I should leave Willy at night, yet. He's had a lot of change and I think it's better if we stick to his evening schedule."

"You could bring him with you."

"Oh, right, to an engagement party at your mother's house. It would be like bringing a screaming alien to the opera."

"My parents have seen babies before. My mother even gave birth to a couple."

"Yes, but you and your brother probably never had colic, and never cried for more than five minutes and slept through the night as soon as she came home from the hospital. I'd put money on the fact that you weren't allergic to disposable diapers."

"And we never spit strained peas when nanny used the silver spoon to put them into our perfect little mouths," he said, mocking her assumptions.

"You said that. I didn't." She shrugged, a wicked visual of his near-perfect naked body floating through her mind.

Moving his near-perfect body close to hers, he picked up her hand and rubbed his thumb over the place that betrayed her skipping pulse.

"I wonder what it takes for you to tell the truth," he said. He lifted her palm and pressed his mouth against it. "I wonder why it's so important to me to get the truth from you."

"Me too," she managed and pulled her hand from his, barely able to resist the urge to rub his kiss from her palm.

"We've already established that I'm not your kind and you're not mine."

"If that's true, then why do I think about you in the middle of when I'm lecturing?"

"Because you're speaking on a very boring subject," she said bluntly.

He chuckled. "Maybe. But if I'm not your kind of man, then why were you reading a book about opera?"

Delilah stared at him. Her brain locked. She felt stripped, deeper than her skin. But her skin burned worse than the time she'd blistered swimming in the lake when she was a kid. How horrid. She was blushing. She swore.

"My clients discuss opera," she mumbled, wishing for that telephone genie Benjamin had mentioned moments ago.

He shook his head slowly. "How can I not be fascinated by a woman who rescues me, takes on the care of a baby that's not her own, and secretly reads a book on opera."

Her heart twirled and thumped at the expression on his face. "It obviously wasn't a complete secret," she grumbled. "Don't take it personally."

"I do," he said. "But why'd you choose a book for dummies when you're no dummy?"

Delilah tried to steel herself against his effect on her, but her insides were feeling suspiciously goocy. *Because I don't want to feel like a dummy*, she thought, but couldn't bear to say it aloud.

He could see it though. She knew by the look in his eyes.

"You're not," he said in a low voice.

She held her breath at the emotion that surged through her. It was so sweet and sharp it brought tears to her eyes. This was the closest a man had gotten to her in maybe forever. Benjamin was different. Being with him made her feel differently about herself. Being with him made her think differently. In secret moments, she'd watched him hold Willy and wondered how it would feel if he were the father of her child. She wasn't sure she liked the direction her head and heart were taking her. She knew she didn't like it. Surely sex was less intimate than this.

Inhaling to steady herself, she caught a whiff of a slightly pungent scent. She wrinkled her nose, trying to place it when she heard Willy make a grunting noise.

She shook her head. Rescued by a poopy diaper. Who'd have thunk it? "I believe Willy has answered nature's call and he'll definitely need a diaper change." So *vamoose, go*, she silently said to Benjamin.

He didn't budge, so she walked through the foyer and opened the door. "Sorry I can't help you with that party. Thanks for thinking of me," she lied.

Benjamin strolled toward her and she told her heart not to jump. "Let me know when you finish the book," he said. "Graduation will be me taking you to the opera."

Not in a million years, she thought. "Good night," she said and closed the door.

Standing beside Robert, Lilly accepted congratulations and best wishes from the top twenty-five relatives and friends on the Huntingtons' *list*.

"She's lovely," one woman said, shaking Robert's hand. "I can tell she'll be an asset to you."

"That she will, Mrs. Oliver," he said. "I'm glad you could make it tonight."

"Thank you," Lilly murmured as the woman shook her hand and walked toward Robert's parents.

"How are you doing?" Robert asked in a low voice.

"Fine," she said. "But I need cue cards. How will I remember all these names?"

"Try to repeat their name three times when you speak to them and find something about their appearance to associate with their name," he told her.

Impressed, she smiled at him. "How did you know that?"

"I read it. I was horrible at remembering names and knew I'd have to improve if I was going to run for office."

She nodded. "How did you remember Mrs. Oliver's name?"

"I have to swear you to secrecy."

"Consider me sworn."

"O for owl," he said.

Lilly laughed because the woman had resembled an owl. Chuckling, Robert snagged her hand and she felt a tiny bit of the connection she craved with him.

The evening wore on and she and Robert became separated. The women's smiles all began to run together. Robert's father's laugh sounded a little too loud, a little too hearty. She felt like she was on display in a carnival.

"Lilly," a male voice broke through her daze.

She glanced up into Robert's brother's eyes and felt a thump of disappointment mixed with relief.

"Come and let me get you a glass of wine," Benjamin said. Lilly had met Robert's brother a few times before. He had a confident, intelligent air about him and from what Robert said, he didn't bow to family pressure very often. He was his own man. Even at this party, something about him set him apart from the crowd.

Feeling claustrophobic, she gladly allowed him to lead her away from the cackling crowd of women. "Thanks," she murmured. "Where's Robert?"

"Surrounded by some of his benefactors," he said dryly. "White wine or champagne? My father will be making a toast soon."

"Champagne," she said. "I may as well gear up."

"Are you okay? You looked a little woozy over there," Benjamin said, taking a glass of champagne from a tray and offering it to her.

Lilly swallowed a long sip of the bubbly liquid and prayed it would go to her head. She had thought she would feel ecstatic. She had thought that once she got engaged to Robert, she wouldn't feel lonely anymore, but she felt just as disconnected as ever. "I guess the hot air got to me," she managed with a smile. "It feels a little like a circus."

"And it's just starting," Benjamin warned her. "Don't get pushed into anything you don't want to do."

"I want to marry Robert."

He nodded, but remained silent.

"Sometimes I'm not sure about him," she confessed, then abruptly stopped, embarrassed at what she'd revealed. "I'm being silly. I'm sure it's all the excitement," she said. "Look, there's your father signaling for the waiter. It must be toast time."

"Lilly, come out of that corner and stand here with Robert," Mr. Huntington said in a booming voice.

Taking a deep breath, she walked toward Robert. He offered her his hand, thank God. Hers was trembling. "My wife and I are delighted to announce the engagement of Robert Huntington and Lilly Bradford. May theirs be a match made in heaven."

"Here, here," several voices echoed and Lilly gulped her champagne. She squeezed Robert's hand and prayed that tonight he would stay all night.

* * *

Just as Willy began to drift off while Delilah rocked him, the doorbell rang. She scowled at the intrusive sound. She knew it couldn't be Benjamin because he didn't ring the doorbell. He just walked in as if he owned the place. Oh wait, she reminded herself. He *will* own the place.

Carefully shifting Willy to her shoulder, she put him down in his crib. The doorbell rang again and she snarled, rushing through the foyer. She looked through the peephole and blinked in shock.

Nicky Conde stood outside her door, shifting from foot to foot. Delilah tried to imagine why Willy's mother would be there, and none of the reasons that came to mind were good.

Her stomach twisting viciously, she reluctantly opened the door.

Nicky bit her lip. "I made a mistake."

Chapter 15

*D*elilah stared at the girl in disbelief. "Which mistake would that be?" It seemed to Delilah that Nicky had made one mistake after another. Getting pregnant by Howard Bradford, abandoning her baby, taking off to be a model in Paris.

"I want Willy back," Nicky said.

Nicky's statement hit her broadside. Delilah had expected a request, something along the lines of money, but not this. "Excuse me?"

Nicky sniffed and her eyes filled with tears. "I was crazy to go to Paris. I missed Willy the whole time. I thought I could leave him with you, but I couldn't. I love him too much."

Delilah felt as if she'd been hit with a concrete block. "But what if you change your mind? He's not a ping-pong ball. He's a baby."

"I know he isn't," Nicky said. "I won't change my mind. It'll be different this time."

"How?" Delilah demanded, an odd, but strong panic seizing her. Outraged that Nicky felt she could waltz into her condo and pick up the baby as if Delilah had merely been a temporary baby sitter, she grappled with her feelings of anger and shock. "How will it be different? You're still not even twenty years old. You're still alone."

"I'm not alone. I called my mama and she said we could live with her. I'm going to go to the community college and get a nursing degree." She chewed on her lip again. "It's not really about the money because Howard gave me a bunch of money for Willy. I forgot to tell you before because I was in such a rush."

Forgot my ass, Delilah thought, anger rising inside her. "You signed all custody rights over to me. I can't give him back to you. You might change your mind again."

"I told you I'm not gonna change my mind. I'm his mother," she wailed. "He should be with me."

Delilah felt ripped in half. Two weeks before she would have gladly given Willy back to Nicky, but now , , Now she couldn't imagine it. He was a part of her. She couldn't possibly let him go. She had begun to visualize what he would look like as he grew older and the things they would do together.

She shook her head. "I don't know. This is happening too quickly. I'm going to have to think about it."

"What do you mean you're going to have to think about it?"

"I mean, you dumped this baby on me over three weeks ago like he was a toy you'd gotten tired of playing with. And now you're popping up saying you want to play with him again. You signed the guardianship for him to me. That means you asked me to make all the important decisions about his life. I have to think about this. I can't make an instant decision. This is too important."

Heart-wrenching fear crossed Nicky's face. "You would really consider not giving him back to me even though I'm his mother."

"Nicky, I have to think about what's best for Willy."

"But I'm his—"

Delilah held up her hand. "I know. I need to sleep on this."

Nicky took a shaky breath. "Well, can I at least see him?"

Delilah felt pulled in ten different directions. She felt protective of Willy, but Nicky was his mother. Willy had burrowed his way into her heart in no time, so she could imagine how much Nicky must have missed him. "He was just falling asleep, so you'll need to be quiet," she said and led the way to the room she'd converted into a nursery for the baby.

Nicky looked into the crib with longing eyes. "He's grown," she whispered in surprise. "And look at his Santa pajamas." She extended her hand and lightly touched his back. She wiped her cheek with her other hand.

"You should go," Delilah said, a horrible knot of dread forming in her chest. "We can talk tomorrow."

Three hours later, after she'd nearly paced a hole in her carpet and could stand the feelings clawing though her no longer, she knocked on Benjamin's door.

Dressed in partially fastened jeans, he stared at her, his eyes squinting against the light. "What's up?"

"I'm sorry I woke you," she said, incredibly uncomfortable. She hated asking for help.

He shrugged. "What do you need?"

"I, uh—" She swallowed, fighting the impulse to run back to her own condo and endure her torture all by herself.

"Is it Willy?"

"Sort of," she confessed, lacing and unlacing her fingers.

"You want to come in?"

"No. I need you to come over to my place," she said, nearly choking on the words.

He nodded. "Let me get my key," he said and disappeared for a moment. When he returned, he pushed his arms through the sleeves of a shirt. "Is this going to involve another middle-of-the-night drive?"

Delilah shook her head and they walked down the hall to her condo. He opened the door for her and followed her into the den. She felt him studying her. His gaze was so calm, so steady. So strong. Everything about him said *I can handle anything.*

Her emotions reacted like a volcano, erupting inside her. To her horror, she burst into tears.

Everything blurred after that. She felt sobs wracking from her and tried to squelch them, but couldn't. Benjamin pulled her against him and she buried her face in his chest. He was warm and strong and she could count on him. At least, at this moment.

She felt him rub her back the same way she rubbed Willy when he was upset. She was so confused she didn't know what to think. She took several deep breaths and finally quieted. Still not trusting herself to speak, she remained encircled in Benjamin's arms, breathing in his scent.

"Okay," he said. "I'm ready when you are."

Delilah took another deep breath and pulled away slightly. "Nicky showed up tonight."

"Who's Nicky?" He loosened his arms just a little.

"Willy's mother."

She felt him look down at her. "What did she want?"

"She wants Willy back," Delilah said, hating the tremble in her voice. Embarrassed by her crying jag, she mentally gave herself a shake and told him the rest of the story. The *real* story, without revealing Howard's name. He quizzed her about her previous inconsistencies and she had to come clean, but she still didn't tell him who the baby's father was. Benjamin had his own strange connection to the Bradfords through Lilly now.

Sometime during their conversation, he led her to the couch. He listened intently and waited until she stopped. He tented his fingers. "Do you want me to tell you your legal options?"

Delilah nodded.

"You can give Willy back to her and keep the papers she signed and tell her that you'll be watching to make sure that she takes care of Willy."

Delilah frowned. "But—"

"Or you can take her to court and have a messy, expensive, long, ridiculous court battle after which time you will still end up giving Willy back to her and she'll never let you see him again."

"But she signed those papers."

"But she only abandoned him for three weeks. The court would consider that an aberration and require her to get counseling and be under the supervision of a social worker with a heavy caseload who will put this priority at the bottom of the list."

"But she signed him over to me," Delilah protested. "She dumped him at my door and went to Paris."

Benjamin heard the longing in her voice, saw the despair she was trying to hide. "You went and fell in love with Willy, didn't you?"

She opened her mouth in surprise. "I, I—" Her face crumpled. "I did."

He felt a surge of sympathy and pulled her into his arms. "Oh, Delilah, you poor thing."

"I'm not a poor thing. I'm just a stupid thing," she protested, but her voice was wobbly. "He was such a little pain in the ass. How did he become so important to me? I don't want to give him back He's my baby now. I would rather cut off my arm."

Benjamin tightened his arms around her. "You're not stupid, but you'll have to give him back."

She sighed, her breath sweet against his neck. "This sucks."

He smiled. "Yeah, it does. You want me to stay the night?"

She sighed again, "No If I had sex with you again, you would be so blown away, you wouldn't be able to think straight enough to teach class the next day."

"Promises, promises," he said, but each day he was unwinding another of Delilah's secrets, and each day she left him wanting more and more.

Lilly was in a horrid mood.

Robert had *not* stayed with her last night. He'd said his father said it wouldn't look right. She bared her teeth as she jerked a brush through her hair. Looking closer into the mirror, she scowled. Was that a fever blister erupting on her mouth?

She wouldn't be surprised. To say she was stressed would be an understatement. Plus she was premenstrual. Give her a gun and she had enough frustration and energy to bring in the FBI's ten most wanted criminals. Dead, of course.

She took a deep breath and resolved to take her energy to the spa. She wouldn't get a soothing massage or facial. She would give Delilah hell and hopefully push her closer to the edge. Lilly still wanted that woman out of her life. Out of Houston if she could manage it.

Her doorbell rang and she glanced at the clock. Who could it be? It wasn't even seven A.M. Maxine raced downstairs and barked. Shrugging, Lilly walked to the front door and looked through the peephole. A man. No one she recognized.

"Hush," she said to Maxine, stroking the dog's head. She pressed the intercom button. "Who do you want to see?"

The man lifted his head and looked the door up and down as if he were trying to find the speaker. "Lilly Bradford. I knew her father."

"How did you know him?"

"Oh, I knew Howard for many years," he said in an affectionate tone.

Something about the way the man looked put her off, but the mention of her father reminded her how much she missed him. She could talk to the man on the front porch. She wouldn't let him in. She opened the door and stepped outside with Maxine's breath steaming up the storm door.

"I only have a moment. I have an early appointment this morning. I'm Lilly Bradford," she said, extending her hand. "And you're?"

"Guy Crandall." He smiled and the gesture somehow combined oily nervousness. "Your father and I had a special arrangement. I knew things about him no one else did. I knew he had a son."

Lilly blinked and jerked her hand away from the man. "My father didn't have a son."

"Yes he did, but I figure with your engagement to a politician, you probably wouldn't want that news to get out. I can make sure of that," he said. "For a price."

Stunned, offended, she grasped for a response. "You're insane."

He laughed. "Not insane. I just want to be paid."

Disturbed and ready to slam the door in his face, Lilly put her hand on the doorknob. "This is ridiculous. If you keep spouting these lies, I'll have my attorney call you."

"Not so fast, Miss Lilly White," he said, wrapping his hand around her wrist like a snake.

Sickened by his touch, she jerked away again. "Don't ever touch me."

"Just pay me. Listen, if you don't believe me, go ask Delilah Montague. She knows the whole story."

Everything inside her turned completely red. Delilah Montague was behind this sordid story. She shouldn't be surprised.

Delilah told Maria the perfect nanny that she wouldn't need her to take care of Willy anymore. She decided to take the morning off and spend it packing all the things she'd bought for Willy. She cried at the oddest things. The cloth diapers she'd cursed. Strained peaches. Willy loved peaches. His baby cookies.

She had hardly slept during the night, but Willy was still peacefully sleeping in his crib. When he awakened, she would feed him the last time. Lord help her, she was maudlin.

Her doorbell rang, followed by a loud knock. Surprised at the early time, she quickly flitted to the door. Benjamin walked in with his key, so she knew it wasn't him. Glancing through the peephole, she was stunned to see Lilly Bradford. She quickly opened the door.

"Lilly," she said, unable to keep the surprise from her voice.

"You slut," Lilly said, fire darting from her wide blue eyes. "You tricked my father into getting you pregnant and—"

"Pregnant?" Delilah echoed, backing away from Howard Cash Bradford's irrational daughter.

"Well it sure as hell couldn't have been immaculate conception if you were involved," Lilly said and gave her a shove.

Stunned by the move, Delilah gaped at her. "What on earth are you talking about?"

"I was told my father has a son and you're at the bottom of it, you white-trash slut . . . " Lilly ranted as she shoved Delilah again.

"You've gone crazy," Delilah said, shoving her back. "I didn't have your father's baby!"

"It had to be you," Lilly shouted. "He wasn't involved with anyone else half as trashy as you!"

Watching in disbelief as Lilly lifted her hand in a telltale slapping motion, Delilah reacted instinctively. She grabbed Lilly's hair and jerked it hard.

Lilly screamed. "You bitch. You—"

"What is going on here?" Benjamin asked from the doorway.

"She tricked my father into getting her pregnant," Lilly said hysterically, still trying to slap her.

Keeping a firm grip on Lilly's hair, Delilah dodged Lilly's hand. "She's insane. I never had sex with Howard. He was impotent."

Lilly shrieked. "He couldn't have been impotent. He

was a womanizer," she screamed, her face red with fury. She swiped her perfectly manicured nails across Delilah's arm.

"Ouch!" Delilah cried, kicking Lilly's shin and pulling her hair harder.

Lilly screamed. "You made me lose a nail!"

"That's enough," Benjamin said, stepping between them while Lilly's arms flailed around him. "Enough of this catfight," he said sternly, pushing Lilly away from Delilah.

"Benjamin," Lilly said weakly as if she'd just seen through her haze of fury. "What are you doing here?"

"I live next door."

"To her?" Lilly asked, looking at Delilah in scorn. "You have my sympathies."

Delilah bared her teeth at Lilly, resisting the urge to tell her that Benjamin had been more than neighborly.

Lilly glared at Delilah.

"Lilly, why in hell are you acting like a fishwife?" Benjamin demanded.

Lilly shook her finger at Delilah. "It's all her fault. She got pregnant and had my father's baby."

Benjamin looked at Delilah with what she suspected was his lawyerly interrogational expression.

"I did not," Delilah said.

"She did. She's a slut," Lilly interjected.

"Shut up," Benjamin said to Lilly.

Delilah took her first breath in two minutes. "Howard Cash Bradford was impotent. To compensate, he liked having young arm candy. He charmed me into being arm candy, gave me gifts and became my best friend before I realized I wouldn't ever be going to bed with him. He taught me about business and gave me career opportunities I couldn't have imagined."

"That's an understatement," Lilly muttered in a low voice, glowering.

The insult stung. "You're so right. I didn't have any of the educational opportunities you had when I was growing up. Even my father said I was white trash."

Lilly stared in silence.

"I'm sure you remember that your father was very clever, even manipulative at times."

Lilly opened her mouth as if to protest, then closed it, folding her arms over her chest.

"After his last visit to the hospital, I visited Cash at home and he made me promise to look after you if anything happened to him. He also said he wanted me to do one more thing, but he never got to tell me because we were interrupted and he died that night. Willy's mother showed up on my doorstep three weeks ago and told me Howard had promised I would take care of him."

"Willy?" Lilly echoed, her brows furrowing. "Is that the baby you had at the spa?"

Delilah nodded.

"Now some sleazeball named Guy Crandall is trying to get me to pay money to keep him quiet about this," Lilly said.

Delilah swore. "I've already written three checks to the guy." She felt Benjamin's gaze on her and tried not to squirm.

"That's extortion. Is that why you wanted to sell the condo?"

"That and for the baby. Nicky neglected to tell me how to receive financial support for Willy when she left for Paris."

Lilly stared at her in amazement. "You were going to sell your condo to pay Guy Crandall?"

Delilah shrugged. "I hated to do it, but I didn't see any way out. You were going to get engaged to Robert any day and—" She broke off, watching Lilly turn white.

"Omigod, Robert will break our engagement if he hears about this," Lilly whispered.

Delilah searched Benjamin's face and his impassive expression made her stomach knot. "I'm sure he won't," Delilah quickly said, although her voice sounded unconvincing to her own ears.

"Yes, he will," Lilly wailed, grabbing Benjamin's shoulders and shaking. "What are we going to do? I've got to pay him. I've got to or Robert will dump me. You know he'll dump me. He may like me, but he doesn't need me."

"I don't know that," Benjamin said, prying Lilly's hands loose. "I think Robert does believe he needs you or he wouldn't have asked you to marry him."

Delilah turned to Benjamin. "You have to swear not to tell Robert about this."

He shook his head.

"You have to swear," Delilah said. "You owe me."

He narrowed his eyes. "How long are you going to keep extracting favors from me?"

"Owe you?" Lilly said. "Why does he owe you?"

Delilah waved a dismissing hand, but kept staring at Benjamin. "I helped him in his hour of need. Benjamin, you have to agree not to tell Robert."

He raked his hand through his hair. "You can't continue to pay this Guy—guy."

"We're not talking about payment at the moment. I want your word."

"Okay," he said. "I won't tell Robert, but you can't keep paying Guy. He'll keep asking for more. He will get out of control."

A wail sounded from the nursery. "Willy," Delilah said, automatically heading to collect him. She picked him up from his crib and cuddled him close. "Good morning, Mr. Sunshine." Her heart twisted as she recalled again that this would be the last morning she would greet him this way.

Delilah closed her eyes against the spurt of pain, refusing to cry. She felt a hand on her shoulder, a comforting squeeze.

"You okay?" Benjamin asked in a low voice.

"Don't be too nice to me," she whispered. "It'll make me cry."

No way around it, sex in a closet will be murder
on someone's knees. But you'll never be forgotten.
—DELILAH'S DICTUM

Chapter 16

"**S**o this is really my half-brother," Lilly said as she stared at Willy.

"The ears are a dead giveaway," Delilah said, stroking the baby's soft ears that stuck straight out.

Lilly touched her own ears self-consciously.

"Your father's ears were like this," Delilah said.

Lilly let out a slight breath. "I guess you're right."

An uneasy silence settled between the two women and Lilly cleared her throat. Benjamin had left after extracting a promise that there would be no more hair-pulling, clawing, smacking or kicking.

Lilly cleared her throat again. "I suppose I owe you an apology."

Delilah gave a wry smile. "Kinda hard to do when you're bearing a grudge the size of your native state."

Lilly sighed. "He was always out with you. And when he wasn't out with you, he was talking about you."

"Really?" Delilah felt a dart of pleasure. "I didn't know that."

"Well, he did," Lilly grumbled. She gave her a curious glance. "What's the story with your parents?"

"I prefer to say I was hatched," she said. "But the truth

is that my mother gave birth to four children by four different fathers. My father is an evangelist and he regards me as the daughter of a she-devil."

Lilly looked at her for a long moment.

Delilah's stomach tightened. "Don't feel sorry for me or I'll have to stomp on your foot."

"Benjamin said no kicking."

"He didn't say no stomping and he didn't say I couldn't rip your hair out by the roots."

"You must think I'm a spoiled brat," Lilly said.

"Have you given me reason to think anything else?"

Lilly paused and looked away. "I guess not. So why did you pay Guy Crandall?"

"Why do you think?"

"Because you made a promise to my father?"

Delilah nodded.

Lilly looked at Willy and shook her head. "My father could really be an ass sometimes." She extended her hands to the baby. "May I hold him for a minute?"

Delilah handed over Willy's warm, squirmy body. He immediately wrapped his hands around Lilly's hair.

"You're a cutie, aren't you?" Lilly said to the baby then looked at Delilah. "Will you be keeping him?"

Her stomach twisted. "No, but that's another story. His very, very young mother dumped him on me, but she has decided she wants him back."

Lilly looked at her in disbelief then closed her eyes. "This whole situation is crazy. What are we going to do about Guy?"

"Pay him until we figure out how to neuter him," Delilah said.

"Neuter?"

Delilah shrugged. "Neuter. Neutralize. Same thing. Any chance you can make this a short engagement?"

Lilly's eyes filled with misery. "It'll be very short if Robert finds out about this. Every decision he makes is affected by his run for office. Even sex. He won't even stay—" She broke off as if she just realized what she'd confessed. Her face flamed.

"Are you saying that you and Robert haven't had sex?"

If possible, Lilly's face turned brighter red.

"Are you?"

Lilly closed her eyes and nodded. "He said his father said it wouldn't be good if a reporter saw his car staying at my house overnight."

Delilah groaned. "So? You don't need a bed to have sex. You only need a man and a condom."

Lilly opened her eyes "What are you suggesting?"

"Go to his office, lock the door and have your way with him."

"I never thought of that."

"Well maybe you should. Women who say that the way to a man's heart is his stomach should look a little lower."

By eight o'clock that evening, Delilah felt like a used tissue someone had tossed on the ground and ground into the pavement. Giving Willy to Nicky had ripped her in half. She felt so full of unshed tears that she was sure she was going to burst any moment, but she was determined not to cry.

She looked at the spot where she'd kept the playpen and sucked in a deep breath. "No crying. Crying doesn't solve anything," she whispered.

She was so upset she didn't even feel like getting in the Jacuzzi. The last champagne she'd bought had gone flat and turned to vinegar, so she couldn't even have her favorite cocktail. She was out of M&Ms too.

She felt so lost. Maybe if she went to bed she would fall asleep and the horrible knot in her chest would go away. She heard her door open and looked up to see Benjamin enter.

He glanced around the condo. "Did Nicky come for Willy?"

She nodded, her throat tight with misery.

"Did you work out an arrangement to see—"

"I don't want to talk about it," she said, biting her lip to stave off tears. In fact, she'd promised Nicky that she would rip her into little pieces if she didn't take good care of Willy.

He nodded, taking a breath and putting his hands on his hips. "You'd rather talk about Guy Crandall and why you lied to me."

Ouch. The accusation pinched. "Not really."

"You didn't really lie?" he asked, his voice rising.

"No," she said, looking at the leather cushion. "I meant I wouldn't rather talk about Guy Crandall." She could feel the anger rolling off of him. His displeasure bothered her. She was a survivalist. She'd been through tough times and she'd had to do things she wasn't necessarily proud of to get through them, but she didn't like what she was feeling right now. She hated disappointing Benjamin.

She felt like a piece of crud.

He sat on the cushion that she'd been intently studying. His thigh blocked her view. "Why did you lie to me?"

"I couldn't tell you the truth because of your brother."

"That's no excuse. You had every reason to trust me," he said and she heard more than injured male pride in his voice.

Delilah felt even more like crud. Nothing like being caught between a rock and a hard place. Jeez, that was where she lived. She met his gaze. "How hard for you was it to promise that you wouldn't tell Robert about Willy?"

"Difficult, but—"

"Exactly. If I'd told you earlier, then it would have been even more difficult. You have this huge sense of integrity and it would have suffered. Your integrity is suffering now."

"Doesn't yours suffer?"

Delilah fought the guilty feeling. Her father had spent a lot of time trying to make her feel guilty. The trouble was she wasn't just feeling guilty because she hadn't told Benjamin the whole truth and nothing but the truth. She felt guilty because she sensed she'd hurt him. "I do my best and I do what I have to. I know I'm not perfect and never will be."

"I hate for people who are important to me to lie to me."

Her heart dipped. Was she that important to him? *No*, she insisted. "I did what I had to do."

Benjamin stood. "Damn it, you should have trusted me, Delilah. I was willing to buy this friggin' condo from you. That should have given you a sign."

She gnawed on her lip. "Yes. That was very nice, but blood is different. You can't tell me you're not protective of your brother."

"Of course I'm protective of my brother, but—"

"But nothing," Delilah interjected. "You feel torn now. You would have felt torn then."

"What's it going to take for you to trust me? When are you going to admit that there's something between us?" he demanded.

Delilah was oh-so-tempted to close her eyes, cover her ears and sing la-la-la so she couldn't hear him. "I don't have a lot of experience with trusting people."

"Maybe you've been hanging around the wrong kind of people," he said, his voice edged with a sexy roughness.

"Maybe," she admitted, her heart jumping.

"Do you want me to stay tonight?"

Yes. No. Yes. No. She felt raw and vulnerable. He could get to her tonight. He could get to her in ways she wasn't sure she wanted to be gotten. He already had.

"No," she finally said.

"Okay, good night," he told her in a voice so cold it gave her a chill. She blinked and he was gone, and she was even more miserable than before he'd visited her.

The following morning, Delilah felt lost. She kept going into the nursery and inhaling the baby powder scent of Willy. She called Nicky to find out how Willy was and learned that he'd had a restless night. Although deep down, she knew Willy would adjust, Delilah knew she had been altered, and she wasn't sure she could go back to being the person she'd been before Willy had shown up on her doorstep. Irritated with her misery, she left for the office early and resolved to catch up on everything she'd set aside during the last few weeks.

Midway through the day she came upon an invitation to a cocktail party from one of the spa's most influential clients, Iris McLanahan. Delilah chuckled at the scribble at the bottom of the invite, *No need to RSVP. You will attend! Bring a gorgeous man.*

Delilah thought of Benjamin, and immediately shook her head at the image. She heard the low chuckle of Paul

Woodward in the outer office and liked the idea. She had noticed that Paul and Sara were getting along much better lately. What a relief. Sara had been so stiff and uncomfortable around him for a while.

Rising from her chair, she peeked into the outer office. "Hey big boy, I've got a special request. Are you up to it?"

The slightest trace of discomfort crossed his face. Glancing at Sara, he winked then lifted his lips in a boyish smile. "You know I've always been up to it," he flirted back at her. "What do you need?"

"Are you available tonight?" she asked.

His jaw dropped and he darted another quick glance at Sara. "Uh—for what?"

"Business acquaintance obligation. Iris McLanahan has summoned me to a cocktail party. She's also ordered me to bring a gorgeous male. You fit the qualifications, so you're elected if you can make it."

"I, uh—"

"I'd really appreciate it if you could do it," Delilah confessed. "I don't feel like doing this one alone."

"Okay. Just tell me what time and I'll pick you up."

"Eight o'clock." She smiled. "I'll try not to keep you out too late."

Hours later, Delilah was putting the finishing touches on her makeup. She was dressed in a purple curve-loving designer dress and she looked pretty damn good if she did say so herself. She remembered her mother had always said that if you felt depressed, you should dress up. It would make you feel better.

Delilah had to confess that she did indeed feel a little better, not a lot, but enough. She hadn't attended an adult event since Cash's funeral, so she supposed it was time.

Her doorbell rang and she couldn't help smiling. Paul. He was gorgeous. He was safe. Perfect combination for tonight. Grabbing her purse, she opened the door and thoroughly approved his well-cut suit. She let out a whistle. "You look better than I do."

"I'm blushing," he lied.

She rolled her eyes. "You never blush."

"Under the right circumstances with the right woman," he corrected, escorting her to the elevator.

"Have you found her?" she asked, curious.

"Who?" he asked, seeming a bit distracted.

"The right woman," she said as the elevator whisked down to the garage.

He was silent for a long moment.

"Paul? Are you okay?"

He nodded. "Yeah. I just have something on my mind, but don't worry. I'll put on my party front at Iris's."

"You don't have to go," she said, feeling guilty for having pushed him into going with her.

"No." He lifted his hand. "This is fine. It's good."

"Good for who?" she asked doubtfully.

"For several people," he said in a mysterious voice.

"What have you got cooking on the back burner?"

"Front burner. She hasn't taken me seriously yet. My instincts tell me she may after tonight."

"Poor woman," Delilah said, making a clucking sound as he led her to his car.

"Poor me," he corrected.

Two-and-a-half hours later, Delilah had loosened up. After two champagne cocktails and two of Iris's secret cocktail dubbed *Knock-out punch*, she felt as if she were walking on a ship. The walls were moving. The floor definitely shifted when she tried to put one foot in front of the other.

She nodded and smiled at everyone who spoke to her, but she couldn't have repeated what they'd said. Hearing Iris's trilling laughter from the next room, Delilah saw an anniversary clock on a table and squinted to make out the time. She couldn't resist the urge to put her hands on either side of it to make it stay still.

"What are you doing to that clock?" Paul asked, appearing by her side.

"I can't read it when it's moving," she said.

He chuckled. "Definitely time to go."

"Ya think?"

"Yeah. Let's say goodbye to Iris."

Delilah thanked Iris then leaned heavily on Paul as he helped her into his car. She leaned her head against the headrest and fell asleep on the way to her condo. He helped her into the elevator and tried to help her to get into her room, but she couldn't find her key.

"I know it's here somewhere," she muttered and dumped the contents of her purse onto the hallway floor in frustration. "Do you see it?"

Paul lifted a key. "Is this it?"

Delilah shrugged. "Probably. Try it."

Pacing his condo, Benjamin heard odd sounds in the doorway. He'd just returned from a family dinner where he'd watched Lilly nearly have a meltdown. His father was pissed because Benjamin had told him he was going into business with a friend. The evening had been so awkward it had made his teeth ache. And Delilah weighed heavily on his mind.

Hearing another sound from the hallway, he impatiently opened the door and spotted Delilah sitting beside her door doing something with her purse while a man messed with her doorknob.

An ugly bitter taste filled his mouth. Wearing an unbuttoned coat that revealed her shapely legs, Delilah was dressed to slay armies, and although he didn't swing that way, he suspected the guy standing beside her didn't have a hard time keeping his bed occupied.

If he had any sense, he would close his door and forget Delilah Montague, but Benjamin was pretty sure he'd lost most of his sense the day she'd rescued him.

"Need some help?" he asked, stepping into the hallway.

Two heads turned in his direction. The male looked somewhat relieved. Delilah looked dazed and disheveled.

The man cleared his throat. "We can't seem to find her key," he said.

"Benjamin has one," Delilah said, scooping up the contents of her purse.

"Benjamin? I'm Paul, Paul Woodward. I work at the spa with Delilah," he said, extending his hand.

Worked with her? Or *on* her? Benjamin grudgingly accepted the man's handshake.

"Thanks for your help," Paul said. "I think Delilah needs to get to bed."

Benjamin pulled her key from his pocket and unlocked the door. Paul made no move to go inside.

Benjamin relaxed a millimeter.

"Thanks for being my escort for the party," Delilah said, kissing Paul on the cheek. "Sorry I got wobbly. I think Iris's *Knock-out punch* was really a knock-out."

"No problem," Paul said. "Sleep a few extra winks."

He turned to Benjamin. "Thanks again."

Delilah tottered into her foyer, weaving from side to

side. She leaned a bit too far and collided with the wall. He heard her swear under her breath and bit back a chuckle.

"You okay?" Benjamin asked, closing the door behind him.

"I'll be fine as soon as everything stops moving. Iris thought she was so cute with that *Knock-out punch*. Geez, I wonder what she put in it."

Benjamin took her arm and led her to her bedroom. He pushed her into a sitting position on the bed. She kicked off her shoes.

"Who is Paul?" he asked, still feeling an itchy tension.

"Everybody's favorite massage therapist. Isn't he gorgeous? And he's not too smart."

Benjamin ground his teeth. "He meets your qualifications."

"Yeah." She sighed and fell back on the bed. "Except he seems like a brother. Damn shame, isn't it?"

"Sure is," he lied, lifting her slightly to remove her coat. Her arms were dead weight. She offered little help. "Why didn't you ask me to escort you?"

She rolled her eyes. "You're a Huntington. Everyone would whisper, whisper, whisper. What's a Huntington doing with that skanky Delilah Montague."

"You're not skanky," Benjamin corrected. "You just give the false impression of being a bad girl."

"How do you know it's false?"

"Because I've seen you be good."

She waved her hand. "You're making my head hurt," she said her eyes smoky, her mouth pouty. "Thanks for using your key."

He pulled her up the bed so that her head rested on the pillow.

She shook her head at him. "Just because I had too much of Iris's punch doesn't mean you're going to get any from me tonight."

Benjamin cleared his throat to cover a chuckle. "I've never been into the idea of necrophilia."

She frowned. "What's that?"

"Sex with dead people."

"I'm not dead," she said and closed her eyes. "I'm just dizzy. And sleepy." Her voice slurred together.

For his own amusement, Benjamin silently counted to fifty-three before Delilah's snore interrupted him.

You know you drank too much when you wake up the next morning and you're still wearing your control-top pantyhose.

—DELILAH'S DICTUM

Chapter 17

*J*ust before midnight, Sara's doorbell rang. Her heart jumped in her chest and she bit her lip. With her luck, it would be a ring and run.

Paul had promised he would come see her after he delivered Delilah to her condo. She'd told him it wasn't necessary. They hadn't made any promises. No strings, no commitments. Just friendship and amazing sex.

She'd told herself that all evening as she'd gnawed her fingernails down to the quick. He was almost ten years younger than she was. He couldn't be that attracted to her. He couldn't want her exclusively. He couldn't, even though he insisted that he did.

Pulling her terry robe around her, she cracked the storm door and saw him standing in all his gorgeousness on her front porch. Her heart danced again. He smiled, revealing his ladykiller dimple, and she opened the door.

"As promised," he said, stepping inside.

"Unnecessary," she said, though she was thrilled to see him.

"I disagree," he said, pulling her into his arms. "I'm

here to make a late-night delivery." He lowered his mouth and kissed her.

The room began to spin.

"Let me move in with you," he coaxed between kisses.

Breathless, she shook her head. "You're crazy."

"It's crazy for me to keep driving back to my place at night when I want to stay with you," he said, sliding his mouth down her neck and pulling at her robe.

"This is insane," she said, helping him with her robe and tugging at his shirt. "I thought you would be tempted to stay the night with Delilah."

"I told you Delilah just flirts with me because I'm safe." He chuckled. "Poor thing. She got drunk. She's gonna have a headache the size of the Grand Canyon tomorrow morning."

Sara felt a twinge of sympathy. "She must be upset about Willy."

"And maybe some other stuff. I don't know what. Right now, I just want to be with you," he said, cupping her breasts. "In you."

Sara's knees wobbled. "Oh, Paul, what you do to me. I'm shameless."

Paul shook his head. "I love you. I want to ask you to marry me, but I know that'll scare the hell out of you."

Sara gasped. "Marry!"

"Yeah, but I can wait." He picked her up and carried her to the bedroom. "I just wish you'd let me live with you so I can prove how indispensable I am."

Sara fought a lump rising in her throat. "I'm just so afraid it won't last. That you'll wake up one day and realize you don't want to be with an older woman."

"Sweetheart, I've proven to you over and over that I'm no baby." He paused, sliding his finger from her lips, down her chin and throat to her breasts. "But I'd sure like to give you a baby."

He couldn't have said anything more perfect. He couldn't have said anything that would touch her deepest longings more. Her chest tightened and her eyes filled with tears. Her husband hadn't wanted children and she'd just assumed that her chance for a baby had passed her by.

Oh, Lord, was it possible? Was it wise? How could she possibly say no? She looked into his gaze and the expression in his eyes silenced the voices of doubt that crowded her head. "You're making me fall in love with you."

"Lady, I've just gotten started."

Delilah awakened the next morning to a ringing sound. It felt as if it originated inside her head. She shook her head and winced. The ringing continued. She slowly opened her eyes, which was difficult to do, because she hadn't removed her makeup last night and her eyelashes were sticking together. The ringing stopped. Squinting her eyes, she looked from side to side. A sliver of relief slid through her. Her bed. She was in her bed by herself.

So she hadn't been totally stupid. She thought of those last two drinks and cringed. Just partly stupid. She had a vague memory of Benjamin helping her to bed. It seemed he was rescuing her all the time lately.

She frowned. Her mouth tasted as if something had crawled inside and died. She lifted her head and her stomach turned over. She immediately sank back onto the pillow.

She realized she was still dressed. That was good and bad. Geez, she hadn't even ditched the shaper pantyhose, she thought, feeling like a thousand rubber bands were wrapped around her waist and thighs. She lay still for a moment and had an odd feeling that something was wrong. What was it?

Her brain bumbled along until it hit a speed bump. Willy, she thought. Willy was gone. She closed her eyes at the pain that twisted through her. What was she going to do without him? She felt so empty.

The ringing began again. The phone, she realized and carefully rolled to her side to retrieve it from her bedside table. "Hello?"

"This is Guy."

Delilah's stomach heaved. She closed her eyes and took a careful breath. "How did you get my home number?"

He laughed. It was an unpleasant sound. "I'm resourceful. I talked to Miss Lilly White."

"You leave Lilly alone," Delilah said, nausea rising to her throat. "Can't talk. I'm sick—" She dropped the phone and raced to the bathroom, making it just in time. Rinsing her mouth and brushing her teeth, she swore at her reflection. She stripped off her clothes and took a quick lukewarm shower, scrubbing her face and body. Pitifully weak and exhausted afterward, she sank onto the top of her bed, naked.

When she felt a chill, she climbed under the covers. Catching sight of the phone on the floor, she stretched until her fingers grasped it and pulled it on the bed with her. She stared at it for a few moments, locked in internal debate. She hated to ask for help. She despised needing help.

Sighing in surrender, she punched out the number for her sister Katie. At the sound of her sister's voice, she felt her heart swell. "It's Delilah. I need your help. I need Michael's help."

After a flurry of phone calls, she and Katie learned there were no seats available on any flights departing Philadelphia for Houston due to the Thanksgiving holiday. Katie was so upset she wanted to charter a jet, but Delilah persuaded her to wait until after the Thanksgiving weekend.

She just had to last until Monday after next, she told herself. Just until Monday. She wouldn't answer her phone until then. Today was Saturday. Nine days. She could do it. Sure she could.

The phone rang again and she started to sweat.

By Saturday evening, Delilah regained some of her appetite. She scrambled eggs and buttered some toast. The condo was way too quiet. Feeling fidgety, she turned on the television. *The Wiggles* appeared on the screen, causing a knot of loneliness in her chest. She quickly changed the station to a cooking show.

Just as she finished her last bite of toast, Benjamin walked through the door. Her heart bumped at the sight of him. He walked through the foyer and stood in front of her, studying her. "You look like you feel better."

"Than last night?" She gave a wry laugh. "I was feeling no pain. It was this morning that—"

"I checked on you before I went to class to make sure you were still breathing," he interjected.

Delilah cringed. "You saw me this morning. Ewwwww."

He glanced at her plate. "I was going to ask you to join me for dinner."

"Too late. I'm all done."

"Would you go and sit with me? I'll buy you a drink."

His invitation sent a weird rush through her. She realized no one had asked her on a real date in a long time. But he was a Huntington. "Better not," she said, surprised at the sting of disappointment she felt. "I don't want to ruin your rep."

"You think I can't handle the gossip?" he asked, his gaze solid.

Her heart fluttered again. He was a big boy. He could probably handle anything, and that was part of his attraction. Still, she wasn't dying to cause him trouble. Someday he would come to his senses and start dating a woman with great bloodlines and impressive education, get married and have babies. He would be a terrific father, she thought and sighed. She didn't want to be a skeleton in his closet. "I didn't say that. I was planning on staying in tonight. And I plan to abstain from any alcohol until I completely forget how awful I felt this morning."

He raised his eyebrows. "Abstaining from alcohol and sex. Your father would be proud."

She narrowed her eyes and scowled at him.

He tugged at her hand. "Fix me something to eat."

"What?"

"I don't care. You're watching a cooking show," he said, pointing at the television. "Fix what he's fixing."

Delilah laughed, but allowed him to drag her to the kitchen. "You don't understand. I watch these shows with the idea that someday I'll cook like that. Do you know when someday is for these kinds of things? Never. I'm warning you I don't have much in my cupboard."

"I'm easy," he said, his voice silky with suggestion.

She shot a quick glance at him, but his eyes were wide with innocence as he leaned against the refrigerator with one lifted arm. His stance emphasized his broad shoulders, the developed muscles of his chest and flat belly. She was tempted to allow her gaze to venture further down, but decided she would be asking for trouble.

"Hamburger it is," she said, pulling a frozen patty from the freezer. She defrosted it in the microwave then fried it, put a slice of cheese on top and added condiments per Benjamin's instructions.

He downed it with her last beer in no time.

"Should I have fixed you two burgers?"

He shook his head. "That took the edge off. I didn't eat lunch. You know how that goes. If you haven't eaten in a long time, you eat fast because you feel deprived." He fiddled with the cuff of her blouse, dragging his finger against her inner wrist. "Then you can slow down."

The sensual gesture reminded her of how he'd touched her that night they'd made love. His expression told her he was remembering the same. Delilah felt her body temperature crank up another degree.

She cleared her throat, shook her head. "I'm not going to bed with you again. Been there, done that. Got the tattoo."

"I don't remember seeing any tattoos," Benjamin said.

"It's an expression." She pulled her hand from his.

"I didn't ask you to go to bed with me."

"Not in so many words," Delilah said. "But you were thinking it."

"How do you know what I was thinking?"

"I could tell," she said, lifting her chin.

"Well, you're wrong. I was thinking I'd like to dance with you."

She blinked. She hadn't expected that. Her stomach turned a little flip.

"What kind of music do you have?" he asked, heading for her entertainment center.

"No opera," she retorted, following him.

He chuckled. "That's okay. I wasn't looking for opera." He pulled out a CD and put it in the player. "This'll work."

Delilah felt oddly nervous. "I didn't say I would dance with you."

The smoky voice of Norah Jones filled the room. Her favorite. He was a beast, she decided.

He extended his hand to her. "Dance with me."

Her feet moved forward of their own volition. "You didn't really ask."

"Okay, do you want to dance with me?" Before she could answer, he pulled her into his arms and covered her mouth with one index finger. "Honest."

When he looked at her that way, it was hard to muster a defiant lie. She closed her eyes and sank against him, letting her body talk. It was just dancing. It wasn't sex.

As the notes flowed into each other, she inhaled his scent and savored the moment. His body and hers worked well together, no surprise there. His movements were smooth, not fussy or overdone. She liked that. He held her just tightly enough, provided just the right amount of lead to make dancing with him a pleasure.

One song slid into another, then another. Toward the end, they were barely moving, just swaying, his thigh between hers. She could feel his heat. There was no mistaking the evidence of his arousal pressing against her, and yet there was no pressure, just anticipation. It clung to her like humidity on a hot summer day.

His lips brushed her forehead. The sweet caress touched her in a dark, secret place. It was gentle, almost protective. It had been such a long time since someone had been protective of her.

She wanted to kiss him. She wanted to taste his lips and inhale his breath, touch his naked skin and take a bath in his strength. The need was strong, the want was fierce. A vague, primitive need crystallized inside her. She wanted to mate with him. She wanted to have his baby.

The shocking thought stopped her breath. Oh, hell. She must be crazy.

With her heart hammering in her chest, she took a careful breath, steeling herself against the knee-weakening effect of his scent. She bit her lip. "That was really nice," she said.

"But you want me to leave."

She smiled at the wry note in his voice.

She looked up at him. "How did you know?"

"Every time I get close, you tell me to leave."

"I won't ask you to come to bed with me," she said, a knot rising in her throat. Why did he affect her so strongly?

"You don't have to," he said.

"But you're hard."

"And you're aroused too. It doesn't mean we have to have sex right this minute."

Even though she wanted to. She just thought it would be smarter for her to stand on the highest point of a golf course pointing a golf club to the heavens during an electric storm.

"I am going to kiss you, though," he said and lowered his mouth to hers, leaving her no time to refuse.

She wasn't particularly inclined to refuse his kiss. It seemed sort of safe, like dancing.

From side to side, he rubbed his mouth against hers then slid his tongue across the seam of her lips then rubbed some more.

Delilah swallowed a *mmmmm* sound. He drew her bottom lip into his mouth and ran his tongue over her soft inner lip. Following his lead, she joined in the seductive rhythm of his caress, although he kept in control, the same way he had when they'd danced.

If she thought about it, it was the same way he'd lightly kept control when they'd made love.

He tilted her head for better access and explored her recesses more deeply. Her head felt light, her knees buttery, her skin hot and other various parts swollen and achy. His mouth moved in a way that reminded her of sex with him, provocative and consuming, making her want more.

When he finally pulled back, he inhaled with a ragged breath. She did the same, unable to look away from the deep, drugging intimacy in his dark eyes.

He inhaled again, his gaze still holding hers. He lifted one finger to her still-buzzing lips. "Have you even been courted?"

She shook her head, not sure what was happening between them, inside her.

"Maybe it's time you were." He leaned forward to kiss her forehead and pulled back. "Good night."

Unable to respond, she watched him as he walked out of the condo. Courted? How strange. Her heart felt all squishy and her stomach was jumpy. She felt like a little girl again, just jerked from her mother's custody and living with her father. New home, new school, no friends. She was gawky, raw and vulnerable. Hopeful that someone would like her. Hopeful that someone would approve of her.

She'd been hoping that for years. That was why Cash had been so important to her. She closed her eyes and slid her fingers through her hair and tried to tell herself that she was an adult and she didn't need anyone's approval, especially Benjamin Huntington. But she couldn't totally extinguish that little girl hope.

Robert still hadn't made love to Lilly. She was ready to tear her hair out. Stifling the urge to tap her toe in impatience, Lilly bided her time during the dreadful rubber chicken dinner at the Kiwanis Club meeting. She'd figured out what she needed to do. She needed to thoroughly disrupt Robert. Subtlety wasn't going to work.

As she sat in the large gathering room provided by the library, she toyed with her food. She hated to admit it, but she'd used Delilah as her guide. If Delilah had wanted to get a man's attention, what would she do? How far would she go?

Further than Lilly would go, she suspected, fighting an anxiety attack. If the elderly man seated beside her knew what she had planned, he would keel over with a heart attack. That meant she needed to make sure that Robert was the only one who heard what she planned to say to him.

She downed a sip of iced tea and wished it was alcohol. Wondering if she should have brought a tranquilizer with her, she mentally slapped herself. *What would Delilah do?* she chanted to herself. Delilah would get a huge kick out of her secret. She would smile and laugh at herself.

Lilly needed to go to the ladies' room.

She rose. "Excuse me, I'll be right back." Taking her courage in her hand, she bent slightly and cupped Robert's ear. "I'm not wearing any panties." She counted to three. "What are you going to do about it?"

Her face flaming, she quickly walked to the rest room before her bladder finished the job of embarrassing her to death. After using the bathroom, she washed her hands and fanned her face to bring down the color. She took a deep breath, reassuring herself that she wouldn't have to deliver on her dare until after Robert had given his speech. She still had the last course of partially frozen Sara Lee cheesecake to bolster her nerves. She just hadn't known that going pantyless would feel so, well, breezy.

Pulling open the door, she stepped outside and nearly walked straight into Robert.

"Whoa." He caught her with his hands.

"Oops. Excuse me," she said, feeling her throat tighten with embarrassment.

He drew her to the side of the hallway and cleared his throat. "I think I didn't hear you correctly a few minutes ago."

Lilly wanted to seep into a crack in the floor. She couldn't say the words again, especially not in the bright light of the hallway, directly to his face. She swallowed over her dry throat. "I said excuse me."

He shook his head. "No. You whispered something to me right after you got up from the table."

"What did you hear me say?"

He paused, his gaze meeting hers. Then he chuckled. "I want to hear you say it."

Do I have to? She bit her lip. She glanced both ways and whispered, "I'm-not-wearing-panties-what-are-you-gonna-do-about-it?"

He cupped his ear and drew closer to her, his mouth twitching with telltale humor. "Excuse me. I think you said it too fast."

At that point Lilly knew he was teasing her, pulling her leg, as her father used to say. She narrowed her eyes. "You know what I said. You know what I asked."

He raised his eyebrows. "There's nowhere to meet your

challenge. We're supposed to meet my parents at their house for a drink after the meeting."

"We can be late," she said defiantly, crossing her arms over her chest.

"But where?" he asked wearing a surprised, but intrigued expression that gave her hope.

"There's a room that's being renovated at the end of the back hall."

"Here?" he asked, incredulous. He lowered his voice. "In a library?"

"Only if you're up to it," she said, packing her words full with double entendre. "We should get back to the meeting." She skimmed her hand down his red power tie. "You can think it over during your speech. And for the record," she said, as she cupped his ear again, "I'm on the pill."

*On Virginity: Take heart. The second time is usu-
ally better than the first.*

—DELILAH'S DICTUM

Chapter 18

*I*f her father knew what she was doing, he would roll
over in his grave ten times. After she and Robert returned
to the table, she asked herself the question again, *what
would Delilah do?*

When Robert walked up to the podium to speak, she
moved her chair to the front, so that no one stood between
her and Robert's vision.

He glanced in her direction and she crossed her legs.

He paused an extra beat and continued to speak.

Oh, yes, the man was smooth. It would take quite a bit
to ruffle him.

He looked again in her direction and she uncrossed her
legs, discreetly, of course.

He paused again, this time clearing his throat.

He continued to speak and every time he turned his
head in her direction, Lilly crossed or uncrossed her legs.
By the end of his speech, she counted eight coughs and ten
forehead touches, as if he were trying unsuccessfully to
keep his head from turning in her direction.

She was amazed at how powerful she felt, and all she
had to do was move her legs and wear no panties. Techni-
cally, she could have just *said* she wasn't wearing panties.

Robert concluded his speech and everyone applauded. Standing, she waited for him to shake hands with the crowd of people who had rushed up to speak to him afterward. Several moments passed and her feeling of euphoria began to wane. By the time he finished glad-handing, she wondered if he would remember her dare and her pantyless state.

A few more moments passed and she wandered to the water fountain for a sip of water. Lowering her head, she took a long drink. Just as she was ready to lift up, she felt a hand over hers on the lever for the fountain.

"Better drink up," Robert murmured. "I want you to give me a private tour of the library renovations."

Lilly nearly strangled over her drink of water. She met his gaze and he looked more determined than she'd ever seen him. Her heart hammered with a combination of an ticipation and trepidation. A quick slice of panic raced through. Omigod, could she do this?

She had to. She glanced behind him. Several people still milled around in the large meeting room, but no one appeared to be looking.

"Hurry," she whispered, snagging his hand and urging him down the hall with her. She guided him around another turn and down an unlit hall to a door with a sign that read DANGER: RENOVATING. NO ADMITTANCE ALLOWED.

Lilly pulled out a key and opened the door.

Robert stared at her in amazement. "How did you get that key?"

"I asked for a tour of the library earlier today. After the librarian finished, I asked for a key to get a second look at the renovations." She slid the key into her purse. "I'll return it tomorrow."

"You planned this," he said, shaking his head in disbelief.

"Are you complaining?" she asked in what she prayed was a sultry voice as she stepped inside the darkened room where she would finally lose her virginity.

"Not at all," he said, following her in and closing the door behind him. He reached to turn on the light and she covered his hand.

"There's a frosted window on the door. A light will draw attention."

"How do we see where we're going?"

She took his hand. "It's not that far. I set out a dropcloth this afternoon."

He gave a low chuckle. "You surprise the hell out of me. I would have never guessed you could be so—"

"So what?" she asked, eager to know what he thought of her. Eager to know that he thought of her at all.

"So wild," he said, pulling her against him. She could barely see his face, but his warmth and nearness felt so good, so comforting. "Who would have thought little Miss Lilly White could be so wild? Sweetheart, you don't have to do this. We can wait if—"

She shook her head at the mere suggestion of waiting and wrapped her arms around him. "I've told you I don't want to wait any longer, Robert. I feel like I've waited my entire life for you."

He brushed his hand over her hair in a gesture that calmed her. "You're so sweet. And so hot," he said, lowering his voice. "You keep surprising me. So when are you going to prove to me that you didn't wear any panties?" he asked, his voice low and sexy.

Her heart skipped in her chest. "You can find out now."

He lowered his hand to her thigh and nuzzled her nose

with his. He slid her skirt upward and she felt a cool draft of air. Suddenly his warm hand was on her bottom.

"Oh, Lilly, you feel good," he said, and she was very glad that she had exfoliated her entire body this morning in the shower.

"You've got such a nice little ass," he whispered and took her mouth in a french kiss.

She felt herself grow warm from the inside out. The indolent stroking of his hand on her bare skin made her feel sensual and a little bit bad. He lowered his other hand to her thigh and skimmed it up her thigh and across her femininity. The quick intimacy took her by surprise. She gasped.

"Mmmm. Your legs feel so silky and you taste so good. I wonder how you taste all over," he said, taking her mouth in a deeper, more carnal kiss.

He slid his hand between her legs and softly stroked her. Lilly forced herself to relax and concentrate on the seductive touch of his fingers.

Their pants of breath mingled in the still air and he gave a low groan as he rubbed against her. She could feel his erection through his dress slacks.

"Touch me, baby," he told her.

Eager to hide her lack of experience, she slid her hand over him, cupping him, listening carefully to his tone to guide her caresses.

He rubbed her faster and she echoed his movements. She felt herself buzz in all her feminine places.

"Oh, Lilly, you feel so good." He plunged his finger inside her. The movement took her by surprise. "That's what I want to do," he muttered. "Get inside you."

His dark needy tone was a visceral turn-on. She unzipped his slacks and touched his bare erection.

He swore under his breath. "Where's that dropcloth?"

She guided him a few feet further into the room and knelt down on the carpet. He followed her down and pushed his slacks to his knees. Shoving her skirt up, he pushed her thighs wide apart and thrust inside her.

Pain seared her. She felt too-stretched, totally invaded and not in a pleasant way. She lay beneath him frozen.

"God, you're tight. Are you sure you're not—"

Self-conscious, hurting, but determined not to die of embarrassment, she pulled his mouth down to hers and kissed him.

The kiss must have done the trick because he started moving again, thrusting and moaning with pleasure. It didn't hurt so much now. She might could even like it, she supposed, feeling as if she weren't really participating. He thrust again and let out a long moan.

"Oh, baby, you felt so good." He kissed her cheek. "So good." He kissed her other cheek. "I wish I could have lasted longer, but oh, you felt good."

She felt warmed by his gratitude. She couldn't remember him acting so grateful. Her feminine places burned and she felt vaguely dissatisfied. She shrugged. Oh, well, the deed was done.

"Was it good for you?" he asked, pulling back and zipping his fly.

"Sure," she said, pushing down her skirt and sitting up. She felt a sticky spot on the drop cloth beneath her and made a face, thankful for the darkness.

"Are you sure?" he asked. "I mean did you come?"

"Of course," she said, knowing she hadn't, but didn't want to over think right now.

"Lilly," he said, moving closer to her, wrapping his

arms around her. "I have a feeling you're not telling me the truth."

She tensed. "What do you mean?"

"I mean I have an awful feeling this was your first time."

Her cheeks heated. "Well, why would you think—"

"Lilly." He squeezed her. "Tell me the truth."

She closed her eyes. The darkness wasn't enough. "It was my first time," she whispered. "But I'll get better. I just need more experience."

"Better?" he echoed in disbelief. "You were so good I couldn't last once I was inside you." He reached for her hand. "I'm the one who needs to make it better for you, but I'm not sure this is the place."

Her heart softened at his eagerness to please her. Maybe he did care for her more than she'd thought. "I want to be so good for you. I want to be perfect for you."

"You are, sweetheart. You couldn't be better." He gently pulled her upright. "Lilly, you amazed me tonight."

His tone made her feel happy, but something else didn't seem right. She rubbed her legs together and felt uneasy at the damp sensation. She didn't want to act like a scared, inexperienced virgin. "I want to please you."

He gave a dirty chuckle. "Well, darlin' you really pleased me tonight." He sighed, kissing her forehead, making her feel cherished. "It's a shame my parents are expecting us."

Lilly couldn't face Robert's parents without taking a bath and putting on underwear. She just couldn't. "Listen, would you mind terribly if I called a raincheck tonight?"

He skimmed his finger down her cheek. "Not what you expected, was it?" he asked, his voice full of regret. "I'll make it better for you next time. I promise."

Trying to pull herself together, she dipped her forehead against his chin. "Maybe it's like pancakes," she said.

"Pancakes?" he echoed.

"My housekeeper used to say that the first batch of pancakes never turns out because you're in such a rush."

"And you definitely put me in a rush."

She felt a trickle of relief at his desire for her.

"Next time, we'll take it slow."

Robert drove her home and walked her to the door. "I wish I could stay," he said, and kissed her. "Remember I'm golfing tomorrow, so I'll see you Monday night."

"Monday night," she echoed, eager to get inside the safe comfort of her home. "Good night."

Maxine greeted her and followed her upstairs while she soaked in a soothing bath and tried to answer the question of whether she liked sex or not. Ticking off a comparison on her fingers, she decided she liked getting Robert rattled, she liked him to hold her, and she liked having him grateful. She hadn't liked the messy part, and going pantyless in November was insane.

Emotionally, it had lacked something. She had expected to feel swept away, yet totally enveloped by Robert. She'd expected to feel safer, yet more excited than she'd ever dreamed possible. She'd expected to feel reassured about Robert's commitment to her.

She did. And didn't.

She wondered if this was one of those times when sex wasn't the answer after all. She wondered if the situation with Guy Crandall was clouding her judgment, muddying her vision of Robert's feelings for her. Maybe she needed to take a deep breath and believe Robert had strong feelings for her and would stand by her. Maybe she needed to believe that deep down, he really did cherish her.

Petting Maxine, she drew comfort from the dog Robert had given her. She would have never predicted how much comfort the dog brought her. Still, their lovemaking had left her feeling empty. She went to bed wearing comfortable pajamas and cotton panties with a little pain in her chest. She closed her eyes and tried not to think about it.

When Lilly rose the next morning, she moved gingerly, but was pleased that she wasn't as sore. Starving, she bounced down the stairs to grab the Sunday paper from the front porch and enjoy it with her breakfast. She opened the front door and found a bouquet of red roses on her front porch.

Delighted, she picked them up, along with the paper. She opened the legal-sized envelope and read the note scrawled by Robert.

Dear Lilly,
*   I will never be able to think of library renovations in the same way. Thank you for an amazing evening. I'll be thinking of you today.*
*   Yours, Robert*

She smiled inside and out. He must have delivered them on his way to play golf. It was the first time he'd given her flowers. She often wondered if he thought of her when she was with him, let alone when they were apart. Knowing he'd gone to a little extra trouble gave her hope.

Sniffing one of the roses, she removed the tiny bottles of water at the base of each stem and arranged them in a crystal cut vase. She put a frozen waffle in the toaster and opened the Sunday paper.

Another envelope fell on the table. Lilly picked it up and felt her blood plunge to her feet. It was addressed to

Guy Crandall. Her fingers shook as she opened the un-sealed envelope.

Send $10,000 in the enclosed envelope for wedding expenses. You do want to get married, don't you?

Lilly crumpled the note and threw it in the trash can under the sink. Her waffle popped up in the toaster, but her appetite had disappeared.

"Come out to dinner with me," Benjamin said to Delilah.

She shook her head. "No thanks. I've worked at home most of the afternoon and I'm going to treat myself to a take-out chili dog from that place down the street."

"You'd rather have a take-out chili dog than go to a nice restaurant?"

She nodded. "I've been good all day. Now I want something bad and messy."

I could give her something bad and messy that would last all night, he thought, feeling himself grow hard at the prospect. Lately he felt like he spent half his waking and non-waking hours hard. Now he could add heartburn to the mix, but he was determined to prove to Delilah that his interest in her was legitimate. He knew she was trying to hide her sadness over Willy's absence. He also knew she needed to get out of her condo.

"Okay, grab your jacket and let's go," he said.

"You'd rather have a take-out chili dog with me than go to a restaurant with someone else?"

"I'd like to do both, but since you have a prejudice against my family name, we'll take the low-profile route." He helped her put on her leather jacket.

She frowned at him. "I'm not prejudiced."

"Yes, you are."

"Am not."

"Are too until infinity," he said.

She shot him a double-take, her lips twitching. "Am not."

He opened the door and motioned for her to proceed. "What kind of work were you doing today?"

"Crunching numbers," she said as they walked to the elevator and got on. "I want to add self-tanning showers. They're showers that spit out a fine mist of self-tanner solution so you don't end up with an uneven tan. We have tanning beds, but there's no way around the fact that they're bad for you. Our chief esthetician is always hanging an OUT OF ORDER sign on the doors for the tanning beds. I think these new showers will go over like gangbusters. They're just not cheap."

"You want the spa to be state-of-the-art," he said.

She nodded. "And still keep some of the older services too."

"Sounds like Howard left the spa management in good hands."

She shrugged and they walked out of the elevator. "He taught me a lot."

"Oh, you're not going to go humble on me, now, are you?" he teased. "Who would you say is honestly the best person for your job?"

She shoved her hands into the pockets of her black leather jacket and made a face. "Me, me and me. Satisfied?"

They turned a corner and strolled toward the tiny restaurant. "Not by a long shot," he muttered more to himself than to her.

"What about you? What did you do today?"

"Played golf with my brother, father and the state attorney general."

"Power golf."

"Not exactly. My father wasn't speaking to me for half the round. He's still upset that I'm not joining his firm."

"Nothing personal, but your father sounds like a prick," Delilah said as they entered the restaurant.

Benjamin chuckled. "You're not the first to say so."

"I don't understand his problem. You graduated in law with honors. You're gainfully employed and getting ready to start your own practice. What's not to like?"

"Control. He likes to have control."

She made a face. "That would drive me nuts. How does your mother handle it?"

"She takes anti-anxiety medication and is in ten bridge clubs."

"But you want a different life," she said, studying him.

He nodded. "I always have. It just took me awhile to figure out exactly what that was."

"And exactly what is that?"

"Aren't you the curious girl. Let's order," he said and they did. Two hot dogs loaded, chips on the side and sodas. The restaurant provided complimentary mints.

After they got their dogs and Delilah grabbed a stack of extra napkins, they sat at a corner table. "I'm not letting you out of it that easily. What exactly do you want?" She took a bite of her hot dog and gave a moan of approval.

Benjamin couldn't help remembering how she'd moaned when they'd made love, but he dragged his mind away from the images. "My own practice where I can negotiate the ground rules with a reasonable partner. I want to be with people who aren't with me just because of my name."

"Interesting," she said. "It's sorta the reverse of my situation." She ran her tongue along the edge of the bun. "So that's part of the reason you spend so much time with me? Because I'm not bowled over by the Huntington name."

"Partly," he admitted. "I'm waiting for you to admit that you're bowled over by me."

She widened her eyes in surprise then made a *tsk*ing sound. "Careful. Your family arrogance is showing."

"It's not arrogance," he said, taking a bite of his own hot dog. "You like having me around, but you're afraid that all I want is sex with you."

"And you don't want sex with me?" she asked, her voice full of skepticism

"I want that and more," he said.

Silence fell between them and she concentrated on consuming her hot dog. "Why?" she finally asked in frustration, breaking the silence. "Why? Why? Why?"

"Because you're an original. You'll go to the wall to keep your promises and protect those you love. I've been around enough to know that's rare."

She sighed, setting down the tiny corner of her bun. She looked as if he had discovered her secret and she wasn't sure she was pleased about it. "I don't love easily."

"I know," he said, but he suspected she'd never come up against his brand of determination.

She threw down her napkin. "I don't know why we're talking about this. You'll change your mind."

The accusation irritated him, but he let it pass. "What are you going to do to entertain me now?"

She blinked. "Me entertain you? Why?"

"Because I bought you this scrumptious meal that is guaranteed to give me heartburn."

"So I owe you?"

"We can go back to your place and dance again."

Her eyes widened and she shook her head. "Okay, I'll take you to my favorite tourist site in Houston. You drive."

Several minutes later, Benjamin illegally parked near the famous water wall. Delilah grabbed his hand and dragged him into the center of the sixty-plus-foot waterfall. The roar of thousands of gallons of water surrounded them.

"I haven't been here in a long time," he said.

"I go at least once a month." She stepped closer to the falls and closed her eyes.

He'd never seen her look so peaceful. He'd never seen any woman he'd been involved with so delighted by something so inexpensive. He stepped closer to her.

She opened her eyes and leaned against him. "The world fades away in here." Her eyes turned sad. "I was planning to bring Willy here when he started to walk."

"You still can," he said. "Nicky will let you, won't she?"

"I think so," she said. "I just thought things would turn out differently. I miss him like the dickens."

"He got into your heart," Benjamin said. Like *he* planned to.

"Yep, he did."

He slid his arm around her and stood there with her for several moments. The pounding water seemed to wash away his frustration.

"I read something about this place in the paper recently," he said.

"What?" she asked, curiosity lighting her eyes.

"It was voted the number-one most romantic place to kiss."

"That isn't why I came here," she told him, returning her gaze to the wall.

"You sure?" he taunted. "You've been determined to have your wicked way with me since that night we spent together."

"My wicked way," she protested. "You're the one who was such a stickler for that three for me and one for you rule. Control freak."

"You didn't like it," he said, pulling her closer to the wall so that they felt the mist on their faces, and the force of the water sounded like thunder.

"I didn't say that," she said, stretching her hand out to touch the shimmering wall. "How many women have you kissed here?"

"None. How many men have you kissed here?"

She shook her head and met his gaze. "None, but you'll do," she said and lifted her mouth to his.

Benjamin took her lips and felt the magic swim around them. Her lips and face were damp and cool from the mist, but they quickly warmed. She pressed herself flush against him, as if she couldn't get close enough. He sensed her release a fraction of her reserve toward him. He could feel she trusted him a little more today than she had yesterday.

She pulled back, breathless, and her eyes were filled with wary wonder, as if she was finally feeling the power that flowed between them. Maybe she was finally getting the message.

The right man is like WD-40: He keeps his woman . . . well, you figure it out.
—DELILAH'S DICTUM

Chapter 19

*O*n Monday morning, Delilah peeked out of her office to ask Sara for a file and spotted flowers on her assistant's desk. Paul stood in the doorway chatting.

"Lovely flowers, Sara. Who are they from?"

Sara colored prettily and shot Paul a furtive glance. "I, uh—"

"They're from me," Paul said.

Surprise raced through her. "You?" She looked at Sara in amazement. "When did this happen? I must express my complete approval. Is he as good in bed as he looks?"

Sara opened her mouth then closed it and cleared her throat. "As a matter of fact, he is."

Delilah chuckled. "Is this serious?"

"I'm trying," Paul said. "Trying to get her pregnant."

"Paul!" Sara said. Their feelings for each other were obvious. Delilah was flabbergasted. And envious. *Now, that's stupid*, she told herself. The last thing she needed was romance or a baby. She thought of Willy and felt a twinge of pain. Delilah gave herself a hard mental shake. What she needed was to get Guy Crandall neutered and to purchase a self-tanner shower.

Lilly Bradford burst into the office suite with a desperate expression on her face. "I need to talk to you," she said to Delilah.

Sara shot Delilah a questioning glance. Delilah just nodded. "It's okay. Come into my office. Sara, please hold my calls." She glanced at Sara and Paul and smiled. "Congrats."

Lilly looked at the flowers. "Oh, they're pretty. It must be in the air. I got some yesterday," she said as she followed Delilah into her office. As soon as Delilah closed the door, Lilly's composure slipped. "Guy Crandall left a note on my front porch yesterday!"

Delilah scowled. "He called me the other day, but I was sick so I had to hang up on him."

"We've got to do something or he's going to destroy my chances of marrying Robert," Lilly said, her eyes filling with tears.

Delilah sighed. "I'm working on it. I really am. Next Monday I'm getting some help and—"

Lilly gasped. "You're hiring a hit man?"

"No," she said. "Although I've fantasized his demise using several horrible, painful methods." She studied Lilly. "Any progress with Robert? Any chance you can move up the wedding date?"

Lilly sighed in disgust. "We haven't even set a wedding date. His father wants it to be the social event of the year."

"Yeah, Benjamin told me he's a prick."

"Benjamin said that?"

"No. He just described him and I sorta filled in the blanks." Delilah thought of possible solutions. "Maybe you could get pregnant."

Lilly's eyes popped wide open in horror. "How?"

"The usual way," Delilah said.

"I'm on the pill."

"Damn, so you've finally done the deed. Was he any good?"

Lilly opened her mouth and worked her jaw, but made no sound.

"That either means it was really good or really bad," Delilah concluded.

Lilly pushed her blonde hair behind one of her ears, a sure sign she was flustered because Lilly *always* covered her Dumbo ears. "I suppose it's a matter of perspective," she said with a sniff. "Robert left roses on my front porch before he went golfing yesterday."

"Hmm," Delilah said, studying Howard's daughter. "But how was it for you?"

"It was fine," Lilly said a little too quickly. "Fast, but fine."

"It's none of my business—"

"Exactly," Lilly said, getting a snippy tone in her voice.

"A quickie may be fine every now and then. Exciting, forbidden. But it's better not to make a habit of it. It's better to make them work for it, to put some time into it. That way, you get what you want and he gets that juvenile rush of making a touchdown."

A knock sounded on the door and Sara looked inside. "No telephone call, but I didn't think you would mind these," she said, bringing in a beautiful bouquet of red-tipped ivory roses. She set the vase on the desk and waited expectantly.

Lilly made an *oooh* sound. "They're gorgeous. They remind me of those rare roses named after a celebrity. Who sent them?"

Surprised and self-conscious, Delilah pulled the card from the bouquet. No one had sent her flowers since Cash. She opened the note and quickly scanned it.

These are a rare hybrid of roses. Beautiful, original, rare, like you. Benjamin

Oh, wow. Her heart turned over at the message. Feeling Sara and Lilly's curious gazes, she cleared her suddenly tight throat. "Thank you so much for fitting me in to the Botox party," she invented. "You saved the day. Ciao, Iris."

Sara's face fell. So did Lilly's.

"Botox. How unromantic," Lilly said. "What a waste."

Sara sighed. "I had hoped that you were finally—"

Delilah shook her head. "There's enough of that going around between you two and your boy toys."

"Boy toy," Lilly echoed. "I can just imagine what Robert would think of being called that."

"He can be taught," Delilah said slyly.

Lilly stiffened and glanced at Sara.

Sara, ever gracious and intuitive, took the hint. "I'll leave you to your meeting. If you need anything, call me."

As soon as Sara closed the door, Lilly turned to Delilah. "How are we going to handle Guy?"

"Well, I have personally decided not to answer my phone or be alone here at work until after next Monday."

"What's happening on Monday?" Lilly asked impatiently.

My big sister and her husband are coming and they're gonna beat him up. "A securities specialist that I trust is coming to town."

"Are you sure you can trust him?"

"Totally."

Delilah listened for Benjamin to walk through her door that evening. As she paced her living room, it occurred to her that this had become a routine without her realizing it. Somehow in the middle of caring for Willy they'd begun sharing their evenings together and never stopped. She should probably put a stop to it now.

Yeah, right. Stop the flowers, stop the kisses, stop the good feelings. Maybe next week, she thought, glancing at her nails. At that moment, her door opened and Benjamin appeared. Her silly heart hiccupped.

"Hi," he said.

Her heart sped up. Oh, this was silly. Just the sight of him and all he had to do was say hi and he was the sexiest man on earth?

"Hi," she said, resisting the urge to kiss him. Instead she inhaled his scent and allowed herself to feel a little dizzy. He had the same effect on her as drinking two champagne cocktails on an empty stomach. "You were a bad boy today."

"Me?" He shot her his innocent, but sexy look. "What did I do?" He headed for her kitchen and she heard him open the refrigerator, probably intending to drink one of the Coronas she'd bought yesterday.

"You sent me beautiful roses and they arrived when Lilly Bradford was there."

He returned with beer in hand. "Bet she was envious."

She chuckled. "A little. Both she and my assistant were very curious about who sent them."

He nodded. "So was I a massage therapist trying to get in your pants or a customer you rescued from hair emergency?"

He knew her a little too well. "A customer thanking me for fitting her in to a Botox party."

"Botox," he said, grinning. He leaned against the back of the couch. "That was pretty good."

"You really shouldn't do things like that. If it got out, people might get the wrong—"

"Or right idea," he said, snagging her hand and pulling her against him. He nuzzled her nose then drew back. "Did you like them?"

Her heart tightened. "Of course I did. They were beautiful. I've never received such beautiful flowers, but you need to be—"

The phone rang and she broke off. She tensed and walked over to check the caller ID. The number was blocked. She held her breath for four more rings.

"Why didn't you pick up?"

"I'm not picking up if it's a blocked number or if I can't identify the number until Monday."

"Does this have something to do with Guy Crandall?"

"I don't want to talk about it," she said, turning away from him.

"I've done some checking on him."

Delilah whipped back around to face him. "No! Don't do that. That's exactly what I don't want. I need to keep this very low profile. You are very high profile."

"I'm not high profile. I'm just—"

"A Houston Huntington," she said, rolling her eyes. "With standing reservations in all the best restaurants in town, a membership at the best country clubs, and season tickets to the opera and every sports event."

"Guy gambles."

Realization instantly dawned. "So that's why he's upped the ante lately. Calling me, leaving notes for Lilly."

Benjamin's face turned deadly serious. "He's been calling you?"

His expression was so fierce it almost frightened her.

`"Well, just once that I know of. But that was when I had a hangover, so I had to hang up on him."

"You can't keep paying him."

"Well, if your brother wasn't such a weenie, we might not be in this mess."

"What are you talking about?"

"I mean if anyone was sure that Robert really loved Lilly, then we wouldn't have to be so careful about keeping this quiet. But we don't know for sure that he loves her enough to stand firm with her if there's some controversy, do we?"

Benjamin sighed. "I don't know. It's hard to read him. My father's got the screws so tight on him sometimes I'm not sure when I'm talking to Robert or my father's mouthpiece."

"That's why I called my sister for help."

Benjamin wrinkled his brow in confusion. "Your sister?"

"My sister is married to a securities specialist. They're coming on Monday."

"I could have handled this for you," he said, his hurt expression pulling at her.

"Yes, except if you hired a private investigator, it would probably show up in the newspaper and the mess would be even worse. You may not realize it, but people watch you."

"Not as much as you think."

"Uh-huh," she said in disbelief.

"Let's go ice skating at the Galleria."

She got whiplash from the change of subject. "I'm not a very good skater."

"Good, that will give me an excuse to hold you. Up,"

he added as an afterthought. "I'll wear a stocking cap, so no one will recognize me. C'mon, don't be a sissy."

Nobody called her sissy and got away with it.

Hours later, after they'd skated and she'd fallen too many times to count, they'd grabbed a bite at The Cheesecake Factory and arrived back at the condo.

He followed her inside and toured all the rooms while he talked with her.

"What are you doing?" she asked when he opened her closet.

"Just checking to see which of your underwear will fit me," he joked.

She couldn't help laughing at the image of him in her red teddy. "Nice try. You're making sure Guy Crandall isn't hiding under my bed."

"Hey, if I'm not getting any, then he's not getting any."

She lightly punched him. "Guy's too chicken to show up at my condo."

He shook his head and pulled her against him. "Not if he's desperate."

Disliking the thought of Guy Crandall invading her space, Delilah sank against Benjamin and savored his strength. "Does this mean you'd be willing to guard my body?" she asked, trying to pull back the lighter feeling she'd enjoyed with him all evening.

He pulled back slightly. "Your body, heart and soul," he said. "You want me to sleep in the extra bedroom?"

No, I want you to sleep with me all night long and chase away all the boogey men. Surprised at the power of her desire for him, she gave herself a hard mental shake. *Buck up, girlfriend. This isn't like you.*

"That's a very nice offer. Can I have a raincheck?"

He nodded. "Yeah. Bang on the wall if you need me."
He turned to leave and she grabbed his hand.

"You forgot something," she said.

"What's that?"

"You forgot to kiss me," she told him.

"Oh, so you *want* me to kiss you?"

"As long as you're not going to act all cocky a—"

He pulled her into his arms and stopped her words with
his kiss, knocking the breath and sense out of her. Oh,
wow, she was going to have to put a stop to this. Next
week. Or the week after.

As Robert rubbed one hand over her breast and drew
her hand to his crotch, Lilly arched against him and
rubbed him intimately. He groaned with approval and she
rubbed some more then drew back slightly and sucked in
a deep breath.

"I think we're steaming up the windows," she murmured.

"You're steaming up more than my car windows," he
said.

"I wish we had more time," she said, rubbing her
mouth against his jaw. "We could do more." She slid her
hand to his thigh, struggling with the desperate feelings
that had plagued her all day. "I wish you could stay."

"I do too." He groaned, this time in frustration. "I'm
going to have to do something so we have some more
alone time together."

"That would make me happy," she said. When they
were alone, she believed Robert would stand by her.
When they were alone, she believed he almost needed her.

"You've been a little quiet, tonight. Anything wrong?"

Lilly tensed. She had been counting on Robert's absentmindedness to cover her turmoil. "Of course not. What could possibly be wrong? I'm engaged to the man I love and steaming up his windows . . ."

He chuckled and hooked his thumb under her chin. "Are you sure you're okay?"

She held her breath. "Very sure."

"If you need anything, you should let me know," he said.

"I just need your love, to be your wife."

He stroked her cheek. "My mother and father suggested a June wedding date. What do you think?"

"That's a long time," she said, thinking about the ticking time bomb of Guy Crandall.

"I agree, but my mom says it will take at least six months to plan everything. It sounds almost as involved as running for election."

"I guess. Do you mind walking me to the door?" she asked, still spooked by the appearance of Guy's note on her front porch.

Robert escorted her up the steps. "I'd love to go inside with you. You remember I'll be picking you up for Thanksgiving dinner with my folks?"

"I couldn't forget it." She pressed her lips against his. "Good night, darling."

She stepped inside her door and bit her lip. How long could she keep hiding her father's secret from Robert? How long did she want to? She was ready to bite her acrylic nails to the quick.

She loved Robert and wanted to be with him. She wanted so badly to be a part of his family that it possessed her, but she was tired of pretending she was perfect when Lord knew she wasn't. Sighing, she triple-bolted the door and climbed the stairs to her bedroom.

She still wasn't sure he really loved her. The doubt taunted her. What if she was fighting for something that was never going to happen? What if he was never going to love her?

Stepping into her familiar bedroom decorated in the Queen Anne cherry her mother had given her when she'd moved to New York, Lilly kicked off her shoes. What if she wasn't able to keep the secret until she and Robert were married? June, she remembered him saying and her stomach turned. She would have to lie until June.

What if he hated her for keeping the secret from him? What if the press found out at an awkward time? Then both Robert and his father would hate her.

Lilly groaned as she unbuttoned her blouse. She wanted to be the woman he needed and loved. She wanted to be the woman he turned to. She wanted to be part of his family. Even though his family was a little dysfunctional and her future father-in-law was the most controlling man in the universe.

Discouraged down to her bones, she hung up her clothes and put on her pajamas. She went through the motions of removing her makeup and brushing her teeth and slid under the covers. Needing some extra warmth tonight, she turned on her electric blanket. Reaching out to turn off her bed lamp, she caught sight of her engagement ring.

She knew the diamond was real. A Huntington would do no less. She just wished she knew if their marriage would be real.

On Wednesday during lunchtime, the front entrance receptionist paged Delilah at her desk. "I'm sorry to bother you, Miss Montague, but there's a young woman here who says she has an appointment for services, but she's nowhere on the books and you know how slammed we are. She insists on seeing you."

Delilah rolled her eyes. Probably some prima donna college girl on break. "What's her name?"

"Lori Jean—"

Delilah smiled. "I'll be right there."

She told Sara to hold all her calls until further notice and continued to the front desk. Her youngest sister, Lori Jean, dressed in designer jeans stood at the desk, her eyes dancing. Her long blonde hair silky straight, she cocked her head in subtle warning toward a big, beefy man standing in the background.

"What services had you arranged?" Delilah asked.

"Oh, the works. I'm on break from college and I need a beauty SOS," Lori Jean said.

"I'll take care of this," Delilah said to the receptionist. "Please come this way."

"See ya later, Chucky," Lori Jean said to the beefy guy at the door. "Bodyguard," she whispered to Delilah. "Pain in the ever-lovin' ass. My father is damned and determined to make sure I don't lose my virginity until I get married. I swear he'd put a chastity belt on me if he could."

"How did you manage this?" Delilah asked, well aware that Lori Jean's father, Harlan Granger, had done his best to sever all of Lori Jean's ties with her half-sisters. Katie's husband, Michael, had brought them back together two years ago and they'd vowed to keep in touch ever since. It was toughest for Lori Jean because her father freaked out at the mention of Katie and Delilah's names, plus he had a heart condition. "Your father wouldn't allow you within five feet of me."

"He doesn't know you're the big cheese here. I told

him that since he has stuck me in the middle of nowhere at the women's college he insists I attend, the least he can do is allow me a little relief at the best spa in Texas. He grumbled, but allowed it. I can't stay long, though. His jet's taking me back to Dallas in three hours."

"And you're supposed to get the works?" Delilah asked, leading her into her office.

As soon as she closed the door, Lori Jean threw herself into Delilah's arms. "I'm so glad to see you!"

Delilah's heart melted at her sister's effusive affection. "Me too. It's a good thing you're so inventive or I'd never get to see you."

Lori Jean pulled back and frowned. "Yeah. I just wish Katie could be here."

"She and Michael will be here on Monday," Delilah said, and immediately regretted it.

"Monday? Damn," Lori said. "I'm going back to school on Sunday. Why are they coming?"

"Something with Michael's job," Delilah manufactured.

Lori sighed. "What a bummer. At least you get to see them. Maybe we can work something out for Christmas."

"Maybe. So do you want a facial?"

"A trim for my hair would be nice," Lori said then smiled. "It's been a while since you cut it."

Delilah laughed, remembering how she'd butchered Lori Jean's hair when they were little girls. Her mother had been furious. "Are you sure you trust me?"

"Totally," Lori said. "But just the ends."

"Five inches, right?" Delilah joked then trimmed her youngest sister's hair and gave her a manicure and pedicure. She fed her M&Ms from her secret stash and they talked about Lori Jean's college life.

"Your fingernails are a mess," Delilah told her after she finished a topcoat.

"I break them at the barn," she said and shrugged.

"Buying you a horse is one good thing Harlan has done for you."

"Katie was partly responsible for that. She pretty much pushed him into it the day he picked me up. But Harlan's been good to me. He tells me I'm the sunshine in his day and he treats me like gold except for the overprotective part." She glanced at Delilah. "How often do you see your father?"

"Never," Delilah said as she applied polish to Lori Jean's toenails. She knew she hadn't done well in the father lottery. "It's better that way. Howard was a great friend."

"I'm so sorry he's gone." Lori Jean made a sympathetic sound and reached out to touch Delilah.

"Don't you mess up your nails," Delilah fussed.

Lori Jean smiled. "Oops. Almost forgot. Well, how are you really doing? Your emails don't reveal much."

"Things at the spa are going pretty well. It got a little sticky for a while, but it's better now. If everything goes well, we'll be adding a second location in Dallas."

Lori Jean's eyes widened. "That would be great! I'd get to see you more often."

"Maybe," Delilah said with a smile as she finished painting Lori Jean's pinkie toenail. It surprised her how much she was enjoying this. Crazy.

"But what about a man?" Lori Jean asked. "Or two? Or three?"

"Don't have time right now," Delilah said.

Lori lifted her eyebrows in disbelief. "You told me there's always time for a good time with a man."

Delilah smiled. "That was when I was young and ignorant. Now I'm old and swamped."

"So there's no one? No one at all?"

For some insane reason she couldn't quite explain, Delilah wanted to confide in her sister. She sighed. "Okay, there's this man who lives near me."

"And?" Lori asked, wiggling her toes in impatience.

"Be still," Delilah said sternly as she finished the second coat. "And he's—" She searched for the right words. "He's nice."

Lori made a face. "He's nice? But is he hot?"

Delilah nodded. *Very*, she thought.

"Have you uh gone—"

"He's a friend," she said, feeling an unusual slice of self-consciousness. She usually joked about sex, but with Benjamin it felt different.

"A friend," Lori said, underwhelmed. "Like Howard Bradford."

Delilah shook her head. "No. He's a different kind of friend."

She felt Lori studying her for a long moment and could practically feel her sister's curiosity popping in the air.

"I bet he's more than a friend," Lori said in a sing-song voice. "I bet he's knocked you on your butt."

"I bet you better shut up or I'll cut off five inches of your hair," Delilah warned. Her sister was just a little too close to the truth.

*A mental trip to the Caribbean can save your sanity.
And it's free.*

—DELILAH'S DICTUM

Chapter 20

*D*elilah turned down three offers for Thanksgiving dinner. The first, from Benjamin asking her to join him and his family, made her roll her eyes every time she thought about it. Lilly would have needed tranquilizers. A client had invited her to a large gathering which Delilah had politely declined. Sara and Paul had invited her to join the two of them. As much as Delilah loved both of them and was delighted with their romance, she didn't think she could bear witnessing their lovey-dovey expressions and eat at the same time. Sara and Paul made her think about things she shouldn't want. Like babies. With a man like Benjamin. Dangerous thoughts. Very dangerous.

She should have gone somewhere in the Caribbean, she thought. If only she wasn't being blackmailed. She called Nicky and checked on Willy. His gurgle on the telephone both reassured her and made her miss him more. He was happy and safe and with his mother. That was what was important, Delilah told herself.

After eating a turkey sandwich in honor of Turkey Day, she decided to treat herself to a visit at the water wall. With most people immersed in family gatherings, the wall wasn't likely to be crowded.

She parked illegally like she always did and rushed over to her little mecca in the city. She went directly inside and felt the same thrill she felt every time. The water had such power that it washed away everything that bothered her. Guy Crandall, missing Willy, never pleasing her father, missing Cash, worrying about Lilly, wanting Benjamin.

Her heart jumped. Oh, well, it didn't quite eliminate that last one, but everything else faded away. Heedless of the cold concrete, she sat down, folded her arms over her knees, and just stared into the rushing water. Thirty minutes passed and she felt as if her mind had been totally cleansed.

"I thought I might find you here," Benjamin said from behind her.

She felt her pulse race at the sound of his voice. "What are you doing here?" she asked without turning. "You're supposed to be indulging in gluttony with your family and watching football until your eyes fall out."

He sat down beside her. "I ate and ran."

"How rude." She took in the sight of his dress slacks and camel hair sports coat. "You'll mess up your nice clothes," she warned.

He shrugged and looked at the falls. "This is nice. Glad to see me?"

She hesitated a half-beat, but she couldn't deny her pleasure. "Yes," she reluctantly admitted.

His lips twitched and he met her gaze. "So hard to admit you like me."

"I keep telling myself that we have a very bad habit of spending so much time together and we are absolutely going to have to break that habit."

He slid his arm around her shoulder and the simple gesture felt so good. His presence just felt good.

"Next week," she added. "Or the next."

He nodded. "Or the next. Let's go back to your place and watch football."

"Why didn't you watch football with your father and brother?"

"You know why. I missed you."

His honesty continued to knock out her defenses. God, it was silly, but his showing up here today made her feel thankful on Thanksgiving. Her chest felt tight and achy. "I really shouldn't tell you this, but you made my day."

"It's a secret?"

He smiled gently and brushed his fingers over her cheek. "You can tell me secrets anytime you like. Delilah I won't tell."

And she thought he might just be telling the truth. They returned to her condo and sat on her couch and watched football all afternoon. She got hungry and thought about fixing spaghetti, but she felt lazy.

"What did you have for lunch?" he asked.

"Turkey sandwich."

He looked at her, appalled. "On Thanksgiving? You didn't have dinner?"

"It was an excellent sandwich," she said defensively. "I ate a fudge-covered Oreo for dessert."

He rolled his eyes. "You've got to let me take you out tonight," he said firmly.

She shook her head. "Absolutely not."

Her stomach growled.

He pointed to her belly. "You can't say you're not hungry."

"Trust me. I won't croak from skipping a meal. Besides, we've discussed this before. I'm not going out in public with you."

"No one will be at these restaurants tonight," he said, dismissing her concern. "Think about it. If people are going to eat out on Thanksgiving, they eat out at lunch."

"It's still a bad idea."

"It's a great idea. What do you want? Steak, seafood, ribs?"

Delilah's mouth watered. Her stomach growled again.

He shot her a *gotcha* glance. "Get dressed and I'll call a restaurant."

Feeling herself weakening, she frowned at him. It was weird as all get out, but the idea of going out with him tonight gave her a forbidden thrill. "You're being very pushy."

"You're being argumentative for no good reason. If you go tonight, you can get me off your back for a good week."

She weakened further. "Promise?"

Minutes later she pulled on a little black dress, black stockings and her favorite killer heels and she and Benjamin left for a cozy restaurant downtown.

She breathed a sigh of relief when she saw the light crowd. If she was lucky she wouldn't run into anyone important to Benjamin. He plied her with wine, food and conversation. She liked the way he looked at her, as if nothing could divert his attention from her. She liked the gentle way he teased her, but didn't let her get away with anything. She liked far too much about Benjamin and for all her good feelings, she had the uncomfortable niggling sense that it could all come crashing down around her if she weren't careful. But tonight, she wasn't going to think about that.

"Uncle," she said and pushed the chocolate dessert they'd shared away from her. "I'm glad you talked me into this, but you may have to wheel me home. Excuse me while I go to the powder room."

She felt his gaze on her rear end as she left the table and couldn't help smiling. She was still smiling when she exited the powder room.

"Well, well, well, if it isn't Howard's sweet young thing," a male voice said. "God rest his soul."

Delilah whipped her head around to see one of Howard's business acquaintances leering at her. She'd never liked this man. She could have stood his pot belly and thinning comb-over, but his manner gave her the creeps. More so now that she'd spent so much time with Benjamin. She would have to think about that later. "Happy Thanksgiving, Mr. Winters," she said politely, but didn't extend her hand.

"I haven't seen you out and about in a long time, Delilah. Howard wouldn't want you to waste away. I'd be happy to take you out to dinner sometime if you need some comfort," he said and tried to hand her his business card.

"Oh, I couldn't do that," she said. "Absolutely couldn't."

Winters raised his eyebrow. "Found a new sponsor already?"

She fought a burning need to grind her heel into his groin. "No, I'm sponsoring myself. I like it better that way."

"Well, if you change your mind . . ." He dangled the business card.

"I won't," she said flatly and headed back to the table.

She tried to appear calm, but Benjamin must have

sensed something was wrong. "The powder room not to your liking?"

She smiled despite her tension. "No. The powder room was lovely. I just ran into someone I don't have on my count-your-blessings list. Could we please go?"

"Fine with me. I've already paid the check."

He ushered her to the car and she felt a whisper of relief when she got inside, but she was still bothered. What if Winters had seen her with Benjamin and started talking? What if he talked to Benjamin's potential clients? She castigated herself the entire way back to the condo.

Benjamin pulled into the garage and cut the engine. "You haven't said a word out loud since we left the restaurant, but I'd swear you talked a blue streak to yourself. You want to tell me what's going on?"

"I shouldn't have gone there with you tonight. All it takes is running into one wrong person, one gossip, and then you'll be stuck with a hot potato."

He looked at her in confusion. "What are you talking about?"

"I'm talking about ruining your reputation. That's what I could do. Potential clients, potential friends, they could all be negatively influenced if they knew you were involved with me."

"I don't care what people think."

"That's what people say who have never had to deal with being snubbed or having business taken away or being the subject of nasty whispers due to rumors being told about them."

Benjamin turned quiet. "How long have you had to fight off the rumors?"

She laughed, but felt no humor. "Since I was born. My mother was eccentric. When she ran low on money, she won wet T-shirt contests to buy groceries. I never fit in at my father's house. Then when I moved to Houston, I was nobody until Howard took me under his wing. Now I'm Howard's former arm candy."

"You could try to be uglier," Benjamin suggested.

Delilah reluctantly smiled. "I'm trying to be serious here. Serious about saving your future, saving your reputation."

His eyes glinted with recklessness. "Maybe I don't want my reputation saved. Maybe I'm more concerned about what I think about you than what other people think about you." He paused a half-beat. "Maybe I'm in love with you."

Oh, wow. Delilah couldn't breathe for a full minute. She shook her head. "No, you're not. You're just confused because we had really good sex and because I'm different. I'm a novelty. You're used to Waterford crystal and I'm Tupperware."

"We did have really good sex and you are different, but I'm not confused. I want you. Not just at night under the covers. I want you outside in the sunshine, in front of crowds. I want you and I don't want to keep it a secret."

Delilah swore under her breath and covered her eyes with her hand. No, no, no. "Benjamin, you really don't love me."

"What if I do?"

She felt as if she was going to hyperventilate. He couldn't. It was a terrible idea. She'd loved every minute they'd spent together, but she'd always known nothing would come of it. "You don't," she insisted.

"What if I do?"

"I don't love you," she said and felt a horrible tearing sensation inside her at the way the light went out in his

258 *Leanne Banks*

eyes. "I'm sorry, but I don't," she said and scrambled out of the car to the elevator.

She broke a nail slamming her hand against the button and rushed inside when the elevator door whooshed open. Even after she sank against the side of the elevator, she felt as if the hounds of hell were nipping at her. She felt as if she'd committed some horrible, horrible sin, more horrible than any she could have imagined when she'd lived at her father's house.

Benjamin just didn't understand. Yes, he was an intelligent man, but his only reference point was that of being a Huntington. How would he feel if people talked about him behind his back? How would he feel if he found out clients decided to take their business elsewhere because of his association with Delilah? How would he feel if his family turned on him?

She couldn't bear the thought of any of that happening to him. He was one of the few good men she'd met on this earth and she was damned if she was going to mess up his future.

The elevator doors opened and she ran to her condo, praying he wouldn't use his key to get to her tonight. She ripped off her dress and put on her flannel pajamas, propped a chair under the doorknob and turned out all the lights.

A knock sounded at the door and she covered her ears. She put on headphones and listened to Alicia Keyes. When she couldn't bear the soulful strains of the singer's voice any longer, she removed the headphones.

Silence.

She felt an odd mixture of relief and nauseating disappointment. Then the phone started to ring. She glanced at the caller ID. Benjamin Huntington. She pulled the cord out of the wall.

Lilly strode up the steps of the Huntingtons' estate and rang the doorbell. The housekeeper greeted her and invited her inside. She bit her lip and rotated her engagement ring around her finger as she waited for Robert to appear.

She'd been mulling over her situation since Thursday, but she knew the moment she'd made the decision. It had been during Thanksgiving dinner, just as the pecan and pumpkin pies were served and Benjamin excused himself.

Robert had covered her hand with his beneath the table then lifted her hand to his lips. The gesture had surprised her. His words had knocked her off her feet, *"You've made this Thanksgiving special for me. I want to be the one to make all of yours special in the future."*

So he really did care for her, deeply. Perhaps he even loved her. Lilly twisted the ring again. It wouldn't make sense to a lot of people, but Lilly had known at that moment that she should break the engagement.

Joining Robert and his family for the holiday meal, feeling included, feeling cherished by Robert, had been her dream come true, but she'd felt like a fake the entire time.

Robert's feelings for her were genuine. How shallow was she to cause him to risk his dream of getting elected or tainting his clean reputation? If she really loved him, if she really wasn't a spoiled conniving bitch, then she would protect him.

Learning all Delilah had done to try to keep her promise to Howard had provided Lilly with food for thought. Delilah might joke about the things women should do to keep a man in line, but when it got down to the nitty-gritty, she'd been strong enough to make sacrifices for someone she loved.

Did Lilly love Robert enough to sacrifice?

"Lilly, what a pleasant surprise," Robert said with a smile as he descended the stairway. "I was thinking of you between every other line of the speech I was writing."

Her heart turned over at the sight of him, and she saw something she hadn't noticed before, the gentle growing light of love in his eyes. She'd been too frantic and bent on *catching* him to notice it before. She saw commitment.

He lifted his hand to her jaw and slid his fingers through her hair. "You're cold. Take off your coat and I'll get you some hot chocolate."

Something inside her twisted. "I can't stay. I just needed to see you for a few minutes." She glanced around. "Is there somewhere we could talk alone?"

Robert's smile faded. "Of course." He guided her toward a small parlor. "Is there something wrong? Is Maxine okay?"

Lilly laughed, choking back a spurt of hysteria. The dog was the least of her concerns. "Maxine's fine, but I, uh—" Her voice broke and she stiffened her spine. "I've been thinking." She twisted her ring again and looked away from him, trying to form the words. She'd practiced, but her mind suddenly went blank. She cleared her throat.

It's like ripping off a band-aid, she told herself. *Do it fast.* Ripping her ring off her finger, she shoved it into his hand. "I can't marry you. I'm sorry."

He stared at her in shock. "Why?"

She shook her head. "I just can't. I can't explain it, but you just need to believe that it's the best thing for you. It really is." Her voice wavered. "I'm sorry."

Robert reached for her, but she pulled back. Hurt and confusion darkened his eyes. "Lilly, you're upset. We have to talk about this. I can't stand for you to be this upset."

She shook her head again, tears welling in her eyes. "I can't talk about it." Her throat was too tight with misery. "I just can't. I'm sorry," she said and ran from the room.

Delilah successfully avoided Benjamin for two days. On the third, he burst through her door before she had time to shove the chair under the doorknob.

"Do you ever check your messages?" he asked, looking like a thundercloud.

Her chest tightened like a vise at the sight of him. "I'm waiting until Monday just in case Guy—"

"Well, you might want to listen to one Lilly might have left."

Delilah blinked. "Lilly? I haven't heard anything from her since last week. Did something happen to her?" Panic sliced through her. "Is she hurt?"

"Not physically, but she broke up with Robert."

Delilah dropped her jaw in shock. "I don't believe you."

"Believe it. She broke the engagement last night and Robert is walking around like a dead man. He and my father called me last night. Robert and I went out afterward and drowned his sorrows." He shot her a bitter look. "What did you tell Lilly to do to Robert?"

"Nothing!" Delilah searched her memory. "I suggested she get pregnant, but she nixed that because she was on the pill. She indicated sex hadn't been so great with him, so I told her it's better for everyone if men have to work at it." She met his censorious gaze. "Well, it's true. Usually," she added. "I can't imagine why she would have broken the engagement unless Guy got in touch with her again. You don't think—"

"I don't know what to think," Benjamin said. "I just know my brother is miserable and you made me promise not to tell him about Lilly's dilemma."

"Why did she do this? I just don't understand. She wanted to be Robert's wife so much. She wanted to be part of your family. Your father wanted her to be part of your family. He practically hand-picked her for Robert." Delilah shook her head, at a loss.

"Maybe after she got a closer look at my family, she changed her mind."

"I don't believe that. Your father may be a prick and your mother may be a little over-medicated, but they're still good people." She sighed. "Lilly wanted a family. She wanted to belong, to be needed."

"How do you know?" he asked, his gaze so sharp she felt like her mind was being sliced in half. "I thought you and she weren't close."

"We weren't. I just understand her."

"Why? It wouldn't have anything to do with wanting the same things, would it?"

Delilah didn't want to answer that. "I just understand."

She met his gaze and the turbulence in his eyes grabbed at her. She suspected she was the cause of his unhappiness and that made her hurt all over.

"I'm going to tell Robert about Lilly's secret," he told her.

Delilah shook her head. "You can't. You promised. My sister and her husband will be here on Monday and we might be able to work something—"

"It's time for them to work this out. Time to fish or cut bait."

She felt a lump form in her throat as if Benjamin wasn't just referring to Robert and Lilly, as if he was talking about her. Cutting the lines should be okay with her. It was what she'd planned for all along. *Keep telling yourself that, girlfriend, and you'll be fine.*

"I'd rather you wait until Monday."

"I'll see," he said and walked away from her.

On Sunday morning, Robert didn't show up for his tee time for his game of power golf. His father was going to be pissed, but Robert really didn't care. He had more important things on his mind. Lilly's ring was in his pocket and he had two dozen roses wrapped in green paper on the passenger seat of his car.

Stopping in front of her house, he cut his engine, clutched the flowers in his hand and got out of the car. He walked up the meticulously groomed path to her porch and rang her doorbell.

The dog barked, but Lilly didn't answer.

He wasn't surprised. She hadn't answered her phone during the last two days. He rang the doorbell again.

Still no answer.

He pounded on the door. When she still didn't answer, he proceeded to yell.

"I'm not leaving until you come down and talk to me, Lilly. I'll beat the damn door down if necessary. Come down here and—"

The door whipped open and Lilly, dressed in a long kimono robe, her hair in disarray, stared at him in surprise. She scrutinized him. "Have you been drinking?"

"Not this morning," he said, although he'd tied one on

a couple of nights ago. He'd never known a hangover could last longer than twenty-four hours.

"We need to talk," he said.

She pulled her robe around her tighter and lifted her chin. "We've already talked enough. I told you I don't think an engagement between the two of us is going to work."

"I disagree."

She sighed. "I realize your father probably sent you to try to persuade me—"

"My father expected me to tee off fifteen minutes ago." Robert smiled grimly. "Looks like he'll be the one who is teed off."

She looked momentarily surprised then shook her head. "It doesn't matter. It's not going to work and—"

"May I come in?"

She blinked, shifting slightly so Maxine wouldn't get out. "No."

"If you don't let me come in, I'll cause a scene your neighbors will never forget."

Dismay crossed her face and she sighed again. "Okay, but there's really no reason to discuss this. I've made up my—"

As soon as he stepped inside the door, he pushed her against the wall and pressed his mouth against hers. He pulled back slightly. "I've missed you."

"You have?" she said in a startled voice.

"Yes, I have. I've missed your smile. I've missed you putting up with my boring conversation."

"You're not boring," she said.

"Just self-involved."

"It's the election, isn't it?"

"God, I hope so. I'm going to bore myself to death if I don't find a way to handle this differently."

Lilly gaped at him.

"I missed your ears," he said, touching one that stuck out between blonde strands of hair.

She blushed and tried to cover it.

"I want you back. How do I get you back?"

Lilly gulped and shoved away from him. "I—I already told you I didn't think we suit each other."

"But why?" He followed her into the living room.

"I don't think I would be a good politician's wife," she said, pacing the oriental carpet.

He stepped in front of her. "How can you say that? You haven't fallen asleep during any of my speeches," he joked, trying to unwind some of her tension.

She couldn't meet his gaze.

"Lilly, tell me why you dumped me."

She bit her lip. "Because I have a secret that could be messy." She met his gaze with eyes full of misery. "I can't get in the way of your dream." Her voice broke. "I just can't."

Robert's heart ached at the depth of her pain. The depth of her love rocked him. He hadn't realized how important she was to him, how precious she was. "What is this secret?"

"It's about my father," she said.

Chapter 21

Lilly told Robert about her father and Willy and Guy. She watched surprise cross his face when she told him about Willy. When she mentioned Guy, his expression changed. His eyes turned cold and his jaw hardened.

"Why didn't you tell me about this?" he asked when she finished.

"I was afraid you would break the engagement. Plus, I started thinking about it and Willy is my half-brother. I'd like to have a relationship with him and I don't want to feel like I have to hide it."

He stared at her and shook his head. "You must think I have no backbone at all."

"No. It isn't that. It's just that I know you have a goal of getting elected and every decision you make is impacted by that goal. And there's your father . . ." Lilly stopped, not wanting to criticize Robert's father.

"But I love you. We're supposed to work these kinds of things out."

Lilly's breath stopped in her chest. She lifted her hand to her throat.

"What?" he asked, taking her hand in his. "What?"

She swallowed, feeling herself tremble. "That's the first time you've told me you love me."

He furrowed his eyebrows in confusion. "Are you sure?"

"Yes," she whispered.

He closed his eyes and shook his head. "Oh, Lilly, I'm sorry. I love you and I want you to be my wife." He lifted her hand to his lips and met her gaze. The power of love and commitment in his eyes was a dream come true. She wondered if she should pinch herself.

"Can you forgive me?"

She nodded, her throat so tight she couldn't squeak out a word.

He pulled a jeweler's box from his pocket. "Let's try this again. Maybe I'll get it right this time. I love you, Lilly. Will you marry me?"

She bit her lip, still worried about how her father's scandal might affect Robert. "Are you sure it's a good idea?"

He nodded. "Best idea I've had in a long time."

"But what about—"

He covered her mouth with his finger. "We're going public with this."

Her blood drained to her feet. "Oh, my God, are you sure that's wise?"

"If we go public, the snake loses its venom."

"Or gets neutered," she muttered, remembering what Delilah had said.

"You still haven't answered my question," Robert prompted.

Lilly surreptitiously pinched herself. She kept waiting to wake up from this incredible dream. "Yes. I can't say no to you."

He opened the box and slid the ring back on her finger

then pulled her into his arms. "If something is bothering you, I want you to promise to tell me."

"I will," she said.

He took her mouth in a kiss of commitment and surprising passion. Lilly felt herself melt against him.

"I think I have some making up to do," he muttered against her lips.

"What do you mean?"

"I mean I know our little rendezvous in the library wasn't very enjoyable for you. I want to make it up to you."

She felt a rush of anticipation. "Now?"

"Do you have anything planned for the next twenty-four hours?"

Omigod. By the look in his eyes, he was going to eat her up. "Uh, no."

He smiled like a wolf. "Good."

Hours later, Lilly couldn't walk, couldn't think, but didn't care. She lost count of how many times Robert had brought her to climax.

He kissed her funny ears and ran his hand over her breasts. "I love the way your body responds."

"I had no idea how—" She groped for words. "How good you could—" She broke off, shaking her head. "You always seemed so distracted."

He lowered his mouth to her nipples and she sighed. "I'm not finished."

On Monday, Delilah picked up Katie and Michael at the airport. Katie hugged her tightly, casting worried glances over her during the entire drive to Delilah's condo. Delilah told Michael the whole sordid story and listened while he read her the riot act for giving Guy any money.

"You never pay them. Once you start, they turn into parasites and they'll bleed you dry."

"Same thing Benjamin said," she muttered, pulling into the parking garage.

"What?" Katie asked.

"Nothing," Delilah said. "I just really appreciate both of you coming to my rescue. I'm sorry to have to ask you."

Katie shook her head. "You should have called us sooner." She gave Delilah another fierce hug. "We're family. We should count on each other."

Delilah felt a sliver of relief. "Thanks, Priss," she said, using the name she'd called Katie as a child.

On the way up to her condo, Michael told Delilah what he had already learned about Guy from researching him online. She was stunned with the speed at which he'd gathered so much information.

"How do you know so much?" Delilah asked as she opened the door to her condo.

"The guy surfs the Internet," Michael said. "I hacked into his system."

"What did you find out?"

"You and Lilly aren't the only ones Guy Crandall is blackmailing," Michael said.

Delilah dropped her jaw. "We're not?"

Benjamin appeared in the hallway and her heart dipped to her feet. He was obviously still furious with her. "Is this your sister and your brother-in-law?" he asked in a chilly voice.

She nodded. "Katie, Michael, this is Benjamin Huntington."

A light of recognition glinted in Michael's eyes. "Lilly's your sister-in-law to be?"

He gave Delilah a hard glance. "That remains to be seen. No one has talked with Robert since yesterday morning."

Delilah felt a sinking sensation in the pit of her stomach. "Oh, no."

Katie looked from Delilah to Benjamin and back again. Delilah suspected her sister's intuition was working overtime. "Let's go inside so you can hear Michael's plan."

The four of them walked into the living room and Delilah sat in a chair on the far side and told herself not to look at Benjamin. He made her nervous.

Katie slid her arm around Michael and smiled up at him. "Okay, show them how brilliant you are."

He rolled his eyes, but kissed her. The steady love between them glowed like a light that would never lose its power. Delilah felt a sharp twinge. She was happy for Katie, she reminded herself. Katie had been through a lot of hard years. She deserved happiness. She deserved Michael's love and devotion.

Delilah didn't like to think about what she deserved.

"I hacked into Guy Crandall's machine and found some interesting files. He apparently keeps records of his blackmail on his computer."

"Names?" Benjamin asked.

"Names, dates, amount received, amount owed and a one-sentence explanation of the dirt he has on these people."

Benjamin whistled. "What a racket."

Delilah burned with anger. "What a scumball. And to think I paid him. To think I was willing to give up ownership of my condo."

"I think I can wrap this up by tonight," Michael said.

"How?" Delilah asked.

"He's very good," Katie said.

Michael chuckled. "Since I've acquired this fascinating CD of information on Mr. Crandall's activities, I thought I'd meet him after his poker game tonight and go over the legal ramifications of blackmail."

Delilah shook her head. "He's really a jerk. I'm not sure he'll listen to you."

"He will if I threaten to go to the police with the information."

Delilah began to see the plan. She smiled. "You're going to neuter him."

Both Benjamin and Michael blinked at her. "I hadn't thought of it exactly that way, but I guess so."

"You don't mind if I join you, do you? I know a little about law," Benjamin said.

"A little," Delilah said with a snort. "He graduated with honors with a law degree from Harvard."

Katie looked at her curiously, making Delilah wish she'd bit her tongue.

Michael met Benjamin's gaze. He gave a half smile. "That could make things entertaining. Are you sure you don't mind getting your hands dirty?"

Benjamin glanced at Delilah. "Not at all."

An hour later, Benjamin and Michael were getting along like two peas in a pod. Katie joined Delilah in the kitchen while she made some sandwiches for a late afternoon snack.

"Why do I get the feeling that Benjamin is more than a *neighbor*?" Katie asked.

Because you're a witch, Delilah thought, but forced a

bland smile instead. "I don't know. Could it be your hormones acting up because you're pregnant?"

Katie turned silent. Too silent.

Delilah squealed. "You're pregnant already?"

Katie smiled. She snapped her fingers. "It happened that fast. It was almost like all we had to do was *think* it."

Delilah shot her a look of disbelief. "I know you had to do more than think it."

"Well, yes," Katie said with an expression of supreme feminine satisfaction. "Michael can be a man of action."

Delilah felt another tug of the happy and sad feeling in her belly. "Have you told Jeremy?" she asked, referring to their youngest half-brother.

Katie shook her head. "We haven't told anyone. I wouldn't have told you if you hadn't guessed." She paused a fraction of a second. "But not so fast. I believe we were talking about Benjamin Huntington."

"No, we weren't. You might have been, but I wasn't."

"He seems like a good man," Katie said.

Delilah felt her defenses deflate like a balloon. "He is. He's a very good man and that's part of the reason it's not going to work between us." She lifted her hand to stop Katie's protest. She could see it coming. "I can't talk about this right now or I'll cry. Please just trust me."

Katie frowned in concern. "I hate to see you hurting."

"I hate to see me hurting too," Delilah said.

Katie gave a sad smile and brushed Delilah's bangs out of her eyes. It was the same kind of thing she would have done when the two of them were children. "Someday you'll meet someone who will make you believe that everything your father tried to teach you about how bad you are was wrong."

Delilah didn't hold out much hope for that. "Sandwiches are ready. Let's take them in the den."

Every minute that Benjamin remained in her presence Delilah felt herself swinging from one emotional extreme to the other.

She wanted him to leave. She wished she'd never met him. She wanted to never see him again.

She couldn't keep her eyes off of him. She wanted to drag him away from Michael and Katie and off to her bed. She wanted him to never leave again.

By the time Michael and Benjamin left to meet with Guy, she was ready to scream. Katie laid down for a while to rest and broke the news that she and Michael would only be staying the night. Michael had to get back for a special client, but Katie insisted that Delilah plan to visit for Christmas.

Delilah took a dip in the Jacuzzi and told herself not to think. As the clock neared midnight, she forced herself to go to bed.

The following morning, she'd barely showered when Robert, Lilly and Benjamin burst through her door. She stopped mid-bite of her English muffin.

Robert's hand enclosed Lilly's and Delilah noticed the engagement diamond was winking on her finger. Michael stood. Katie looked at Delilah for an explanation.

Delilah shrugged and made the introductions. "My sister Katie, brother-in-law Michael. That's Robert Huntington and Lilly Bradford, and I believe they are now re-engaged."

"We should have called you yesterday, but we were—" Lilly cleared her throat and her cheeks turned pink. "We were busy working out some things."

"Lilly and Robert have decided to go public about Willy," Benjamin said.

Delilah gasped. "You're kidding. Are you sure?"

Robert nodded. "It's the best course. And Lilly wants the freedom to get to know her half-brother."

"I don't want to feel like I have to hide it," Lilly said with a smile. "And Robert has convinced me that everything will be okay."

Michael shot a glance of camaraderie at Benjamin. "I'd say Guy has been doubly neutered."

Benjamin smiled in agreement, but it wasn't a nice smile. He bared his teeth like a predator, making Delilah wonder just exactly what he and Michael had done to Guy last night. Not her worry. If he was still alive and his genitals were attached, then they had been nicer than she would have been.

Robert and Lilly insisted on giving Michael and Katie a ride to the airport since they had a meeting in that general direction. After a flurry of hugs and kisses and promises to call, her condo was emptied within minutes.

The only ones left were her and Benjamin.

Feeling his gaze on her, she fought the urge to scratch her neck. Surely she wasn't getting a stress rash, she thought darkly.

"It looks like Robert and Lilly found the courage to come out of the closet," he said.

She felt a knot tighten inside her stomach. She nodded, picking up dishes from the hastily eaten breakfast.

"If they have the courage, then—"

"They're in a different situation," she interjected, thinking of Lilly's pampered upbringing.

"And different people," he said.

She heard the slight edge in his voice and met his gaze. "That's right."

"It takes a lot of love to be that courageous. Takes a lot of courage to love." His gaze turned shuttered. "I guess some people just can't."

She watched him leave her condo and knew he wouldn't be walking through her door again uninvited.

*The miracle of love is that it can happen to you
even if you think you don't deserve it.*
                              —DELILAH'S DICTUM

Chapter 22

The M&Ms weren't working.

And he'd ruined the water wall for her.

Delilah had spent the last two weeks burying herself in work at the spa. She hadn't spoken to Benjamin once during that time and she was thoroughly miserable. She kept telling herself it was for the best, but it didn't feel like the best. It felt horrible.

She stared at the expense reports in front of her, but the numbers blurred. She shook her head and glanced at the clock. Six-thirty. She should probably go home. Or go out, she fantasized. Go out and have a wild night on the town.

She'd probably put on her cotton jammies and watch a rerun of *Friends*.

A knock sounded at her door. She tensed, then remembered it couldn't be Guy. Guy was now history, thank goodness.

Helga poked her head inside. "Miss Montague, I must speak with you."

Delilah felt a sinking sensation. Uh-oh. Helga had probably terrorized another assistant into quitting. "Come in."

"Are you sick?" the woman asked bluntly.

Taken aback, Delilah shook her head. "No. Why do you ask?"

"You look like crap. You have dark circles under your eyes and your skin and hair look dull. You're a bad advertisement for the spa. Come now, I will give you a facial and you will look and feel better."

Shocked, Delilah couldn't produce a response. Helga had just insulted her, yet offered to help her feel better in the same breath. She rubbed her forehead in confusion. "I think I've probably just been working a little too hard. You don't have to give me a facial."

"Yes, I do," Helga said in utter seriousness. "You look like crap."

Helga gave Delilah one of her trademark facials and her skin glowed afterward, but she still went home and watched a rerun of *Friends*. She received an invitation from Lilly and Robert to attend a formal holiday party at the country club. Nice gesture, she thought, but there was no way she would attend.

One week later, Lilly called and begged Delilah to attend.

"I don't have a date," Delilah said.

"You don't need one," Lilly said.

"I don't have anything to wear."

"And you don't like to shop?" Lilly asked in disbelief.

"Not during this time of year," Delilah complained, thinking she had a lot in common with Scrooge right now.

"I'm sure you can dig something out of your closet, but even if you can't, it won't hurt you to get something new. It's not as if you're being blackmailed by Guy anymore."

Delilah shook her head. "I don't understand. With the exception of when you were trying to get me to resign from the spa, you have always tried to put as much distance between you and me as possible. What's up?"

A long silence followed. "I like you."

Delilah stared at the phone in shock. "Excuse me?"

"I said I like you. I miss seeing you and talking with you. Okay?" She sounded irritated. "My father was right. You're a really cool person. And you were willing to pay off Guy and take care of Willy so I could marry Robert. You're nicer than I thought you were."

Touched, but wary, Delilah paused for a long moment. "I'm still white trash, though."

"That may be somebody else's opinion, but it's not mine," Lilly returned in a snooty voice.

"People still think your father was my sugar daddy."

"I know the truth and I want you there. There are a lot of people I don't know if I can trust, but I know I can trust you."

Delilah felt a small trickle of pleasure and pride. "I do believe you have changed, Lilly Bradford. I'll think about coming to the party. *Think*," she emphasized.

"Well think hard because I'm putting you down as a yes," Lilly said and hung up before she could argue.

Delilah went to bed that night thinking of Benjamin, as she did every night. She told herself that she had done the right thing, that Benjamin's life would be better without her. The next morning, however, when she saw the announcement of the opening of his new law office and partnership, she couldn't resist sending a gift with congratulations from Lilly.

Lilly would be confused when Benjamin mentioned it to her, but Delilah figured it would take them awhile to be sure who sent it.

Sara and Paul repeatedly invited her to dinner, but seeing their open love for each other just hurt too much. Delilah grew uneasy. It had never taken her this long to get over a man. She hadn't thought about sex at all, except for remembering the night she'd shared with Benjamin. What if she had made a mistake? What if she was in love with Benjamin and there was no cure for it?

Impatient with herself, she booked a trip to Grand Cayman for herself. The day before Lilly's holiday party, she bought an eye-popping red dress and decided to attend. She would see Benjamin and feel horrible, then run away to the islands the next day. It was a perfect plan.

As she drove her car to the valet service, she couldn't help admiring the thousands of white lights decorating the country club shrubbery and windows. She gave her key to the valet, collected her stub and climbed the stairs. A doorman opened the door. She showed her invitation and was directed to a ballroom.

She felt a little tingle of nerves as she stepped inside the sumptuously decorated ballroom. A band played music. Waiters carried trays of champagne and the room was lined with tables groaning with food.

Spotting Lilly and Robert, she smiled across the room. Lilly waved her over and as soon as Delilah was within touching distance, she embraced her. Robert shook her hand and kissed her on the side of her forehead.

"It's so good to see you," Lilly said. "It feels like it's been ages. How is your sister Katie?"

"Fine," Delilah said, still blinking at Lilly's transformation. She had bloomed. Her smile was confident, her eyes sparkled. "You look wonderful."

"I feel wonderful." She smiled at Robert. "I would ask how everything at the spa is, but I know it's insanely busy because even I couldn't get an appointment today."

"That's a no-no. The receptionist should have told me."

"I told her not to bother you. I didn't really need to come in. I think I just had some last-minute jitters." She glanced up. "Oh, here come Robert's parents."

"I'll let you talk to them," Delilah said, ready to slither away.

Lilly grabbed her arm. "Oh, no, I want them to meet you."

Why? Delilah wanted to ask, but didn't have time.

"Mr. and Mrs. Huntington, I'd like you to meet Delilah Montague. She's the director of Spa DeMay."

Mr. Huntington shook her hand in a gracious, un-prick-like way. "Heard that place does a bang-up business."

"We do pretty well. Nice to meet you, sir," she said.

"I've always wanted to go to Spa DeMay," Mrs. Huntington confided. "Do you think they could do something with my hair?"

Delilah swallowed a chuckle. "I'm sure. Your hair's lovely, but if you'd like a change, we have some very talented hair stylists."

"There she is," Mrs. Huntington said, turning her head to the entrance. "I wasn't sure if she would come." She glanced back at Delilah. "Oh, excuse me. My son's fiancée just arrived from Connecticut and I must see her."

Connecticut. Fiancée. Delilah's mind snagged on the words. Her stomach sank to her feet, but she couldn't resist searching the crowd for Benjamin's perfect former woman. Or maybe they'd gotten back together. Her stomach knotted again. Maybe the woman had come to her senses.

She saw the blonde woman dressed in black with her hair pulled back in a classic chignon and knew who she was in an instant. Mrs. Huntington slid into view pulling Benjamin with her.

Benjamin. Her heart rose into her throat. In that black tux, he looked good enough to eat. She had the odd sense of watching her own funeral, but couldn't tear her eyes from the mini-drama playing out across the room.

Benjamin's fiancée smiled and opened her arms. She felt an inexplicable stabbing sensation. He embraced her and brushed a kiss across her cheek. The knife inside her turned.

As if he knew he was being watched and it bothered him, Benjamin glanced over his shoulder and his gaze met hers.

Delilah panicked. "Oh, no. Caught," she muttered, biting her lip. "Definitely time for a trip to the powder room." She moved as quickly as her unsubstantial high heels would permit and tried to exit through a side door. It was locked. She quickly walked to the next one. Locked. In frustration, she eyed the fire exit.

"Hello," she heard from behind her and closed her eyes. Benjamin, of course.

Delilah swore under her breath. She had known she would see him again. She had even hoped that seeing him would help her make some sort of peace with herself. And if not, the Caymans awaited her tomorrow. The Caymans were looking more necessary to her survival every minute.

Taking a deep breath, she turned and stared at his chin. "Hi."

"How did Lilly get you to come?"

Delilah chuckled, feeling awkward. "She played on a soft spot. She said she needed me."

"So the magic four-letter word is need," he said.

She smiled and her eyes met his. "I don't know that it's magic, but it worked for Lilly."

"You look beautiful."

"You do too," she couldn't help saying because he did. She felt as if her eyes were trying to drink him all the way down to her toes. Coming here had been a terrible mistake, she thought. It had been a terrible mistake to ever meet him. The truth hit her hard even though she'd suspected it for some time. She was never going to get over Benjamin.

"I know your secret," he said with a smile.

"Which one?" she asked nervously.

"You sent me a plant for the opening of my office."

"Did not," she said.

"Did too," he said.

"Did not till infinity."

"It was dead."

She dropped her jaw. "It better not have been dead. I told them to send the freshest—" She broke off, realizing he'd just tricked her.

He grinned. "Would you dance with me?"

Her pulse quickened. "What about your, um, date?" she asked.

"I don't have one. Do you?"

"No, but what about your fiancée?" she asked, wondering where the beautiful blonde woman had gone.

"My mother invitèd her without my knowledge."

Delilah made a silent O of surprise.

"She was under the mistaken impression that I was suffering from a broken heart due to my former fiancée. Right about one, but wrong about the other."

Delilah felt a lump in her throat and a horrible longing in her soul. She shouldn't ask. She absolutely shouldn't ask, but she had a devil of a time doing what she should where Benjamin was concerned. "What was she right about?"

"She was right that I've been suffering from a broken heart, but not because of my ex-fiancée."

She could barely breathe. "Oh."

He reached for her hand and she couldn't find the will

to snatch it away. He twined her fingers through his and tugged her closer to him. "Dance with me," he told her.

Her emotions in turmoil, she let him pull her into his arms. "This isn't a good idea."

"It's a great idea," he told her. "Have you missed me?"

She tried to make her mouth form the word *No*, but it wouldn't cooperate. Delilah frowned.

The music was sweet and romantic and he smelled as wonderful as usual. Her pulse was racing like a machine gun as she rested her chin on his shoulder.

"I've missed you," he said against her ear. "But I couldn't keep the secret anymore."

Her throat knotted. "I don't know why you don't understand that a relationship between you and me isn't good for you."

"When did you get into sado-masochism? Or maybe it's martyrdom," he replied.

She pulled back slightly, looking at him in confusion. "I'm no martyr."

"Yes, you are. I want you, need you and love you. You want me, need me, love me. But you deny me and you deny yourself."

Delilah frowned. Unfortunately, she couldn't dispute her feelings for him.

"I love you, Delilah. I need you too."

Her heart hurt at his words.

"Were you happy with me?"

"Yes," she whispered.

"It's time to stop being a chicken, sweetheart." He slid his hand behind the nape of her neck. "My mother and father are watching us."

She stiffened.

"My ex-fiancée is watching."

"Great," Delilah muttered.

"Robert and Lilly are watching."

"Maybe we should—"

"I'm going to kiss you," he said, shocking her spitless. He lowered his mouth to hers and with the first touch of his lips, the crowd was wiped from her mind. The kiss promised eternity, but only lasted a moment.

He pulled back, his gaze full of everything he was feeling. Everything she was feeling too. Taking her hand, he knelt on one knee in front of her and Delilah felt the room begin to spin.

"I love you and I need you," he said. "Will you marry me?"

Holy shit. No genie was going to snap her out of this situation. Scared, oh, so scared, she stared at him and wanted to hit him. And kiss him. She supposed she could walk away.

Actually she couldn't.

Her feet wouldn't let her. She wasn't even certain her knees would allow her to crawl away from him. But the crux of the matter was that her heart wouldn't let her.

She didn't look anywhere except his eyes, but felt a crowd forming around them. Whispers and gasps swirled through the air. The odd thought struck her that she was glad she'd put on a double layer of deodorant because she couldn't remember being put in a more trying position.

When she looked in his eyes, she felt calm. When she looked at his face, she saw forever.

Maybe it was time to stop torturing herself and trust the most trustworthy man she'd ever met. She lowered her head, so she could speak in a low voice. "You do know that you are letting yourself in for a lifetime of all kinds of trouble, don't you?"

"Bring it on, baby."

She smiled and she felt her eyes burn with tears. "Yes," she said. "I'll marry you."

Someone let out a whoop and there was a chorus of applause. She didn't hear more than the first few claps because Benjamin stood and kissed her again.

Two-and-a-half months later, they were back at the country club after she and Benjamin exchanged vows in a beautiful ceremony at his family's church. Robert hadn't stopped grumbling about Benjamin's ability to get around their father. He was chomping at the bit to move in with Lilly. Delilah smiled at Wilhemina and Douglas McGinley; the unlikely pair of heiress and hog farmer were expecting their second child. Katie was also glowing from her pregnancy and Michael had turned hyper-protective. Lori Jean had managed to wrangle permission from her father to attend, primarily because he approved of the Huntingtons. Nicky Conde had brought Willy to the reception and Delilah was amazed at how much he'd grown. She still missed him, but she could see that he was thriving and that Nicky was indeed devoted to him. Her brother Jeremy was trying to steal some frosting off the cake without getting caught. Sneaky little charmer.

Benjamin's parents had surprised her with how warmly welcoming they had been. She had expected them to disapprove. She suspected Benjamin had threatened a Las Vegas wedding if his mother and father didn't show complete support.

Somehow, during the last couple of months, she'd bonded with Benjamin's father. He appreciated her business sense and drive, and his mother was thrilled with the possibility of grandchildren.

After her dry-run with Willy, Delilah didn't feel pressured. She couldn't wait to have children with Benjamin. She knew she would be giving some child the most fabulous father in the world, and Benjamin had convinced her that she could be a good mother. Amazing how that man affected her.

Sipping a glass of champagne while Benjamin spoke with a wedding guest, she smiled. Sometimes she still couldn't believe he loved her, but he never let her forget it. He must have felt her looking at him, because he looked her way and returned her smile. Within a moment, he was by her side.

"I'm ready to leave," he said, pulling her against him.

"Your parents will kill us. The party's only been going for two hours."

He groaned then a glint of sexy mischief crossed his eyes. "We can steal away for a few minutes, can't we?"

"What do you have in mind?"

"Come on," he said and pulled her with him.

"Benjamin," someone called.

"Delilah," Lilly called.

"Be right back," Benjamin said over his shoulder and led her down a hallway then another. After looking both ways, he opened a door and pulled her into a catering closet.

She glanced around at the catering supplies and shook her head. "You bad, bad boy."

"I can be badder," he said, pulling her against him.

"Oh, really?"

He lowered his mouth and kissed her. The last week had been so busy they hadn't had time to be intimate with each other. The touch of his mouth reminded her of all the ways she'd missed him.

She felt his hardness against her and her body heat

cranked up further. He groaned and lowered his mouth to her throat then lower to the top of her breast.

"You look so beautiful you make me want to rip off that dress."

She laughed, but identified his sense of urgency.

"We should have gone to Vegas. This wedding has been a pain in the—" He exhaled in frustration. "Ass isn't really the part of my anatomy that's most bothered."

"If you didn't have that dumb rule about three for me and one for you, we could do something about it," Delilah told him.

He went still. "Like what?"

"There are several things we could do. I could unfasten your pants," she said, feeling wonderfully wicked. "And slide down your zipper."

She could feel him holding his breath.

"And get down on my knees—"

"Oh, hell, don't say that," he said, raking his hand through his hair.

"Why?" she asked, brushing her lips over his as she brushed her hand over his erection.

"Because I'll want you to do it."

The combination of naughty and nice was too delicious to resist. She slid down his body to her knees and it was her pleasure to break her husband's three-for-her and one-for-him rule. She was pretty sure she would remember their time in the closet far longer than she would remember much else about the reception. She was pretty sure he would too.

They kissed each other senseless and he cracked the door of the closet, but someone was standing just outside.

"Where is the bathroom in this place?" one woman asked.

"I don't know. I thought someone said there was one up here. Maybe it's on the next hall. What do you think of the bride and groom?"

"They're in love. They can't keep their eyes off each other."

"I hear they can't keep their hands off each other. Delilah Montague's known as one hot number and that Benjamin Huntington's no slouch. With their reputation, I wouldn't be surprised if she had shown up at the wedding wearing no panties and they consummate their marriage at the reception."

Delilah covered her mouth to hold back a gasp of laughter. The women's voices faded away as they walked down the hallway. As soon as it turned quiet, she and Benjamin burst into laughter. He shook his head and poked his head outside the door, looking both ways. He pulled her out after him. "Just one question. Are you or are you not?"

"What?" she asked, so happy to be with him she thought she would burst.

"Are you wearing panties?"

"Oh, that," she said as they rounded the corner. "I guess you'll have to find out."

He chuckled and swore under his breath. "You are incredible," he murmured in her ear.

"Incredibly good or incredibly bad?"

"Both, thank God."

About the Author

LEANNE BANKS is a *USA Today* best-selling author with over thirty novels and novellas to her credit. She holds a bachelor's degree in Psychology, which she says qualifies her to treat only fictional characters. Winner of multiple writing awards, she never fails to be delighted when readers write her praising her books as fun, feel-good reads. Leanne lives in Virginia with her husband and two children, but can usually be persuaded to take a trip to the beach at the drop of a hat. You can visit Leanne at *www.leanne banks.com*.